D1586004

JASON PARENT

THE APOCALYPSE STRAIN

This is a **FLAME TREE PRESS** book

Text copyright © 2020 Jason Parent

All rights reserved. No part of this publication may be reproduced, stored in a retrieval system, or transmitted in any form or by any means, electronic, mechanical, photocopying, recording or otherwise, without the prior written permission of the publisher.

FLAME TREE PRESS
6 Melbray Mews, London, SW6 3NS, UK
flametreepress.com

US sales, distribution and warehouse:
Simon & Schuster
100 Front Street, Riverside, NJ 08075
www.simonandschuster.com

UK distribution and warehouse:
Marston Book Services Ltd
160 Eastern Avenue, Abingdon, OX14 4SB
www.marston.co.uk

Publisher's Note: This is a work of fiction. Names, characters, places, and incidents are a product of the author's imagination. Locales and public names are sometimes used for atmospheric purposes. Any resemblance to actual people, living or dead, or to businesses, companies, events, institutions, or locales is completely coincidental.

Thanks to the Flame Tree Press team, including:
Taylor Bentley, Frances Bodiam, Federica Ciaravella, Don D'Auria,
Chris Herbert, Josie Karani, Molly Rosevear, Mike Spender,
Cat Taylor, Maria Tissot, Nick Wells, Gillian Whitaker.

The cover is created by Flame Tree Studio with
thanks to Nik Keevil and Shutterstock.com.
The font families used are Avenir and Bembo.

Flame Tree Press is an imprint of Flame Tree Publishing Ltd
flametreepublishing.com

A copy of the CIP data for this book is available from the British Library
and the Library of Congress.

HB ISBN: 978-1-78758-355-9
US PB ISBN: 978-1-78758-353-5
UK PB ISBN: 978-1-78758-354-2
ebook ISBN: 978-1-78758-356-6

Printed and bound in Great Britain by Clays Ltd, Elcograf S.p.A.

JASON PARENT

THE APOCALYPSE STRAIN

FLAME TREE PRESS
London & New York

CHAPTER ONE

Come closer, Papa.

"Repeat last transmission," Sergei Kobozev said into his helmet's comm system. "Sebastian? Was that you? Over."

Sebastian's voice came in loud and clear through the built-in speaker beside Sergei's ear. "I didn't say anything. Over."

"Oh...sorry."

Closer, Papa. Don't you remember me? Don't you want to see me?

Sergei flipped off his comm and froze. "Who's there?" The crisp air was silent and still, dead except for the sound of his breaths humming against the fishbowl enclosing his head. That sound increased in frequency. His body trembled. His heart thudded louder and louder in his chest.

"That voice.... It can't be."

A wave of nausea came over him, and he stumbled forward, bracing himself against a boulder jutting out of the frozen tundra. He took deep breaths, trying to calm his nerves and his stomach. Retching inside his helmet was high up on his list of unpleasant occupational hazards, having experienced it more than once during launch simulation and antigravity training. Even in his thermal linens and wind-resistant, temperature-controlled suit, Sergei could feel the bite of the cold, somehow more vicious than it had been throughout the starless night.

Yes, Papa. Closer.

Sergei jumped, his heartbeat kicking up another notch. He looked left and right, turned completely around, but saw no one. He scanned the vast Siberian ice field that was the Kolyma Lowlands. Had his visor not fogged up, he could have seen a mile in every direction.

He could see well enough. No one was nearby.

A joke? If so, someone would pay dearly for it.

He studied the other members of his team, toiling in the distance: six astronauts and astrobiologists drilling into the Siberian permafrost, a bunch of morons preparing for a mission to Mars's polar caps that would never come.

Not in his lifetime, anyway.

Sergei couldn't tell one member of his team from another in their blue gender-nondescript spacesuits. Except for Alfonse. He was a foot taller than the rest of them and easily twice as brawny.

And twice as full of himself. Not to mention his wicked sense of humor. I wouldn't put it past him to place some kind of recording into my comm or tamper with its filters. Alfonse never took anything seriously unless it could improve his rank, pay, or station. *God, if he is made captain of our crew, I'll....*

He slapped his thighs. *I'll do nothing.* He sighed. Alfonse wasn't to blame if Sergei was losing it.

But that didn't mean he could forgive Alfonse or any of the others if someone was acting out a malicious prank. Sergei's past was no secret. He squinted across the flatland at each of his colleagues, men and women who were supposed to be his peers, his comrades even. They worked at various stations, none paying him any mind, one of them possibly playing him for a fool.

Any one of them could have been responsible for the tasteless joke, so-called intellectuals as ignorant as he had been before he learned what truly had meaning in life, before—

It's me, Papa. The voice resonated through his head again. *It's not a joke. Don't you remember my voice? Don't you remember me?*

Sergei whacked his fist against his helmet, attempting to bite on his knuckle to quell the shriek rising in his throat. He pursed his lips, and his cry, stifled, passed softly between them, a low whimper that trickled into the laughter of a madman.

The voice had seemed much closer, all around him, on top of him – clear and unmistakable. Soft and soothing, barely more than a whisper, it did not belong to Sebastian and definitely not to Alfonse. The voice was female, but it did not match that of either woman on his team. And it hadn't come through his helmet's speakers but rather out of the air inside his helmet itself. He knew that voice, and that knowledge caused his teeth to grind and the hairs on his neck to stand on end.

The voice of a little girl.

You do remember! Oh, Papa, it's me. It's really—

"Enough!" Sergei shouted as he tried to click off his comm again before realizing he already had. He rubbed a gloved hand over the outside of his helmet where the condensation was thickest. It didn't wipe away. *Why is it foggy?*

The little girl he could not see began to cry. *But it is me, Papa. Please, talk to me. Don't leave me. Not again, Papa. Not again.*

Sergei pretended that he couldn't hear the voice, that he hadn't yet lost his mind. "Maybe I've been out in this cold for too long. Is this... hypothermic shock? Fuck!" He turned and headed toward his team's small encampment.

You can't leave me, Papa. More sobs rang through Sergei's ears. *You can't....*

"I must!" he shouted even as he stopped moving. He shook his head and sucked up the snot running down to his lip. Tears stung his cheeks as they iced over. "You're not real. You can't be real."

I am real, the little-girl voice said sharply. It softened. *It's me, your little ballerina. Don't you remember?*

"But...." Sergei opened and closed his fingers. Anger, fear, outrage, frenzy – all welled up at once inside him and boiled over, flooding out and leaving him hollow once more, aching with the emptiness of despair. So many consecutive days had eventually tallied into two years of holding himself together, exerting every effort just to get by. He had wasted away as he pretended to be strong for the sake of a marriage that had failed regardless. The counselors – and there had been many – had told him how difficult it was for couples to move together past the loss of a child, the burden heavier when both parents blamed themselves for the accident.

"It can't be you. I was there. I watched you drown. I...I could do nothing to stop it." He shook his head and gritted his teeth. "Oh God.... I've finally lost it." Tears streamed down Sergei's cheeks. His warm, damp sobs fogged up the rest of the helmet's clear plastic shield.

The condensation forced his scientific mind back into action. Without a sudden drop in temperature, his warm breath would not affect his visibility. Plummeting temperatures *outside* the helmet, where the Siberian cold could kill an exposed man in a matter of minutes, were equally irrelevant. *But if* inside *my helmet, where the temperature is system regulated, were to freeze over....*

He focused on the problem, ignoring the voice as best he could for the moment. The condensation meant one of three things: either his suit's temperature controls were malfunctioning or he was going crazy and hallucinating the frosted plastic and everything he was experiencing or, perhaps even more frightening but not beyond the realm of possibility, some unseen presence, a gaseous, subzero particle with consciousness had coated itself to his visor and—

An invisible hand poked two dots in the condensation. Underneath those dots, a *U* appeared.

A smiley face.

Sergei laughed as he cried, still unable to determine if what he was seeing and hearing was real, his mind twisting in knots he couldn't untie. Part of him knew, even then, that to hear Natalya's voice was madness, but God help him, he welcomed it. He would have gladly given his sanity to hear her beautiful, innocent voice, alive in his fragile mind, if not anywhere else. But sanity yet had a tentative grip.

"Is it…. Is it really you, Natalya? Can it be?"

Yes, Papa. It really is me. I've missed you so much. I've been down here all alone. I miss you…and I miss Mama…and Mr. Snuggums.

Sergei sniffled and snorted out a laugh. "Your precious teddy bear. I still have him, you know? I still have everything. Your room is exactly the same as it was when…."

I know, Papa. It can be like it was.

How Sergei wished that were true. But his mind wasn't so far gone as to believe the dead could live again. The ice beneath his feet was frozen solid even if the ice of his psyche was beginning to spiderweb, intricate patterns of cracks and fissures expanding to the farthest reaches. His thoughts warred against themselves, half grounding themselves in reality, the other half succumbing to a desire to believe in the impossible.

"Natalya, I…I buried you."

I'm still buried, Papa. Just not where you last saw me. Your little ballerina's stuck down here, right here at your feet. I'm scared and alone, Papa. It's cold and it's dark, and I'm so lonely here.

"Where, *angel moy*? I can't see you."

You won't be able to see me. Not at first. I'm alive, just not…all together yet. But all you need is the teensy-weensiest part of me, and we can be together forever. It will all make sense soon enough. You'll see. Then we can both be happy again.

"I'd...I'd like that. I love you so much, my little ballerina."

I love you to infinity, Papa!

Sergei sobbed, his eyes blurring as they filled with fresh tears. The outline of a heart appeared on his visor. His own heart filled with joy.

One eyebrow shot up, and he gasped. "But how will I find you?"

Easy-peasy, Papa. Remember how we used to play Hot and Cold? I'm underneath you, surrounded by ice, so I think we'll play it so that 'colder' means 'closer'. Right now, you're volcano hot, but take just one step forward, and you're already getting a lot colder. And when I tell you you're polar-bear cold, you're right on top of me. That's where you drill your borehole. You won't stop drilling until you find me, will you, Papa?

"I won't."

You promise?

"I promise, my little ballerina. Cross my heart and hope to die."

CHAPTER TWO

Clara St. Pierre had always wanted to make the big discoveries out in the field, exploring hard-to-reach places, studying life – from the simplest organisms to those complex beyond science's comprehension – in all its wildly diverse habitats. She would start with what her eyes could see and, from there, go deeper, smaller, finding whole worlds of life buried within worlds, tiny beings composing the meat and bones of a larger one. In her hand lay a whole cosmos to explore, so long as technology made a microscope powerful enough to define it. Outside her door lay a massive world and the infinity of space beyond.

In her college years, she had dreamed big and small, but her disease had dampened those dreams well before it had confined her to a wheelchair. Her legs had become so weak some days that she might as well have been paralyzed. Those days were blessings, days without pain.

Other days, her bones screamed like metal in a forge. Her muscles toughened and tightened. The multiple sclerosis had ravaged her body, gobbled up a lithe sprinter and swimmer, and shat out a contorted heap of wasted flesh, and worse still, it continued day after day to do so, like a snake eating its tail.

The toll it took on her personality had perhaps been more severe. Clara had been social, energetic, positive, and friendly. None of those traits had survived six months of disease. Six more years had reversed them completely. And though her passion and youthful naïveté had all but been obliterated, her disease sharpened her mind, or at least her will to feed it.

In her discipline, Clara reigned supreme. Medical genomics and bioinformatics required a mind that could deconstruct enigmas and reduce life, even humanity, to its base parts. She'd experienced firsthand just how human existence could break down, and in the genes that engineered her own fall from grace, she searched for the cheat code that could repair what had gone wrong, if not make her invincible. All the accolades she'd accumulated over the course of her life – she'd recently celebrated her thirty-ninth birthday for the fourth year in a row – had failed to bring her a modicum of happiness. She would have traded everything she had, every last euro, to rid herself of her disease.

She spent her days as a professor of microbiology and genetics at Paris Descartes University, but her nights moonlighting as a laboratory consultant, genomics expert, and project leader had gotten her on that plane to the most desolate place in the world outside her heart: the Shakhova-Mendelsen Siberian Research Center, a United Nations-sponsored, state-of-the-art scientific facility. Clara suspected a quiet agreement between American and Russian interests post-Cold War had led to its creation – a place where each country's mad scientists created biological and chemical agents of mass destruction in adjacent rooms. In any event, it had proven a conveniently located structure for the discovery made in the Kolyma Lowlands.

Yeah, perfect. The only thing colder than Siberia is Northern Siberia.

Clara could never rid herself of her sarcasm. That was ingrained, a security blanket that had cloaked her since her disease had set in. But it masked the truth of her spirits that morning, burying all her pain – all her anguish, mental and physical, and all her late-night screaming at a god she might have considered cruel and merciless had she truly believed in him – deep within her subconscious. On that rare day, misery gave way to something surprising.

For the first time in too long, Clara was happy.

The reason for her happiness lay behind the password-encoded door of a refrigerator stationed in a sterilized laboratory, a clean room, which itself was situated behind a heavy, vault-like door that required a keycard to enter. Clara had such a keycard. She knew the nine-digit code for the refrigerator.

And she was on her way toward it.

Do I have everything?

She took in her modest quarters, a dull, uninspiring room that she bet her pampered peers were having difficulty accepting. It was enough for her, having only a cot, a desk, and a bureau for her personal effects, completely unadorned save for a sole picture of Benny, a service dog she'd lost a few months prior and hadn't the heart to replace.

Not yet. Maybe not ever.

When she saw the picture, she winced at fond memories tinged with sadness, times forever lost. She turned away, and her eyes fell upon a small mirror. Looking at herself, frumpy and tired, Clara wanted to spit at what she saw. She bit into her lip and retied her loose, limp brown hair back into a long ponytail. She didn't bother to color over the increasing number of gray hairs or liven up her blotchy skin with a bit of rouge or cover the wells of her tears with eyeliner. No one noticed her. Not in that way.

She let out a long, cleansing breath. *Today is a good day.* Clara nodded at her reflection as if to affirm the thought and pressed her lips flat. Then she turned her chair toward the door.

Before exiting, she stopped to pat herself down. *ID badge clipped to my breast pocket? Check. Lanyard and keycard attached to my belt? Check. Room key? Check.*

Satisfied she had everything she needed, Clara twisted her chair sidelong to the door, reached up for the doorknob, turned it, and spun her chair forward again to push the door open with her feet. She moved out into the hallway.

The acidic odor of cheap disinfectant and stale air made the reticent plaster walls and white tile floor of the research center feel like the inside of a mausoleum. Though dry, the walls always seemed slick, like an in-ground pool recently emptied. Clara wasn't oblivious to the fact that her hands refused to touch them. The place needed color, to look lived in, even if no one wanted to live there.

She looked at the corridor signs. Each hall had a number. She knew hers, and she knew that of the hallway where her precious samples waited. Every day, she would have to guess which twists and turns to make between them. She cracked her knuckles and pushed her chair forward.

I'm coming, Molli.

The giant virus stored in that refrigerator – *Mollivirus sibericum*, which Clara and the other researchers had taken to calling 'Molli' – was the fourth virus to have been extracted from seeds found in an ancient squirrel's nest buried deep within Siberian permafrost for more than thirty thousand years. Millennia upon millennia, a treasure trove of cryogenically frozen life had been stored under their feet, waiting to be rediscovered.

The nest had been found almost completely by accident, so the newspapers had claimed, when a coalition of American and Russian astrobiologists used the tundra to replicate excavation conditions on Mars. The team was credited with the find, but Clara had it on good authority that one man in particular, a Sergei Kobozev, had been the true discoverer. Though she knew all the astrobiologists were present at the Shakhova-Mendelsen Siberian Research Center, she had yet to meet any of them.

She hoped she would meet Sergei. She wanted to shake his hand. His discovery had given her life meaning again. She wiped her eyes quickly, not wanting anyone to see her cry.

A few weeks after that Russian scientist had drilled a hole into a really old ice cube and found life, Clara had been on a flight out of Paris heading to Moscow. There, she met a smorgasbord of leading experts in the fields of microbiology, disease control, bioinformatics, and a plethora of other highly specialized concentrations. They were all ready to work on the discovery of a lifetime, alongside the many other highly specialized and top-secret projects the facility had a reputation for. In addition to the astrobiologists and the genome junkies, the center culled the international *crème de la crème* from a wide array of natural sciences − from botanists studying the seeds and nuts found in the nest to geologists looking for further proof of Pangaea − everyone with an agenda they thought trumped all others.

Clara kept her distance, preferring to work alone. She retreated from her colleagues' company, not out of fear but out of disgust. Like them, she had more letters following her name than all the Henrys and Georges of England. But unlike them, she didn't see herself as any better than anyone else. Her idea of fun was watching classic cinema or reading a thriller with a glass of wine in her hand, not debating evolutionary theory with Christian Scientists and tormenting students with obscure assignments and witless banter. As for her contribution toward the greater good, Clara would gladly show her team spirit by sharing the findings of work done solo.

Yes, Clara hated the academic world. To be fair, though, she hated everyone. At least, she told herself that. A lifetime without truly living had taught her that the world was populated by those who had more than they needed but always wanted more: ingrates and selfish germs deserving of eradication, shit stains on the dirty underpants of a sweaty asshole world.

Of course, that might have been her bitterness talking. Her constant attempts to convince herself of this 'undeniable truth' were undermined by her continual drive to heal all wounds, destroy disease, and remedy societal and individual aches and pains, even those that manifested in her heart.

Those sometimes seemed the hardest to fix, particularly on cold, empty nights when pain twisted her muscles and blissful, oblivious sleep would not come. On those nights, Clara sometimes wished she had a friend to comfort her, maybe even a—

If you don't let them close, they can never hurt you, she reminded herself. She let out a long sigh then forced a smile. *Besides, you do have friends. Four of them, to be exact.*

Lost in thought, Clara had rolled to a stop. Seeing her coattails hanging loose, she tucked them between her legs to keep them from catching in the wheels of her chair, the old-fashioned, hand-rolled kind. She liked it that way. Pushing herself around kept her arms and shoulders strong and able, ready for those times when her legs betrayed her.

Lately, that had been always.

She sighed but fought against her crashing mood. Zigzagging her way through the corridors, Clara passed several labs of varying shapes and orientation. From a central hub, hallways ran like spokes on a wheel, except the spokes had so many bending and winding offshoots that the end result looked like a circle maze. Clara had gotten lost in those hallways more times than she cared to admit.

She looked at a door to her right. *Chem-Lab 601,* she read. *That's new.* She threw up her hands and groaned but pressed forward anyway.

Fortunately, the clean room where she performed most of her experimentation wasn't too far away. A left, a right, then another left down a shiny, over-waxed corridor brought her into familiar territory.

"*Bonjour,* Dr. St. Pierre," a cheery voice called out to her in an almost singsongy way as she approached the biology labs.

Clara stared up into the deep chocolate eyes of a young, shapely Indian woman who was the polar opposite of her in all the ways that mattered to Clara: healthy, happy, and beautiful. Though her heart panged at the sight of so much she couldn't have, Clara didn't resent the younger woman for her blessings. In fact, she even kind of liked her once Clara managed to get past the grad student's endless positive energy.

Clara racked her brain but could not come up with the student's name. *Something like Angie? Angel?* The student worked under that Polish fellow, Dr. Werniewski, but she wasn't from Poland.

"Hi...uh...."

"Anju. Anju Denali. We met at orientation." The grad student's smile was as infectious as most of the known viruses in that place. She had a mouth full of perfect, pearly-white teeth, as healthy as the rest of her. Anju had a lot to be happy about, so Clara forgave the student for whistling sunshine out of her asshole.

"Anju.... Yes, that's right. From orientation." Clara sighed. "I'm sorry. There's just so many people here that—"

"Oh, I *completely* understand," Anju said, bouncing in place. She giggled a chirpy little noise that, like her, was bubblier than shaken soda. "I am...kind of forgettable. You, on the other hand, I could never forget. Your paper on the manipulation of the double-helix formation as an alternative to pharmacology was absolutely instrumental to my research project last spring. There is no ceiling, I believe, to what we can accomplish through gene splicing and genome manipulation. I would love to talk with you about it sometime – that is, if you have the time."

"There's no need to butter me up, kid. I'm nothing like the rest of these stiffs."

"They are a rather lackluster group, are they not? Sometimes I feel like they are afraid to fart for fear of discrediting their own mirages of perfection." Anju chuckled and looked away, covering her mouth as if shocked by what she herself had just said.

Clara couldn't help but chuckle along with her new acquaintance. She decided she liked Anju. "I'll tell you what. You bring me a bottle of decent wine – red wine, *French* wine, not that Californian piss – to that conversation, and we can, as that infuriating American botanist likes to say, 'shoot the shit' about whatever you'd like to talk about."

"Dr. St. Pierre—"

"Please, call me Clara."

Anju smiled warmly, the corners of her mouth threatening to spread beyond her face. Her cheeks curved grotesquely, as if she'd swallowed a boomerang. And still, she was hatefully adorable. "Clara, then." She held out her hand. "We have ourselves a deal."

Clara shook it. "Good. Now, I think you had better run along. If I'm not mistaken, that was Dr. Werniewski whom I just heard break wind, and I suppose he'll be needing a ratchet to seal up that tight ass of his."

She and Anju laughed. Doing so hurt, but it also felt good. Clara couldn't remember the last time she'd been privy to a joke, never mind having made one herself.

Anju had earned herself a spot in a very select group, currently three people at the research center to whom Clara had taken a liking. The second was the charming, if a little hokey, American botanist, Jordan Phillips, who never once treated her any differently on account of her disease than he treated others. When she looked into his smooth, dark eyes, she saw respect, dignity, humanity...not what she had come to expect from her scientific brethren: pity, revulsion, rejection, underhandedness, and worse, false sympathy.

The whole lot of them should take their phony compassion and stick it so far up their asses that no amount of cleansing could ever wash it free.

However, when the good botanist had ushered Clara into his greenhouse to show her some of the flowers his team had nurtured back from extinction from a handful of seeds found in the nest, Clara was impressed with both man and scientist. She couldn't help but admire and, in that moment, share his passion for his work and the many lives he had created.

Focus, Clara. She rolled on. *Best to keep him at a distance lest I give him a chance to prove myself wrong about him.* She sighed. *Men are such shallow and fickle beasts.*

She turned a corner and entered the hall leading to Bio-Lab 347. There, in front of her clean room, stood the third person Clara couldn't help but like. Montgomery Seymour Flint was an Australian national and military type who'd apparently transferred into the better-paying private-security arena. He was a hard-headed, heavy-fisted sort of man, the type typically employed by the Allied Security and Asset Protection Corporation, or ASAP, a privately owned international security company that served as governmental consultants to many of the United Nations members and, Clara suspected, many of those who weren't. ASAP must have had dirt on everyone. Not one country ever made a fuss over the apparent conflict of interest. Clara knew better than to ask questions.

ASAP represented everything Clara despised about the research center, yet she adored Monty all the same – real, sarcastic, and cynical, just like her. In crossing paths with the guard on a daily basis, his post usually being outside the clean room, she had come to know him. Instead of the massive machine guns and thousand-yard stares that plagued many of his comrades-in-arms, Monty, as he permitted her to call him, opted for a much smaller, less-obnoxious firearm, which he kept holstered at his hip. He never, ever, looked past her or down his nose at her but met her eyes and always offered a kindly, sincere smile.

As she pushed her chair toward him, he offered one of those smiles. "G'day, mate," he said, playing up his accent. "A frog, is it? Shall I throw another shrimp on the barbie and mutter something incoherent about dingoes and wallabies on walkabout while playing a three-note tune on my didgeridoo?"

"Why, Monty, do I detect a bit of sarcasm?" Clara smirked. "Is someone here stereotyping you because of your accent?"

"Oh, Christ, Doctor, it's driving me loony." He ran a hand over his finger-length hair, which matched the color of his dandy stubble. "Your friend there – Dr. Werniewski – has a few kangaroos loose in the top paddock!"

Clara looked up at him, eyes squinting. Her left eyebrow shot up. "Top paddock?"

Monty let out a guffaw that sounded a little like a horse neighing. "There I go, proving Figjam right. Dr. W. likes to go all Steve Irwin/ Paul Hogan on me every time he stops by. I swear, if he sings one more Wiggles song, I may have to wiggle his head up his arse...begging your pardon, Doctor."

"No need. He's an associate, not a friend, and believe me, I know exactly how he can be. 'Figjam'?"

Monty snickered. "Uh, yeah, that one's a tough one to explain, maybe. An Australian expression. Anyway, that bloke ain't the only one. You Yanks are all bat-shit crazy. I may have to go Crocodile Dundee on some of your friends here, is all I'm saying."

"I'm not sure if I was born when that movie came out. Anyway, as long as you don't go all *Wolf Creek*, we'll get along just fine."

"Surprise, surprise! The nerd here's a fan of *that* kind of film. You Yanks never cease to amaze me." He rubbed his chin and gave Clara a hard stare before breaking into laughter. "I loved that flick. Classic horror. Now there's an Australian hero I can stand behind."

"Why are you surprised? Is it because I'm a woman or a stuck-up scientist that I can't like horror films? Now who's stereotyping? And stop lumping me in with the Yanks. I know you know I'm French."

Monty shrugged. "North America, Europe.... You're all Yanks to me."

"By that logic – given the circumstances of your country's settlement and unless you're Aboriginal – I'd say you're about as much Yank as I am."

"You wound me, Doctor. Hurtful words you say." Monty pantomimed tears. "So hurtful."

Clara pinched his arm, smirking and almost outright smiling for the second time in one morning. She wondered if one of the viruses had infected her with the smile bug. She hated smiling. It hurt her face worse than frowning did.

She cleared her throat, resurrecting the wall she kept between herself and others of her species. "So, any big plans for the weekend?"

"Weekend? I don't get weekends off any more than you do. Besides, there ain't nothing to do out there but freeze your nether parts off...or drink 'til they're warm again. But I do have a vacation coming up. Me and me mates...ahem, *my mates and I* are having a scrimmage against the blokes who won our ASAP Australian branch league cup last year. It'll start off relatively civil but likely deteriorate into a few black eyes, chipped teeth, and broken noses, I suspect. Good ol' fashioned rugby, like it's meant to be played."

"Sounds...interesting. I'm sure it will be good to get away, especially someplace warm." Clara studied her shoes. She wondered where she would go if she ever took a true vacation. *If I ever had someone to go with.*

"Where I'm from, it's beautiful, Doctor. A small town about sixty kilometers north of Sydney. You ever want to see it, you've got a free place to stay."

Clara considered a fake smile, but that time, she couldn't will it to materialize. "Thanks."

"What about you, Doctor? You plan on sticking around here all weekend, unlocking Pandora's Box?"

"Excuse me?" She huffed. *As if I don't get enough of that crap outside—*

"Ah, I don't mean anything by it. Just something one of the protesters blocking the private road had on his sign. 'Open Pandora's

Box. Release God's Vengeance' or something to that effect. Some freak with a black cross painted on his forehead. I wouldn't have paid him any attention but for the fact he was standing in the middle of the road, so I couldn't get by. Nearly had to run him down to get here." Monty shook his head. "There's more and more of those freaks out there every day, lining the highway and camping closer and closer to this facility. And for what? To freeze their asses off?"

"They just have strong opinions on what we're doing here."

"Yeah, well, opinions are like shit."

"Don't you mean, 'Opinions are like assholes'?"

"No, 'shit'. They run too freely from careless openings."

"That's...not a saying."

"No?" Monty chuckled. "You sure?" He sighed. "Anyway, Hitler had opinions. That guy in *Wolf Creek* had opinions. Some of these assholes with their high-and-mighty opinions might be dangerous."

"Then I guess it's a good thing we're in here and we've got you to protect us." She patted his arm but didn't let her hand linger there. Though Monty was a good guy, she wasn't trying to give him any wrong signals. *Not that he'd answer them if I did.*

Monty clenched his jaw, and for a moment, Clara thought she might have offended him. *Am I that revolting?* She shrank into her chair.

But Monty wasn't looking at her. His lips pursed as his gaze drifted away into nothingness. Ridges formed on his forehead.

He looks...worried? A mischievous smirk twitched Clara's lip at its corner as a realization hit her. *This ought to be good.* "Don't tell me that a big, strong macho man such as yourself is afraid of a few protesters."

Monty's glazed-over eyes filled with awareness. "Hmm?" He met her stare and clenched his jaw. "Nah. That guy's a freak. His long, gnarly hair looked like it hadn't been washed in weeks, and his clothes? Sheesh! They looked like he'd rolled around with a hog in its pen. Probably did, the freak. I could smell his stink just by looking at him." He let out a breath. "Still...the way he looked at me when I blared my horn and told him to get the fuck out of my way…. It gave me the willies."

She sneered and rolled her eyes but then gawped when she realized Monty wasn't chuckling. "You're serious?"

Monty scowled, and his face reddened a little. "You didn't see his eyes. He had this intense stare, the kind that seems to see right through you. He didn't move or say a word, like we were in some twisted game of chicken. And I had a mind to run him down, I tell you. I don't think the sorry whacker would have cared one way or the other. In the end, I backed up and went around him." Monty shuddered and pointed at his head. "He wasn't right up here, that one. I could feel his eyes crawling like sand fleas on my skin as I passed."

Clara tried to stifle her incredulous chortle, but it came out before she could. "I'm...I'm sorry," she said between snorts. "Come now, Monty. Don't you think you're being a bit melodramatic?"

"If you saw this guy, you probably wouldn't say that."

"I think you've been watching too many horror films."

"Whatever."

Clara tsked. "It's this place, Monty. It's cold and desolate, and out there are hordes of people who hate us for reasons I don't think they even understand. The guy you're talking about is probably some vagrant or religious fanatic or both, and probably dangerous. I know I'd keep my distance. But discoveries like this always bring out the lunatics. A tough Aussie like you can't really be afraid of a man armed with markers and poster boards?"

"More like I'm afraid he's right," Monty muttered.

Clara caught it. "What's that, now?"

"Nothing, just...be careful if you leave the base."

"You don't agree with what we're doing here?" Clara pushed.

"My apologies, Doctor. I spoke out of turn."

"Nonsense." Clara leaned in close. "Whatever you say to me stays between us. And you never have to hold back with me or treat me with kid gloves."

Monty let out a breath and relaxed, but only a little. His fingers wagged back and forth at his sides. "It's just that.... Don't you ever wonder if you're messing with something beyond your control or even your comprehension? Christ! The things in that fridge are called giant viruses, a.k.a. pandoraviruses. Personally, I think regular-sized viruses are bad enough."

"The size of the virus doesn't necessarily correlate with its—"

Monty threw his hands up. "I know, I know. But these things.... You know they're dangerous. Tampering with them is just like jiggling the latch on Pandora's Box."

"You sound like those protesters outside, and you were just poking fun at one of them?"

"I don't like them. I know their kind. They take things too far. That doesn't mean I disagree with their message. But shit, I have bills to pay, the same as everyone else."

"We use every precaution, every safety measure imaginable."

"Yes, but—"

"Without risk, we will not advance. Monty, these viruses may be the answer to any number of health conditions. They may be the answer to disease, cancer, death." She couldn't keep her passion and excitement from flowing into her words. "They may hold the keys to the secrets of life itself."

Monty ran a hand down his face and scratched the stubble on his chin. "If God wanted us to know those secrets, He wouldn't have guarded them with something so deadly."

Clara considered that. Science always pushed for knowledge and understanding even in the face of undeniable danger. She could never convince a layman that the potential fruit borne from her research more than justified the risk, even the risk of an epidemic.

Maybe an epidemic is what humankind needs. Hit the reset button on ol' planet Earth.

She shrugged off the thought and offered Monty a nod. "Relax, big guy. If I screw up in there, you'll be the first to know."

Monty chuckled. "Yeah, that's because after you, I'll be the first infected."

CHAPTER THREE

Clara stands at the edge of the pool. Her quads flex as she takes position, the muscles full of strength. Her calves stretch as she rises onto her toes. The feeling is familiar. She remembers her defined swimmer's legs. But these legs are fake, memories of times past. They aren't her legs anymore.

Are they? *She looks down at the water and sees her reflection smiling back. Clara isn't smiling. At least, she doesn't think she's smiling. The reflection is her but not her. It is a mirror's surface of a younger girl, strong, vibrant, and...* happy.

Something she has not been for so long. Too long.

Competitors take their positions beside her. Their faces are wrong, those of her colleagues, not those of the athletes she once knew. To her left stands Anju, wearing a two-piece bathing suit and nothing else under her white lab coat. She offers a nod and a kindly smile.

On Clara's right, Jordan rubs his palms together. He is laughing. "You had better be ready," he says, flashing that uneasy, I-don't-know-I'm-handsome grin of his. His chocolate-sweet eyes are gleaming beneath swim goggles instead of his usual wire-rimmed glasses. He is shirtless, his body toned but rugged – a man's body, muscular and hairy, not like all those boys she swam against and beat.

She bites into her lip, having never seen him shirtless before. She follows a trail of hair down to his black Speedo then blushes as she catches his eyes following hers. His laugh fills with an almost wicked delight.

"I'm going to beat you this time," he says.

"Beat me?" she asks. Her voice echoes. Jordan points to the opposite side of the pool, where a tall, slender woman in her fifties stands with a starter pistol raised high.

Clara narrows her gaze. "Ms. Claverie?" The woman certainly looks like her private swim coach, whom she had trained under well before university, when she was still a little girl.

A ghost from her past.

The acrid smell of chlorine bombards her nostrils. Empty stands along the walls of the hall fill with the sounds of a hundred murmuring voices. Clara straightens her cap and pulls the goggles resting atop her head over her eyes. A slight draft raises goose bumps on her arms. The hairs of her neck stand up. She is suddenly aware that she is wearing nothing but a skintight black swimsuit, replacing the biohazard suit she'd been wearing only moments ago.

Wait. What is this? What's going on?

The pistol fires. Instinct takes over. Clara dives.

She cuts through the water like a dolphin. Beneath the surface, she kicks with the deftness and ability of a pro. The coolness of the water, the heat of muscles in action, the poise and sublime feeling of finding a passion and a calling, the stillness of her breath – sensations she'd missed so deeply – threaten to overwhelm her in their deluge.

She knows it's not real. She knows she has fallen asleep, has found a brief reprieve from the cruelty of the real world. But she will not let go of the mirage, not until some other portion of her brain makes her.

She is at the wall now, flipping, back-stroking back the way she came. Dreams like this should last forever.

"They can, Clara." A gentle voice, female, almost motherly – no, too motherly – echoes in her submerged ears.

"Mom?"

Clara stops racing and treads water in the middle of the pool. The sounds of splashing and exertion have vanished. She lifts her goggles, wipes her eyes, and scans the pool area. She is alone.

"Hello? Anybody here?"

She swims to the pool's edge, pulls herself out of the water, and walks to a nearby bench, where a towel has been laid out for her. She recognizes it immediately: the giant and ever-so-soft plush Mickey Mouse towel her parents bought for her when they took her to Disney World what seems like an eternity ago.

One of her fondest memories, when she was someone else. She frowns. A Disney princess, living a fairy tale.

Clara was only eight when they took the trip, but she kept that towel well into her adult life, until that day three years ago when she buried it alongside her mother.

"You can walk, Clarabelle," a voice, definitely her mother's, says. Only her parents had ever called her Clarabelle. "You don't have to go through life with so much pain."

Clara wraps herself in the towel. She brings one corner up to her nose and inhales deeply, closing her eyes and letting the aromatic smell of her mother's laundry detergent spawn fond memories. She shivers, and her teeth chatter. Her legs are still dripping wet, but she doesn't bother to wipe them, trying to hold on to the moment, unwilling to move for fear of stirring herself from the dream.

"*This can be real, Clara.*"

She hugs the towel close, balling the cloth in her hands. She tries to call out to her mother, but the words catch in her throat. What do I say? What does one say to the dead? *She swallows hard.*

"*I'm sorry,*" *she mutters, not knowing why she says it.*

Her relationship with her mother had always been good, her disease causing no more strain there than it did with her other family and friends. Clara was the one who stopped taking calls, and maybe that is part of why she is sorry. Her mother had been there for Clara until she could be there no longer. Her family had been perfect until she fell into self-pity and her mother died, breaking the tenuous grip her father had on his sanity. Clara wonders if her mom liked the person her daughter had become.

As if reading her mind, her mother says, "I've always been proud of you. I've always loved you."

"*Mom?*" *Clara squeezes the towel more tightly as she looks around for the source of her mother's voice.* "*Where are you, Mom? Are you...real?*"

"*I'm down here, Clarabelle. Don't be afraid. I want to help you. I want to heal you. And I can, Clarabelle. I truly can. I can take away all of your pain.*"

With unsure steps, her knees trembling and legs weakening with each one, Clara creeps to the water's edge. She gasps but is not afraid when she sees her mother standing on the pool bottom, smiling and waving up at her from the depths, looking every bit as lovely as she did in life.

Her mother speaks, but no air bubbles come out of her mouth. "*Let me take your pain away, dear.*" *She beckons her daughter closer.* "*Let me take it all away.*"

"*Mom?*" *Clara begins to sob.* "*It hurts so much, Mom. Every day, living in this...this...useless body, not good for a damn thing. And I'm so alone. You should have lived. I should have gotten the tumor and died. You were always there for me, and when you needed me most, I could do nothing for you. God, I wish I was dead.*"

"*Don't say that, dear. I love you. Your father loves you.*" *Her mother approaches.* "*Come closer, Clarabelle. I can take your sorrows from you. I can make you happy again. Don't you want to be happy again?*"

Clara straightens, tries to be strong, but crumples into her towel. "I don't know how."

Her mother raises her arms toward Clara, and her fingers nearly reach the surface, just a sliver shy of breaching it. "All you have to do is take my hand, and everything will be fine again. Everything will be as it should be."

"I'm scared, Mom. I'm scared to die, but I'm even more scared to live."

"I know, Clarabelle. I know. I'll make everything okay, dear. Just take my hand."

Clara kneels by the pool. Her warm tears form concentric circles as they drop into the water. Slowly, she reaches toward her mother's hand. Only a foot separates her from her mother and the freedom from pain that she offers. Clara leans forward, moving closer.

Her mother doesn't move. She is grinning wildly now, her eyes alive with energy, the look of a fanatic.

Clara's mouth goes dry, and she starts to sweat, but she has gone too far. Over the edge. She can't pull back. She moves closer still.

Closer. Only an inch or two separate her from her mother. If she dares to cross the distance, she will be reunited with someone she thought she could never have back.

A loud rumble courses through the pool area. Clara is shoved backward by an unseen force. She scrambles to her feet as the walls around her crumble. The ceiling begins to collapse. Even the floor opens into great fissures that run through the pool like cracks through a mirror, canyons into infinite blackness.

As the false existence falls away around her, Clara hears her mother howl, not in fright or anguish, but in pure, unadulterated rage. In one split-second glimpse, Clara no longer sees the happy, healthy mother of Clara's swim-meet days wallowing in the deep. Instead, her mother's lips have curled back, and her frame has withered. Clara sees her mother as she had last seen her; the woman she watched die glowers up from the deep through cataract-filled eyes.

*　　*　　*

Clara screamed. A blank, white world engulfed her, the details of which quickly came into focus. She was standing on legs she couldn't feel, her hand hovering over a petri dish partially filled with an odd, purplish growth medium. She tottered a moment then fell backward, lucky that her wheelchair was there to catch her fall.

The clean room? When did I enter the clean room? Her confusion was only slightly allayed by the familiarity of her surroundings. She scanned the gleaming metal lab equipment, machines with sharp angles and hard corners, arranged precisely in a pristine, whitewashed room with immaculate tabletops and a spotless floor. Not a mote of dust, no speck of lint or particle of dirt, marred the confines of the room. The pungent odor of bleach filled the air. Nothing was out of place except the petri dish and pipette on the table in front of her.

And her glove.

She stared at her hand, and her mouth dropped open. Her glove was gone. She didn't remember taking it off. Certainly, she had no reason to. *Why would I take off my glove? And what caused the building to shake? And...was I...standing?*

She shook her head, trying to dispel the many questions, to focus on the present. Her potential exposure to whatever lay in that petri dish was her first priority. Her scientific mind took a backseat to panicked thoughts of disease and outbreak. *I know better. Why would I do this? What sort of madness could have compelled me to take off my....* "*Merde!*" she shouted, staring down at the dish with fire behind her eyes. Her entire body trembled. *Why on earth was I putting my hand into the dish? That was what I was doing, wasn't it? None of it makes any sense.*

She didn't even know where the petri dish had come from, never mind what was in it. Surely, she had been in a daydream. She wondered if people in wheelchairs sleep-rolled in dreams. Even if they did, she never had before.

And sleepwalk? On the rare occasions Clara could stand at all, she'd done so only with considerable assistance. She barely remembered entering the clean room. In her groggy state, hours seemed to have passed. She couldn't have punched in the passcode, opened the refrigerator, pulled out a culture, set up shop, and....

"Oh God, the sample!"

Clara rolled her chair into the table. Just a handful of particles of the wrong virus could cause an epidemic, and she'd tried to dip her fingers into one. The bottle and dropper next to the petri dish, clearly labeled '*Mollivirus sibericum*', represented an unknown quantity, not something to handle frivolously.

And here I am with my goddamn glove off! What the hell was I doing?

What was I thinking?

She stared at the petri dish, remembering vague details of her dream. The solution inside, a growth medium consisting mostly of water and amoebas, rocked gently.

"Mom?" Clara shook her head, feeling stupid. She wondered what had made her think of her mother just then, as if the dead woman's ghost had been standing beside her, whispering incantations in her ear. "Get it together, Clara."

One thing was certain: she had been working with a sample of a giant virus with her hand uncovered. She had to assume the worst-case scenario, that she had been exposed to the virus. The research into Molli was still in its very early stages. She had no evidence to suggest the sample was in any way dangerous to herself or others, but she had no evidence to suggest that it wasn't either. However, her team had ruled out any danger of airborne pathogens at the outset of testing. As long as she and the sample stayed in that room, the rest of the facility would be just fine. She'd have Monty alert Dr. Werniewski and—

"Everyone, please remain calm and return to your rooms in an orderly fashion," a man's voice, thick with a Russian accent and the language's usual solemnity, sounded over a loudspeaker in the hallway outside. An alarm blared. "The research center will be going into lockdown. No one will be permitted to leave or enter the center until we have analyzed the nature of the threat. All external communication devices will be offline."

Clara wondered if her screwup had led to the lockdown until she remembered the earthquake. *An explosion? Fantastic. "Don't panic, everyone. We're only under attack." Brilliant, ASAP, just brilliant.* She rolled her eyes. "And things go from bad to worse."

She figured she would have to rely on Monty to protect her and the samples from any external threats. She had enough problems of her own to deal with. *Yeah, like whether or not you have an unknown, untested virus all over you.* She gathered up her discarded glove, the petri dish, and the dropper and carried them on a tray across her lap to the biohazardous waste-disposal unit, where she dumped in everything, tray and all. Then she rolled herself into the sterilization chamber and activated the system. She breathed in the gas released, hoping the chemicals would cleanse her mind as well as her body.

"Initiating scan for biological contamination," the post-sterilization scanner said.

Clara closed her eyes and relaxed in her chair as the computer inspected her every inch. A series of lenses took thousands of successive photographs, starting with her epidermis, then x-raying and delving deeper and deeper, level by level, until it had scanned her entire body in intervals, the portions spread out like rings of a severed tree trunk.

"Scan completed," the computer announced. "Air quality normal. Biometrics negative for foreign agents. No contaminants detected in room or personnel."

Clara breathed a sigh of relief. With the process complete, she saw Monty peering into the chamber through the small window in its hallway door.

He said into a speaker, "Sorry, Doctor. I can't rely on the scanner and let you out just yet. You know, incubation periods, faulty equipment... you know, just in case the scan is wrong. For the sake of the facility, you're under quarantine, but only until we can get another from your team to come and clear you."

Clara nodded. She hit a button on the intercom by the door. "I expected as much. Can you at least tell me what's going on out there?"

Monty frowned. "I wish I knew, Doctor."

CHAPTER FOUR

He whistled a tune from the opera *Rigoletto*, the name of which he'd long forgotten, as he strolled toward the guard booth. The weight of his backpack caused its straps to dig grooves into his shoulders even through his filth-stained gray vest and black undershirt, but the pain was of little consequence. In the past, he'd shouldered much heavier burdens for much longer distances. Though he took nothing for granted, he thought his present burden would be a weight easily borne.

The guard stationed there, a man of average build in his early twenties, his eyes full of inexperience and doubt, came out of the booth and approached, his hand squeezing the grip of his assault rifle tightly.

The man tossed back his oily black hair, exposing the black cross he'd painted in the middle of his forehead so that the guard might get a good look at it. Also for the guard's benefit, the man wiped his hands on his tattered black pants, which had never been washed, at least not for as long as he'd possessed them. The chilly air made his eyes water as he studied the guard through predatory vision, assessing the ticket puncher's every movement and body language. *At least he hasn't raised his weapon. Not so inexperienced that he's trigger happy.*

"Sir," the guard said, his voice shaking, though he did not otherwise seem afraid.

Cold, probably, the man assumed. Sure, the guard couldn't know who he was dealing with, but he did have the only weapon visible, so the man forgave him his tall stance.

"May I see your badge, please?" the guard asked.

A badge? Why didn't I just get one of those? It would have made this so much easier. He smiled. *But so boring.*

The man with the backpack continued to whistle. He liked whistling, and the song was finally getting to his favorite part. He also kept walking.

"Sir, this is a government-sponsored private facility. Only employees may enter. If you do not have an employee badge, I am going to have to ask you to vacate the premises immediately." The guard raised his gun and held it across his chest.

The man whistled louder. He would not lose his spot in the song and have to start over on account of a blabbering ASAP employee who had no ear for fine music. His whistle crescendoed, and he threw his arms up and stared into the gray, empty sky. "*Bonjour, Rigoletto*," he sang – and well, he thought, though not his finest moment. He smirked with the knowledge that he had chosen to sing the French version of Verdi's opera though, like Verdi, he was from a country famous for its many operas in his primary language.

The guard did not seem amused. He raised his firearm.

"*Ils sont tous de mèche*," muttered the man with the black cross on his forehead. He kept his arms raised, but he lowered his eyes to meet the guard's harried stare. A new song came to mind, one he found laughably fitting. He whistled the tune from an old Western released well before his time, maybe before his father's time, the one with the funny name: *The Good, the Bad, and the Ugly.*

The guard stiffened. "Look, mister, I don't know who you are or what your game is, but I'm not playing it. Last chance to get the hell out of here before I take you in."

The man sighed. *No taste for classic cinema either, I suppose. Ah, Hollywood these days. It's all about bang bang, poke poke, screw screw, boom. Repeat.*

"I do like the boom, though."

"Huh?" The guard's brow furrowed. A bead of sweat ran down his temple. "State your business or leave. If you take one step closer—"

The man took one step closer.

The guard waggled his gun. "That's it. Get down on the ground and…. Wait. First, slide off that backpack. Slowly."

The man complied. He shrugged then relaxed his left shoulder, shimmying the strap off. His hair fell over his eyes, but between the strands, he watched the guard closely. With tortoise speed, the man raised his arm out of the loop formed by the strap and bag. The pack swung loose but remained caught over his right shoulder.

He dropped that shoulder. Gravity and the weight of the backpack sent it careening down his arm. Right before it hit the ground, he grabbed its strap and pendulum-swung the backpack at the guard's face. The pack's inertia shifted violently toward its intended target and collided with his chin. The man let his body follow his arm's movement, pirouetting out of the way of any wild shots the guard might get off.

The gun fired only once, and the bullet hit dirt a few feet away.

Before the guard could recover from the backpack's blow, the man threw a left cross that hit him square in the temple. It drove him to a knee, but he held on to his assault rifle. He was trying to raise it when the man rammed his kneecap into the guard's downturned forehead.

The guard rolled onto his back and lay motionless. His attacker crouched beside him and pressed two fingers into the guard's carotid artery. A strong pulse tingled his fingertips. He picked up his backpack and continued into the parking garage, whistling as he went.

When he reached the bottom floor's center, he picked a row of cars at random. The row he selected began with a Fiat, and for some reason, that felt almost sacrilegious. So he opted for the next row over. That line of vehicles began with a BMW.

He plopped his bag down against the BMW's tire and crouched to open the flap he'd marked with a black cross matching the one on his forehead. He reached in and pulled out one off-white rectangular brick, then another and another, stacking them beside himself as a mason might, ten in total. Carefully measured wire, exactly the distance from the center of one parking spot to that of the one adjacent to it, connected each brick.

He began humming the tune to *NCIS: Hawaii*, an American television show that had played in rerun syndication hell for all eternity in his Campania home outside Naples. With the calm meticulousness of a surveyor taking boundary measurements, he slid the last bar in the chain under the BMW and out the other side. Then he walked around the car and repeated the process under the Lada Kalina parked beside the Bimmer.

He did this seven more times before sliding the brick halfway beneath the final vehicle in the row that his plastic explosives could accommodate. He trotted back to the BMW and gave one last look over the parking garage. It was as empty of people as it had been when he walked in. If security was watching him on its cameras, it had yet to send in the troops.

He listened, trying to detect anything his eyes might have missed. The only sounds he heard were the crunching of gravel under his worn black boots and his interspersed whistling. He had moved on to a popular Italian game-show theme.

He pulled a fuse box from his pack and connected its long wire to the brick under the BMW. He smiled, unable to resist feeling a tad excited. Blowing stuff up was always his favorite part of the job. In fact, it made him want to sing.

So opera it was. "*Anges pure, anges radieux, portez mon âme au sein des cieux!*"

Heh, again with the French. As he ducked behind a fancy-looking SUV, probably belonging to one of those highly paid, think-they-know-everything scientist assholes inside the complex, he stifled a squeal of delight and pressed a button.

Then came the boom.

A powerful blast blew out the SUV's windows and those of many of the vehicles around him. Shards of fiberglass and plastic sprinkled his hair and vest. He stood to marvel at his destruction. Black smoke spread across the garage like heavy fog, rolling over vehicles as if it were a living creature, the kind seen only in horror movies and rare days at Loch Ness. He covered his nose and mouth with his sleeve. The smoke billowed out and up, rising quickly, pushed free from the air upon which small fires below needed to feed, greedy asthmatic flames sucking blissfully at their inhalers.

The man's eyes blurred in the scratching, caustic smoke. Something crashed down beside him that looked like a fender, except it was all twisted and melting and sizzling with heat. Car alarms blared in a cacophony that made his singing sound as melodic as the fattest of The Three Tenors. Still, he stood his ground, beaming as brightly as the fire. Many times, he'd questioned whether he should transition to a more traditional line of work. That moment, however, was not one of those times.

He reached into a pocket and pulled out a Swiss Army knife. He drew the blade and used it to carve '*Sic Semper Tyrannis*' into the SUV's door. *This should throw them for a loop.*

He smirked. The words meant nothing to him. Not a thing. All he cared about was opera, ridding his country of American syndicated television, and blowing stuff up. *And getting the job done.* No matter what the job was, he always got it done.

Still, a little Latin will give those ASAP dumbasses fodder for their idiotic theories if they ever show up. He knew the ideas the phrase might inspire. He had a role to play, and he was going to give them a show. Stealth wasn't an option with the security measures set against him. Misdirection was always an option, as long as it got him inside. And damn, did he love a good conspiracy theory, something almost as bizarre as the truth.

Maybe I should just tell the truth. They won't believe me anyway.

Tires screeched in the distance. *And here they come.* A Hummer and two Jeeps pulled up and jolted to a stop at the front of the carnage. Men with gas masks poured out of each vehicle and began to canvas the area with assault rifles raised. He knew them instantly since they wore the trappings – blue blazers over white button-downs, ball caps, and navy slacks – of ASAP security personnel.

"Mercenaries for hire." The man scoffed. "I should know." He made no attempt to run or hide. "The secrets they must be keeping...."

He said a quick prayer and put his hands on his head just as one of the mercs spotted him. The armed guard pointed his weapon at the man and called over his friends.

"Don't move," the ASAP mercenary said.

But the man with the black cross on his head did move. He raised his arms to the heavens and shouted, "I am Dante, and this is my inferno!"

A moment later, something collided with the back of his skull. His legs gave out. He was falling, his mind going blank as he plummeted into his abyss.

CHAPTER FIVE

"Come on, Monty," Clara begged. "It's me. What happened?"

Monty grumbled but relented without much of a fight. "Reports coming in are saying some whacker blew up the parking garage."

Clara gasped. "Oh my God! Was anyone hurt?"

"Nah, just a lot of property damage."

Clara released a breath. "I guess you were right about the protesters. It had to be one of them, right?"

"Don't know for sure. I'd like to hurt the guy who did it, though. I bet it was the same freak who blocked my car this morning. I knew he was trouble."

"You can't possibly know that."

"You bet I could. The guys are saying he's got a black cross on his forehead. Unless there's more than one of him, or he's in some goddamn cult, it's the same jerkoff." He shrugged and took a deep breath. "Anyway, we've got him, and it doesn't look like anyone was hurt. A lot of people will be speaking with their insurance companies shortly, but the important thing is that sicko didn't injure or kill anyone."

"What will ASAP do with him? Turn him over to the authorities?"

"I don't know, and I don't want to. Some questions are better left unanswered. But in the meantime, we're going into lockdown in case the jerkoff has friends. Just a precaution…like your quarantine." Monty faked a smile an infant could have seen through. "I guess you could say that right now, you're confined to a cell in a giant prison we're all stuck in. I hope you understand—"

"Of course, Monty." Clara winced and looked away, hoping Monty would take her words of understanding at face value. She did understand, and she certainly couldn't fault him for her screw-up. Warmth spread through her face, and she wondered just how red her cheeks had become. *How could I have been so stupid? So goddamn clumsy? Merde! Why do I have to be so goddamn weak and pathetic?*

She closed her eyes and took a breath. "Well," she muttered as she backed away from the chamber, "if I am infected and it's going to kill me, I might as well learn how."

As off-putting as the idea was, Clara just shrugged and sighed. She felt fine – as fine as someone suffering from severe MS could feel, anyway. She was fairly certain she hadn't touched the sample. Even if she had, the sterilization chamber probably would have killed anything on her. Even if it didn't, Molli was probably just another virus with no practical effects, beneficial or ill. And if it did end up being the engine of her demise, death really didn't seem all that bad.

"Everything broken can be fixed," her mother had always said. And for every disease, a cure awaited discovery. Someone smart enough just had to find it or figure out a way to create it.

Someone smarter than me. Clara frowned as she thought back to her experiments.

In its defrosted form, Molli wasn't exactly dormant, but air-quality-control readings and initial testing and observation had ruled out the threat of airborne transmission. If Molli samples contained bacteria that were communicable in other ways – perhaps a contact disease like anthrax, for example – researchers would be better off learning that sooner rather than later. But they were light-years away from injecting it into live subjects, with a mountain of bureaucratic bullshit and three other viruses standing in line in front of Molli, in that regard.

The sample had only been isolated for a few days. Clara was finally getting a chance to study it under something with higher resolution than a light microscope. And since she had time to kill....

She donned a new pair of gloves, a face mask, and eyewear. She opened the refrigerator and took out a bacteria culture and another petri dish containing amoebas used for viral testing. The amoebas were to act like worms on hooks, trapped bait with nothing to do but wait for the big bad virus to come take a bite. The first three viruses had consumed the amoebas at varying intervals and in varying concentrations – nothing surprising or noteworthy. Clara expected much of the same from Molli in the baseline tests.

She reached for a syringe then changed her mind. She opted instead for a larger sample of the virus, contained in a long, flat-bottomed test tube. A rubber plug around its lip fixed an eyedropper to its repository.

The test tube was empty. The long, narrow cylinder of the eyedropper was not.

Giant viruses had earned their nomenclature by virtue of the fact that they could be seen under light microscopes. Clara opted for such a microscope for her first experiment of the day with Molli, hoping to catch any reaction that might occur inside the dish without limiting herself to an area of minute circumference. She monitored the changes in the overall concentration of the petri dish before getting down to the microbiological impacts.

She set a Dictaphone on the table and clicked Record. "Amoeba Test A001, a single drop of Molli from a standard, three-milliliter Pasteur pipette." She slid the entire petri dish underneath the microscope's lens. The lab had been equipped with several microscopes that were adjustable so that their traditional slide table could be removed and lenses lowered to look directly into larger samples. The light source came from special plates built into the laboratory table itself, upon which the microscope and sample were placed.

Having set up the petri dish this way, Clara considered dropping a dash of stain into the clear solution but decided against it. She peered through the scope, made sure everything was aligned to her liking, and removed the eyedropper carrying the Molli sample from its perch. She squeezed the dropper's bulb as she held it over the dish. A single drop of Molli clung like a tear to the end of the dropper then plummeted into the solution.

Not expecting a whole lot, Clara looked away for only a second or two as she returned the dropper to its test-tube stand. When her gaze returned to the dish, she jumped and let out a tiny yelp. The solution appeared to be boiling. It reminded Clara of piranha devouring a cow during a feeding frenzy she'd come across on the Discovery Channel – not quite Shark Week, but still pretty cool, except maybe for the cow.

She didn't dare touch the dish beneath the scope for fear of spilling it. Instead, she stared in wonder as the solution took on a purple hue and released an odor that resembled ethanol but with hints of pine sap.

Clara rubbed her chin. "Pray tell, my dear Molli. What on earth was that all about?" She stared at the dish until her eyes blurred, distracted by the many thoughts racing through her head. "I know one way to find out. But first…." She grabbed the Dictaphone. "Initial results of Test

A001. After sample injected, solution immediately disrupted. Appeared to be boiling. Solution took on a purplish color in less than five seconds. Will study the solution under higher magnification for further analysis."

She clapped and hummed, showing a giddiness that, since her infliction, she felt only when making new discoveries or scientific advancements. Carefully pushing aside the light microscope, she opted for an instrument with considerably more power. She rotated the lenses of the electron microscope until her desired magnification clicked into place. She rolled over to the refrigerator and, in her excitement, grabbed the mother lode of petri dishes, filled with so many amoebas that it looked as if a jellyfish had exploded into countless mini versions of itself, *sans* tentacles. The dish remained steady and level as she transported it to the laboratory station, safely resting on a small tray built into her wheelchair's arm, like those on some airlines.

Clara took a deep breath to steady her hands, which were shaking from a combination of nervousness and excitement. Her heart beat a little faster as she slid the dish onto the table. Despite her eagerness, she didn't spill a drop in the transfer or in positioning her sample beneath the scope.

"Amoeba Test A002," Clara said into the Dictaphone. "Repeat of immediately preceding test. Single drop of Molli from a standard, three-milliliter Pasteur pipette. Higher amoeba concentration. Magnification: transmission electron scope, one hundred thousand X."

Clara assumed the bigger dish and higher concentration of amoebas would slow the reaction time of whatever had happened in the first petri dish. And she couldn't be sure what had happened, anyway. She had several guesses but refrained from speculating until she conducted further experimentation.

"All right, Molli." Clara grabbed the dropper and hovered the end of its tube over the petri dish.

Laboratory microbiology had advanced to the ease of point and click, the microscope being hooked up to viewing screens, scanning devices, and image replicators, as well as computers capable of composite analysis. Clara just needed to know where to aim her scope. She lined up its lens as best she could on the area she wanted to magnify, but under that magnification, the dropper cast a giant shadow over the dish. Under normal research practices, her advanced magnification at such an early stage would have been like trying to find the clichéd needle in the haystack. But given the turbulence she had witnessed in the first petri dish, she figured her haystack was equal parts needles and hay.

"Let's see what you got." With a gentle squeeze of the dropper's rubber bulb, Clara released a single drop of Molli into the mixture. Without removing her eye from the scope, she placed the eyedropper in an empty beaker nearby and prepared to watch and wait.

But she didn't have to wait at all.

The solution instantly roiled like an angry sea. At first, Clara saw nothing except liquid in motion and amoeba moving away, seemingly fleeing as if they were an intelligent species, from the turbulent disruption. Clara chuckled. *They can't be fleeing. Amoebas wouldn't know enough to retreat. They have no instinctive fight-or-flight reactions.* However, watching them move in the same direction regardless of which way the solution rocked made her wonder otherwise.

She dismissed the thought as ridiculous. Then she saw Molli. "There you are, *ma cherie.*" Clara blinked, clearing the blur from her eyes. She pinpointed the organism and upped the scope's magnification, too enthralled to record her steps. "Are you...growing?"

Molli certainly appeared to be, and not just a little. The virus was expanding like a balloon pumped full of helium. Clara stared in awe. She could make out its details with uncanny precision. Her heart thumped, sending pressure pains through her chest.

This is no virus. Of that, Clara was fairly certain, but what to call the life-form in her dish eluded her. "I've never seen anything like this."

Molli's outer boundary, if she could call it that, was constantly changing. It had a sharpened, multi-pointed sickle cell-like shape that was fleeting, the 'virus' becoming amorphous one second then whole again the next, with an entirely new frame. Stalagmites shot out from a bulbous central mass and retracted, only to reappear elsewhere on the single-celled organism's body.

And it had a great many genes, not unlike the bacteria that sat nearby, but Molli seemed prokaryotic, its genes swimming around inside the organism willy-nilly without a central nucleus base. She wondered how the allegedly brightest minds in all of science could have misclassified something so unique, so beautiful, so incorrectly.

"What are you, Molli?" Clara couldn't take her eyes off her test subject. She couldn't possibly fathom what implications the so-called virus would have for science. All she knew was that she was looking at something mysterious and wonderful.

As the cell grew, it formed a figure eight. Then it split into two spheres.

"Binary fission," Clara murmured, working on the assumption that the organism was a prokaryote.

Cell division was happening everywhere under her scope at a fantastic rate. Two were four then eight then sixteen in fractions of a second. Their purplish color tinted the solution.

But the strangest thing Clara noticed concerned their movement: instead of bouncing around in random chaos, every one of the Molli cells beneath her scrutiny moved in the same direction – toward the amoebas – with tiny flagella wagging like happy dog tails, propelling them through the medium.

Then came the slaughter.

"Amazing!" Clara watched like a gambler at a dogfight as Molli overtook the amoebas and consumed them one by one, or so she first thought. However, she wasn't witnessing consumption at all. "It's not destroying them. It's *absorbing* them." She didn't know what to make of it. "Or maybe it's the other way around?"

Molli penetrated each amoeba it overcame and took up residence inside its new....

"Host? Is Molli some sort of parasite?" Clara looked away for a moment, lost in thought. She stared absently into the space in front of her. "No, that isn't quite right." The amoeba retained its essential shape. In fact, it seemed to have grown, appearing healthier, save for its color. The effects of Molli on the original organisms were magnificent, all visible processes seeming to function at higher levels.

She grabbed her Dictaphone and cleared her throat, then straightened and took several long breaths before she was calm enough to push the button and record. "Initial results of Test A002. Under no magnification, results of Test A001 appeared to have been replicated. Solution instantly disrupted, with appearance of boiling and purplish hue."

Clara paused and took another breath. "The organism appears to have been misclassified as a virus. Closer to a bacterium, prokaryotic. Rapidly reproducing. Likely parasitic. The organism has invaded the amoebas, but thus far, no deleterious effects detected. Possibly ameliorative. Amoebas are larger and maintain integrity. At best guess at this early stage, the organism appears to be equivalent to a steroid for cell growth and development."

And how impressive she is! Clara rewound the Dictaphone to record over her last sentence. "What are you, my baby?" she asked the specks in the petri dish.

"Are you symbiotic?" Clara gasped. The ramifications of what she was seeing pushed her normally reserved scientific mind into the realm of speculation.

She couldn't help herself. "What if?" She stared back through the lens as the swells inside the dish settled. "What if this is the missing link? The catalyst for evolution?" Her breath caught in her throat. "The building blocks I've been searching for?"

Easy, girl. Let's not get ahead of ourselves. Clara was nowhere near the point of working with such a profound hypothesis. She rained on her own parade. "Start with the basics. Work from there."

At last, not a single unaffected amoeba remained in the dish that Clara could find. The new organisms congregated in the center of the dish. They arranged themselves into an oval that tapered off at each end. Like an eye.

It blinked.

"*Mon Dieu!*" Clara blurted as she pushed herself back from the table. After a second, she began to titter, low and unsure at first, but quickly building into something strong and real. "For a scientist, you can be so ridiculous sometimes," she chided herself. "An eye...." She chuckled some more.

She wheeled herself back to the scope, her cheeks flushed and her muscles tight. She stared straight ahead, half afraid someone might have seen her silliness even though she knew she was alone. "I knew I shouldn't have had that ham sandwich right before bed."

She looked back into the lens. The Molli-amoebas were still congregating center stage. "You really are beau—"

Glass split. Clara screamed as her view went dark. She fell back in her chair so quickly the front wheels left the floor. She rolled backward, out of breath and trying to catch it. *Did something just jump out of the dish?*

She examined the scope from a distance. If the lens was broken, she couldn't tell. A strand of what looked like chewed gum stretched thin extended from the scope into the dish.

"That…. That's not possible."

A sharp burst came from the hallway. It sounded like a gunshot.

"Monty?"

Something struck the door with a thud then slid down its surface. "Monty?" Clara called again. "What's going on out there?"

A beep emitted from the keycard reader. Clara turned her chair toward the door. "No, don't come in! It's not safe in here!"

But it was too late. The hallway door opened, and a man entered the sterilization chamber. He stared at her with wild eyes, eyes that caused her body to tremble and her stomach to turn, spawning a fear not even the threat of viral death had provoked.

But the man wasn't staring at her. He was staring at Molli.

CHAPTER SIX

The man who called himself Dante sat in a metal folding chair in a room barely bigger than a closet with no windows. His hands were cuffed behind him, the metal clasps secured tightly around his wrists, far too tightly for him to wiggle free. He could probably dislocate his thumb and slide his hand out quickly, a trick that always seemed so easy to do in the movies. But he'd never tried it before and doubted he could pull it off without shattering the joint or causing some other permanent damage.

Times were not yet so desperate. He had a means of escape, albeit a tad more time consuming.

Plus, that has to hurt like a son of a bitch. Why would I want to dislocate my own thumb when I don't have to?

Two burly men with bulging arms crossed over heaving chests stared at him, an aluminum table all that separated them from Dante. They were typical ASAP guards, serious-looking fellows with pronounced jaws and permanently scowling faces. They'd have no trouble dislocating his thumb for him. He thought better of asking.

Stearns and Romanov. Dante read the name tags over their breast pockets. Stearns was even uglier than the photo in Dante's dossier had let on. Romanov was a great big question mark. Dante didn't like question marks. They raised too many questions.

With big, dopey eyes and a sheepish smile that screamed, "D'oh, you boys got me," without saying a word, he stared up at his captors. He offered them a respectful nod then laughed.

As Dante expected, the ASAP men made a tough audience. Stearns grunted and took a seat across from him. The guard clenched his hands together and slid his Popeye forearms over the table toward Dante, who had seen similar demonstrations of strength and authority a thousand times before. He rolled his eyes and snickered.

"You find something funny?" the guard asked, almost barking.

Dante's smile curled bigger. "All of life is funny, my friend. Each of us is caught up in God's ultimate joke: the plight of human existence."

"You hear that, partner?" Stearns asked, glancing over his shoulder at Romanov. "We've got ourselves a philosopher." He feigned a laugh then flipped into a sneer as he slammed a palm onto the table.

Dante faked a shriek then burst into laughter. That part wasn't fake.

"Listen up, you fucking whack job. We ain't exactly the police. We don't give two shits about your rights or that pansy faggot party called the Geneva Convention. We don't give a damn if you're Saint Christopher, Mother Theresa, or the Pope himself." Stearns leaned closer. "We just want to know one thing." The guard drew a large Rambo blade from a scabbard as if he were some kind of pirate. "And I'm going to cut and carve you until you give it up."

"Now, now, Mr. Stearns." Dante tsked. "Children shouldn't play with knives."

Stearns's hand moved with a quickness unbefitting a man his size. With a flick of his wrist, he sent his blade through Dante's flesh.

Though the cut was shallow, it succeeded in souring Dante's mood, if only for a moment. Warm blood trickled down his left cheek. He growled low then checked his anger. *I'm going to kill him for that.* And with that, he let his humor return. "Roses are red. Violets are blue. You'll soon be dead. So how 'bout *fuck you.*"

Stearns struck again, so fast that Dante had barely seen the blow coming. The backhand to his temple rocked his head back and left the room spinning, but he laughed it off.

"Where are my manners?" Dante asked. "That's no way to speak to my gracious host."

"No," Stearns agreed. "It's not. Tell us who you're working with, and you have my word I won't kill you. Or, I'll at least make it quick."

Dante let out a deep breath and leaned forward as if he were about to reveal all the universe's many secrets. "Okay, listen closely. There are seven of them. One of them, well, he can be a bit bashful. I don't know how to get him to talk. Another one, he isn't too bright. Some of the others call him dopey, but I think that's kind of rude. Don't you? Then there's that fellow who won't stop sneezing. God almighty! My house looks like it has been invaded by slugs from outer space. And let's not forget the doc!"

"You finished?" Stearns asked.

"I'm not sure. How many was that?"

Stearns jammed the point of his knife into the table, but as it was also metal, the blade just scraped sideways along the surface with a cringe-inducing sound akin to a nail across a chalkboard. He let it fall from his grip and lunged across the table. His hand clamped onto the back of Dante's neck and slammed the prisoner's face down onto the unyielding surface. Stearns circled the table and lifted Dante by his lapels. The guard gritted his teeth, his mouth so close to Dante's that the latter could smell the eggs his captor had eaten for breakfast.

"You're wasting your time," Romanov said. "He's obviously crazy. He's not working with anyone."

"Oh yeah, smart guy?" Stearns asked. "How many hobos you know that can acquire and wire plastic explosives?"

Dante smirked. Stearns wasn't half as dumb as he looked. *Easy to provoke, though.* He shrugged. It didn't matter what they thought. He wasn't talking.

For a moment, he and Stearns locked stares. Then a gunshot broke the silence.

"Who in the flying fuck is shooting?" Stearns shouted. He glowered at Dante. "If this is one of your guys, I'm going to bring back his head for you. Maybe then you'll talk."

Not one of mine, Dante thought, intrigued by the unforeseen wrinkle. Perhaps he'd finally been given the distraction he needed.

What's going on out there?" Romanov called into his handheld radio. "Someone report. Control?"

"It came from the direction of Bio-Lab 347," a woman's voice blasted back.

"Fuck! The clean room? Where's Flint? Flint, report!"

Only static came back.

"Belgrade, Johnson," Romanov said. "Head there now. Stearns and I will be close behind."

"Sit tight, asshole," Stearns said as he hip-checked the table into Dante's stomach. "I'll be back soon enough…with presents."

"How thoughtful of you," Dante said, grinning through the pain.

Romanov was already out the door with Stearns at his heels, when Stearns turned. "Almost forgot," he said, winking at Dante. He grabbed his knife from the table and was gone.

Dante heard the door lock behind them. As soon as it did, he used the fingernail of his right thumb to begin digging out the pick he'd buried deep in the skin beneath his left. It hurt like a motherfucker, but unlike the whole broken-thumb technique, the pick method of escape wouldn't render his hand useless.

As he worked the narrow, jagged shard of metal free, his thumb's nerve endings sending vicious jolts of pain repeatedly to his brain with every millimeter of movement, he prayed he wouldn't drop it. If he could pick the lock on his cuffs, kicking off the feeble doorknob would take half a second.

Piece of cake. He went to work, whistling while he did.

CHAPTER SEVEN

Papa, why haven't you come for me?

Sergei clawed at his hair. He hadn't slept for weeks. His eyes had glazed over. His clothes hung off his frame, baggy. Colleagues had taken notice, were constantly asking if he was all right, no matter how hard he tried to keep to himself.

He couldn't remember the last time he'd eaten and had skulked into the cafeteria to force down a bite despite not being hungry. After ambling through a short line, he grabbed a tray and pulled a plate of food from under a heat lamp without checking the label over it to see what was on the menu. He started toward the dining area when he remembered utensils, then turned back again when he remembered coffee, which he took black.

Though he often found himself somewhere different from where he'd last recalled being, as if he'd been sleepwalking, real sleep had been a pipe dream – not that he wanted to sleep. Every time he tried, every time he closed his eyes if only to blink, Natalya was there behind his eyelids, just as he remembered her.

Maybe a bit more persistent than I remember her.

Sergei knew his daughter, and what he was seeing and hearing looked and sounded like her – yet not quite her, not quite right, though he couldn't put a finger on what was off. *Probably the fact that she's been dead for two years.*

He laughed shakily then shrank into a seat at the end of one of the dining room's long tables. Several shorter tables and even some two seaters along the walls were more conducive to his desire to be left alone, but he sat where his body had taken him, the cafeteria mostly empty anyway. He chewed his nail down into the quick, barely noticing the pain or the blood. *The question again. Always the same question. Always.*

Papa, where are you? Natalya said through her direct line into his brain. For a second, Sergei thought she was giggling.

"It's not that simple!" he said aloud, pounding a fist into his thigh. He skulked and sneaked a glance to his left, then right, still with it enough to know that others might be watching. He huddled over his lunch like a convict in a prison mess hall, never knowing if someone would make a play for it. He hadn't taken a bite of the roast chicken with biscuits and gravy and didn't want to. Its color seemed gray, like everything else, and smelled of rotting, maggoty meat.

It smelled like death – not just the food, but the room, the air…his own breath. He wondered if it was Natalya's smell.

The intercom announced something about staff returning to their rooms, but Sergei's attention was fixed on his daughter's voice. She talked to him. Nonstop. Every single minute of every single day, without break, without rest.

She was haunting him.

It is, Papa. It is simple. I'm free now. The cripple feeds me, but it's not enough. It's never enough, Papa. I'm dying all over again and just as slowly. And soon, she'll stick me back into the cold. Do you know what it's like to have been trapped in ice for all that time, only to be stuck in a refrigerator the moment you're finally free?

"Like a morgue?" Sergei whispered.

I'm dying, Papa. Dying!

"You can't die, *angel moy*. You're already dead."

You're so cruel, Papa. You've forgotten all about your little ballerina. You don't love her anymore.

Sergei ran his fingers down his face, wiped the crusties out of the corners of his eyes. He sighed. "I do, angel, I do." Her reproach made his heart burn and his head throb. The throbbing escalated into a splitting migraine, the pain manifesting in blinding white light searing into his retinas. "I'm sorry." He cringed as he massaged the middle of his forehead. "I just…. I just can't think straight with you always in my head. You never stop, darling. I can't sleep, can't concentrate. I'm so tired. It's driving me crazy!"

He pounded both fists into the table then glanced around again to see if his second outburst had gone unnoticed, muttering a sheepish, "Sorry."

No one was looking. In fact, no one was there. He wondered how long he'd been sitting in that spot, the breakfast stragglers already having eaten and left. He sipped his coffee, which had gone cold. Even the cafeteria staff had disappeared. He started to wonder where everyone had gone when his thoughts were once again interrupted by her.

Set me free. Set us both free, Papa.

Sergei tasted salt on his lips. "How? I can't get in there. I'm not authorized—"

No, but she is.

An invisible hand lifted Sergei's chin just as Dr. Mary Rose Thomas passed. Mary Rose was the center's esteemed pathologist, part of the microbiological team assembled to analyze the pandoraviruses. Her status seemed more a precautionary measure and probably had more to do with the fact that she was American, a political placement, than with her other qualifications. Still, she was one of the nicest people Sergei had met at the research center, a heavyset woman in her late sixties with platinum-white hair always tied up in a bun. She greeted everyone pleasantly as she passed, acted as though she was everyone's grandmother – never having an unkind word or an overbearing ego – and might have been accepted as such by more than a few. Her kindliness was a lot to expect from a scientist, never mind from an American.

She offered her polite, albeit uneasy, smile then. Sergei returned it with a forced, shark-toothed smile of his own. "I don't want to hurt her," he said as he slipped his fork into his back pocket and rose to follow.

Sergei lost Mary Rose as soon as she left the cafeteria. When he entered the hallway to follow, he found Alfonse and Sebastian standing in his path. He rose up on his toes, trying to see past them and escape the encounter without the mandatory pleasantries, but Alfonse's meaty hand latched around Sergei's arm. The grip was light, unthreatening, but it hurt Sergei all the same as his muscles were weak and achy, depleted of iron.

"*Ciao*, Sergei," Alfonse said. "You don't look so good, my friend."

Sergei forced another smile. "I'm fine. I...I had trouble sleeping last night."

"You sure that's all?" Sebastian asked. "It looks like it's been more than a night. Have you eaten yet? Alfie and I were heading into the mess hall to try and grab some grub to bring back to our rooms. Who knows how long we'll be stuck here? You're welcome to join us if—"

"Can't you see I've just come from there, you imbecile?" Sergei gritted his teeth, and spittle seethed through them. He took deep breaths but couldn't stop his fuming.

Sebastian stepped dangerously closer. "Listen, you little—"

"Whoa." Alfonse squeezed between them. The big man placed a hand on Sergei's chest and gently pushed him back. "We're your friends here…."

She's getting away, Natalya whispered.

Alfonse kept talking, but Sergei heard only his daughter. He slapped Alfonse's hand away and shoved past him then stormed down the hall.

"Asshole!" Sebastian called after him.

Sergei didn't care. He had to find Mary Rose. She was the key. She was what Natalya wanted. He had to get Natalya what she wanted. He had to get her out of his head.

But Mary Rose was gone. He'd lost his chance.

She's heading to her room.

"I don't know which is hers," he snapped. He took off running down the sparsely populated corridors, hallway after hallway, in the direction he guessed Mary Rose had gone. He guessed correctly. "Yes!"

Sergei skidded to a halt. He ironed out the wrinkles in his shirt and began to stalk toward Mary Rose, who stood smiling and chatting with that syrupy, brown-nosed brownnoser that talked like the kid from *Slumdog Millionaire.*

"It's always good to see you, Anju," Mary Rose said. "But we should probably head in." She pointed to the door behind her. "This is me. There's been a rather serious increase in the number of protestors lining up outside. If this is the work of a fanatic, well, I'm afraid these hallways are no place for the likes of us gentler folk."

"Right as always, Dr. Thomas." Anju patted the older woman's hand. "If you need anything, I am right down the hall. Come and get me before heading out on your lonesome, would you?"

"I'm not senile yet, my dear."

"I just meant—"

"I know. I'm just teasing you, dear. And please, don't go out on your own either. As you said, I'm right down the hall."

Anju smiled and gave her elder a slight bow. Sergei waited for the graduate student to walk away, pretending to tie his shoe only a few meters away from them. But Anju lingered. He'd caught her eyeing him suspiciously more than once. He stood, smiled, nodded at the women, and walked on past them. After rounding a corner, he ducked into a supply closet and peeked through a small glass window cut into the door until he saw that caramel-skinned kiss ass go by.

He backtracked to Mary Rose's room and tried the knob. Shut and locked.

He knocked. After a moment, he heard footsteps inside.

"Yes?" the pathologist called.

"Dr. Thomas, it's Sergei Kobozev. I was hoping I might have a word with you. It's about the viruses we discovered."

"Can it wait? We are supposed to be on lockdown, and—"

"It will only take a moment."

A long pause.

Finally, he heard a click. Mary Rose cracked open the door and peered out with her unassuming eyes. "Yes? What is it? This doesn't have anything to do with that explosion we heard?"

Her keycard, Papa. Get her keycard.

Sergei grinned. His gaze fell to the old woman's waist, where the card hung from a lanyard. Then his smile fell from his face as he realized what he had to do. What *she* had always meant for him to do.

He kicked in the door.

Mary Rose cried out in pain when the door slammed into her shoulder. She tumbled backward and fell atop a coffee table, knocking magazines and papers onto the floor.

She started to scream for help, but Sergei leaped on top of her. "I don't want to hurt her!" he shouted as his hands groped their way around her throat. The door slid closed behind him.

"Shh…. Shh-shhh," Sergei pleaded as he strangled a woman who had been nothing but kind to him. He didn't enjoy it, didn't want to hurt her, but he couldn't have her screaming. He would just choke her until she passed out. Just quiet her for a while. She would be fine.

He just needed *her* to be quiet.

"Don't fight. Go to sleep, Mary Rose." His tone was soft, fatherly even. "Just go to sleep, my little ballerina." He looked into the face changing color under him. His daughter's face stared back at him, smiling. He kissed her forehead as his fingers tightened around her neck.

Mary Rose flopped beneath him, clawing at his forearms. Her eyes bulged out of their sockets. It brought tears to his eyes, seeing her terror and knowing he was its cause.

"It'll all be over soon. I promise."

Cross your heart and hope to die, Natalya said inside his mind. He thought he could hear his daughter laughing.

His promise came true. Mary Rose's kicking soon grew sporadic then stopped altogether. She went to sleep. That was all Sergei wanted, for *her* to sleep.

Except her eyes did not close.

Good, Papa. Now, take the keycard.

Sergei grabbed the keycard and yanked it off her belt. The cord connecting the card to the lanyard snapped. He stood with the object of Natalya's desires in his hand, listening to her cheers of approval. He left Mary Rose's room and headed toward Bio-Lab 347.

There will be a guard.

"I know, my little ballerina." Sergei grimaced. He grabbed the fork from his back pocket and slid it up his sleeve.

Sure enough, when Sergei entered the hallway leading to the clean room, a guard was posted at its door. His nametag read *Flint.*

"Please return to your room, mate," the guard said. "The hallways are presently off-limits."

Sergei smiled, but he could feel it shake and twitch upon his face. He wiped his hands repeatedly on his pants, unable to get them dry or clean. *He knows. He can see right through me.*

The guard tensed, his hand hovering closer to his gun.

Sergei wondered what he had done to raise suspicion, as he hadn't even said a word. *He suspects something, Papa. You're so close.*

"I know," Sergei said.

"Good, then," Flint said. "For a moment there, I thought you were going to be tr—"

The fork slid down Sergei's arm and into his hand. Roaring like an animal, he charged.

"Oh, shit." Flint went for his gun and had it drawn just as Sergei jabbed the fork into the guard's eyeball. The gun went off, but the shot went wide, and the bullet buried itself in the wall. Flint fell on his ass, his arms covering his face. Sergei slammed his boot heel into the man over and over again.

Somehow, the guard found an opening and batted Sergei's leg aside. Sergei retained his feet. Before Flint could gain his, Sergei ran for the door and slid the pathologist's keycard through the magnetic-strip reader. The door beeped then unlocked. He slid inside and slammed it shut behind him.

Outside, Flint was groping simultaneously for his gun and the fork stuck in his eye. "Unknown organisms present in laboratory," a computerized voice said through a speaker built into the ceiling. "Air quality normal. Personnel decontamination will now begin. Please remain still and upon completion of the decontamination process, proceed with caution." A white gas billowed over Sergei, followed by intense UV brilliance as the sterilization process went through its various stages.

When it was over, he walked through the entrance to the laboratory. Natalya sat waiting.

CHAPTER EIGHT

Clara knew crazy. Her father had lost his mind after watching his wife waste away. She'd cared for him until he'd become more than she could handle. She'd taken a sabbatical, done all she could for him even while largely confined to a wheelchair, until his dementia and violent confusion brought out one attack too many, sending her to a hospital with a couple of broken ribs and him to a home where she thought he would receive the care he needed.

Each time she had visited him thereafter, which wasn't as often as she should have, her father would stare at her through eyes filled with contempt. He seemed to blame her for his dementia and worse, for his wife's death.

He got worse. Obsessed with clean skin, he wouldn't let anyone touch him, especially not Clara, who played with cancer cells all day. One night, her father had become convinced that fire would sterilize him. The orderlies heard him screaming well before they were able to kick in his door and douse the flames. No one ever told Clara how he'd gotten the gasoline and matches. They said he'd been screaming for help that would not come in time, for someone who had moved far away to escape the insanity, the living nightmare.

Screaming for Clara.

She saw him before he died, third-degree burns covering most of his body. One eye had been left unmarred, flesh having melted the other one shut. She was spared the sight of most of his burns due to his substantial wrappings – damn near mummification. But that one exposed eye, high on morphine, seemed already dead until it noticed her. It woke up then, filled with fire of its own, wide and terrible, a piercing gaze that had shot daggers into her heart.

When she looked at the man who'd entered the lab, she saw her father's wide-eyed lunacy in his eyes. She saw her father's fanaticism in that man whom she did not know. She saw danger, recklessness, fear, and madness – a volatile cocktail that could explode without reason or notice.

Clara's first thought was to protect Molli. The thought of protecting herself took a distant second.

And seconds were all she had.

The stranger charged at the petri dish just as Clara snagged it from the table, his intentions unclear. Her hands were quick, and she counted herself lucky not to have spilled the dish's contents. She held it aloft as the man studied her, feinting one way then the other but not moving in for the kill.

Clara didn't dare move at all.

Who is he? Sickness rose in her throat. It threatened to curl her up, distracting her from the disheveled waif of a man who bore her unknown but certainly ill intent.

Or, if not her, perhaps Molli. Perhaps that desperation she saw in his twitching, bloodshot eyes was meant for grander deeds, inconceivable acts involving a viral outbreak of biblical proportions – if her own clumsiness and stupidity hadn't brought it about already. *I should have asked Monty to shoot me, just to be safe.*

"What do you want?" she asked, a scolding bite to her tone. "The virus? It's worthless. Didn't you know? A great big dead nothing."

The man didn't respond, instead regarding her with that same manic, unstable glower. Every part of him jittered and twitched. His irises shot upward as if the voice of God were calling to him from above and only he could hear Him. When he listened to whatever he was listening to, his fidgeting and shuffling worsened. He looked like a man with bugs crawling all over his skin and no hands to swat them off.

A syrupy stink wafted into Clara's nostrils, and her nose crinkled. She heard a sizzle and looked down to see the water in the dish roiling as if composed of a thousand molecule-sized Mexican jumping beans mid-fiesta. Despite the stranger who had invaded the laboratory, Clara watched the dish with car accident-gawker fascination. Somehow, each purple-plasmid drop landed safely back into the dish.

Until the lunatic seized the growth culture from her hands.

His thumbs disappeared into the test medium, splashing it and sending amoeba-Mollies bouncing over Clara's cheek like barefooted children on hot pavement. The lines between the man's fingers and the contents of the dish blurred.

The liquid tingled like soda on Clara's skin. She winced, expecting burning, irritation, something. Down the bridge of her nose, she saw a single drop hanging from the outside of her nostril. It clung there until she felt it roll up her nose and slip into her eye.

The liquid on her cheeks likewise defied gravity. It *moved* into her eyes – crawled or slithered like something living, breathing, and conscious.

Something evil.

It spoke to her. *I am this one now.*

Clara screamed. She could feel the entity pulsating through her body, vying for control of her mind. *My mind, for Christ's sake!* It was the only thing of value she had left.

That and her eyes, which seemed okay, but some chemicals didn't burn right away. She rolled to the eye-washing station and forced her eyes to remain open as she shot water up into them, trying to flush out whatever had gotten in. She blinked out the water and wiped her cheeks with a paper towel.

Through her haze, Clara watched the frail man. *Sergei! His name is Sergei!* How she knew that, she did not know. She knew more too: how he'd lost a daughter to an accident and a wife through divorce; how he'd been hitting the bottle hard lately; and how he was the same Sergei she'd heard had discovered Molli. She knew everything there was to know about Sergei Kobozev. The only thing she didn't know was why.

In the grand scheme of things, none of that mattered. At least, not at that moment. What mattered was the fact that Sergei was raising the petri dish to his lips, and – as certain about it as she was of all else she knew of the Russian astrobiologist – Clara knew he meant to drink it.

"No!" she screamed, her hand clawing through air as she reached for him. Pity smote her fears, an empty longing to save a man she didn't know from self-destruction.

But what can I do? Stuck in her wheelchair, she felt useless. She couldn't even stand. Her legs were....

Different? Clara could swear she felt them. Feeling...that alone was something. No time to think about it – she threw herself up, out of her wheelchair, and onto her feet.

She immediately fell forward and collapsed at Sergei's feet. Her chin smacked hard against the floor, and she bit into her tongue. Sergei downed the wretched concoction as if he hadn't even noticed her. Her legs had failed her. No surprise there. That wasn't the first time. Except, for a moment there, she thought they might actually hold.

Clara didn't bother to rise. The damage had been done. Whatever tricks Molli had up its dress, the pseudovirus would visit them upon Clara and her new roommate as it saw fit. She recalled how Molli's cells had joined with the amoebas and considered her fate. *Would it be mutation, disease...death?* She smirked. *Or perhaps evolution.* Molli wasn't like any of the girls she knew. Clara couldn't begin to conceive of a countermeasure while the organism remained so dreadfully untested.

She laughed, and her injured mouth spat hot blood onto the floor. *Well, testing should move forward more quickly now that we have a couple of human guinea pigs to evaluate.*

Sergei started to seize. He dropped to his knees next to her, clutching his throat as white foam fizzled over his lips. Still twitching, he fell onto his stomach. After a few minutes, the twitching stopped.

Clara slid toward him and checked his pulse. Nothing. *So much for evolution.*

The clean room went silent. A clamor struck the hallway outside, bangs and thuds and other sounds Clara could not investigate. She was stuck where she was, helpless, confined with a dead man.

CHAPTER NINE

If people only knew how their offering-plate contributions were spent.

Dante had studied the center's blueprints his organization had provided him. It had paid a small fortune to obtain them, leveraging an inside source at a Scandinavian architectural firm who had it under lock and key. His outfit was proficient at acquiring things that even professional thieves, con artists, and others in his line of work considered impossible to procure. He doubted he would have had any difficulty getting it. Where others used finesse, stealth, and cunning, which was all well and good for certain jobs, Dante would have used force – as much as needed to get the job done.

He hummed the tune of the latest La Bella Tarantella radio hit, catchy and poppy with no lyrical substance whatsoever, hating himself for it. He couldn't understand why opera wasn't on mainstream music-provider channels: its power, precision, and beauty – all art, none of the fluff. The stuff he did hear on the radio just solidified his view that the world was mostly composed of stupid people.

And the scientists in the research facility were the worst of the worst. Sure, they were book smart and could probably rattle off pi to the eighteenth decimal point – he could only get to 3.14159 – but did they know anything beyond their areas of study? Anything of art, music, philosophy, philanthropy, community, faith, humanity? *To them, the world is a specimen on a slide. They see one finite detail clear as day but fail to see the bigger picture.*

He loathed their tampering with the natural order. But that was a feeling he easily suppressed. The job came first.

Dante had memorized the plans to the facility, and assuming they weren't forgeries, he probably could have found the clean room easily enough on his lonesome. The sounds of a man screaming and cursing kind of eliminated all guesswork.

He pulled out a long, narrow shiv he'd embedded along his jacket's zipper. He'd designed the weapon to bypass metal detectors that, if set off, would simply alert their human counterparts to the zipper. It was thinner than a chopstick, but its point was much sharper. He hurried toward the sounds of agony, peeking around corners before rushing down hallways.

As he ran, he assessed what lay ahead. *No way in or out of the clean room except its front door and an air vent barely big enough to fit a rabbit. No other places of ingress or egress in the corridor, no places to hide. Offensive measures will be likely.*

He approached a hallway marked Bio-Lab 347 and pressed himself flat against the wall. He listened as he tiptoed closer to the turn.

"Take him to the clinic," a voice commanded.

Dante recognized the gruff American's voice from interrogation. *Stearns.*

Whoever had been screaming had stopped, but someone was groaning. Footsteps came toward Dante. Silent as a cat, he pounced down the hall to an inlet leading to another laboratory. He waited and watched as three men appeared, all security guards. One was on each side of the third as they held him up and led him, Dante guessed, to the infirmary. Something jutted from the injured man's eye like a diving board.

Is that a fork? He couldn't help but smirk. He waited for the three to shuffle out of sight, thankful the infirmary was in the opposite direction, before heading back to the intersection.

"Doctor, are you okay in there?" Stearns called. "Nod if you can hear me." A pause. "Good, good. How about Dr. Kobozev? Is he alive? Oh. Sit tight. We'll get—"

Dante ran the point of his shiv along the wall. *Screech.*

"What was that?" Romanov asked.

"I don't know," Stearns responded. Then softer, "Check it out."

Dante smiled and wiped the end of his weapon on his pant leg, flecks of paint falling to the ground under the line he had scraped into the wall. He slid the shiv between his teeth.

Romanov's arm swung into view. His black-leather-gloved hand was holding a pistol. His other hand was supporting his wrist and his aim in textbook fashion. Dante used it to his advantage.

He leveraged the guard's momentum, sidestepping and hooking

underneath the guard's arm with his own. He slammed it into the wall with all the force he could muster. The guard grunted but held fast to the pistol. One, two, three times, Dante pulled back the guard's hand and slammed it into the wall until the gun dropped.

When it did, Romanov came with a hard left to Dante's cheek. He followed with a vicious boot into Dante's hip. Dante groaned, the force sending him stutter-stepping backward. He barely recovered in time to duck under Romanov's next strike.

As Romanov's punch sailed over him, Dante swept the guard's legs out from under him. Romanov crashed down on his back. He hurried to his feet, but Dante was quicker. He circled the guard and pressed the point of his weapon into Romanov's neck.

Romanov jerked, but Dante's left arm hooked around the guard's neck. His chest pressed flat against the guard's back. "No, no, my friend," Dante said. "Don't move. Don't go for your knife. Don't so much as twitch, or Mr. Pointy enters your jugular vein. And I'm sure I don't have to tell you what kind of mess that will make."

"Why?" Romanov growled. "Are you working with that asshole? What is it you want?"

"I'm afraid I could spend all day trying to explain it to you and you would still be asking me questions at the end of it."

"Do you have any idea what you risk releasing? How many deaths you might cause?"

"Millions. Maybe billions, but that's exactly what I'm trying to avoid. Believe it or not, I'm here to help."

"Help who? Are you some kind of terrorist? Religious nut?"

"Something like that." Dante nudged the guard toward the intersection of the hallways. "Get moving, but keep it nice and slow."

"We'll never let you get the viruses. We'll die first, and we'll take you and this whole facility down with us if we have to."

"Now why would you say such a thing? Let's hope it doesn't come to that. Besides, I think such passion is lacking among many of your coworkers. Now, move."

As they entered the corridor, Stearns was waiting with pistol raised high, the AK-47 still slung over his back. *Looks like Stearns isn't ready to make things messy.* Dante shielded himself behind Romanov.

"Are you okay?" Stearns asked.

Before Romanov could respond, Dante said cheerfully, "I've had better days, but I've got my health, and that's what's important."

"I'm unharmed," Romanov said.

"Release your hostage and raise your hands where I can see them." Without taking his eyes or gun off Dante, Stearns pushed a button on the radio pinned to his shoulder. "Code 32. Repeat, Code 32, Bio-Lab 347. Proceed with caution."

"Hmm.... No. I don't think that works for me." Dante nudged his human shield closer to Stearns, who took a step back. "Allow me to counter offer. Drop your gun, open the door, and step aside, or your friend dies."

"Open the door?" Romanov jeered. "And risk a full-fledged outbreak? Are you crazy? No one opens this door for any reason. Period."

"Better to have an accidental viral attack now than a controlled one later, right, Stearns?" Dante asked.

Stearns tensed. "I don't know what you're talking about."

Dante took a deep breath. His patience was running thin, and in a few moments, the hallway would be crawling with security. He pressed closer. "Open the door, Stearns."

"Are you not listening?" Romanov sneered. "He can't open that door, even if he wanted to. We're not authorized—"

"Oh, but Mr. Stearns here has the override code, don't you, Stearns? And not just for that door, but for the refrigerator as well. His employer, and by that I don't mean ASAP but his *real* employer, has offered a heavy payday for anyone who can obtain those viruses. Research on the second giant virus discovered, probably leaked by you fine ASAP personnel, has garnered the attention of several interested parties notorious for Geneva Convention violations and broadcasted testing of militarized biochemical agents. It may be innocuous in its present form, but apparently somebody out there thinks it can be manipulated."

"That's insane," Stearns shot back. "Our security is impenetrable. Our people are vetted, and—"

"You say that as I stand before you." Dante tsked. "And your people are only as good as their weakest link, Mr. Stearns. My sources tell me that's you." He stepped closer, leaving only two meters between them and backing Stearns into the door.

A scream came from inside the clean room. Stearns glanced back, but only for a second, long enough for Dante to seize his opportunity.

He horse-collared Romanov while blocking the back of his hostage's knees with his leg. As Romanov hit the ground, Dante hurled his mini javelin at Stearns, who squealed when it punctured his left wrist.

Stearns's right hand held on to the gun.

Dante bore down on him like a charging rhino. Stearns wasted time trying to refocus his aim, and by the time he did, Dante was baseball-sliding under it. His heavy boots crashed into Stearns's shins and sent the guard tumbling forward. Dante's inertia carried him into the door. Stearns landed on top of him, driving an elbow across Dante's nose and a knee into his groin.

The first shot was briefly disorienting, the second gut wrenching. Dante fought through the pain and nausea and boxed Stearns's ear with his palm. Stearns rolled with the strike, and Dante rolled with Stearns until their positions had reversed. After poking Stearns in the eyes, Dante had little trouble wrestling the gun free.

And not a moment too soon. Out of the corner of his eye, Dante noticed Romanov had disappeared, but he returned in a flash. Having obtained his gun, he fired it around the corner.

"Fuck!" Dante rolled onto his side. A bullet grazed the side of his head and dug a nasty groove. The rest buried themselves in the tile or ricocheted off the metal door behind him, their trajectory luckily not bringing them into contact with his back or skull. Stearns shrank into a fetal position, covering his face with his hands.

As he rolled, Dante fired, only one shot not intended to hit the guard. But it was enough to send Romanov hiding back behind his side of the wall. Dante couldn't know how long the guard would stay hidden before he conjured the chutzpah to try again.

"Get up," he said as he stood over Stearns. The guard didn't move, so Dante put a bullet into the floor right beside the grounded man's cheek. Debris shot up from the floor and exploded into Stearns's face. He squealed. His right eye instantly looked raw and irritated. Rivulets of blood ran down his cheek.

"I don't have time for this!" Dante shouted. "Get up, or the next one is in your forehead."

Stearns slowly rose. His face flushed red, and his nostrils flared, his look so full of rage that Dante thought he could feel its heat. In case the guard was thinking of trying something, Dante whacked him in the ear to keep him off balance. He bounced Stearns face-first against the wall then pulled him close. He backed himself into the corner beside the keycard reader, directing Stearns to the nine-digit punch pad below it.

"Punch in the override code," Dante ordered.

"I don't know any code," Stearns said.

Dante shot him in the foot. "Wrong answer," he said, holding up the squirming guard. Romanov rounded the corner but had no clear shot. Dante took one of his own for good measure. "Stay where you are. I don't wish to hurt you, but I will if you force my hand."

Dante didn't really expect the innocent guard to understand, assuming he actually was innocent. He had no intel on Romanov, which was either a good sign or Romanov's people were better at keeping secrets.

Dante sighed. *Maybe I should just kill them both.* The governments of the world would each be sending in their Stearnses. Sure, he could kill Stearns number one right then and delay the inevitable, and he was confident the man deserved a whole lot worse. But someone else would send somebody else soon enough. The only question: Who would do the sending? The Americans? The Chinese? The Russians? In the wrong hands, the viruses had the potential to upset the shaky balance of peace.

Since he couldn't take out all of the interested parties, the next best option, the only true option, was to destroy the problem at it source: take out the viruses themselves and eliminate the threat. He ripped the needle out of Stearns's wrist and jammed it into his thigh. Stearns cried out, but Dante was well beyond the point of caring. "Open this fucking door, or I'm putting a bullet up your ass." He pressed the barrel of the pistol into Stearns's tailbone.

Stearns began to whimper. "Even if I know the code, I can't open the door. The two inside have been exposed to direct contact. Letting them out could kill us all."

"Who says I'm letting anyone out?" Dante jammed the barrel harder into the guard's tailbone. Stearns would open the door if it meant his life not to. A man who had sold out millions of lives for personal gain would do so again in a heartbeat. He just had to convince Stearns that the threat of his death was real and imminent. "Open the fucking door. Please, don't make me ask again."

"I—"

Dante grabbed the hair on the back of Stearns's head and drove his face into the wall.

The guard's nose crunched satisfyingly.

"Open. The fucking. Door."

Blood dripped down the front of Stearns's shirt. He reached up with a shaking hand and punched in a number sequence.

"Override initiated." A computerized woman's voice emanated from the intercom near the card reader. "Unknown biological agents present. Recommendation: abort override." After three seconds, the door began to open.

"Stearns?" Romanov called. He stood in the hallway, palms outstretched. "What's going on, Stearns? Was he telling the truth about you?"

Stearns didn't answer. He couldn't answer after Dante cracked the butt of his gun into the guard's head, payback for whichever asshole had done the same to him in the parking garage. The motorized door to the clean room whirred as it continued to creep open. He slid inside and tried to push it closed when someone slammed against the other side.

Romanov.

The guard collided with the door a second time, breaking through it like a battering ram. Dante fell against the opposite door of the sterilization chamber. Before he could get up, Romanov's gun was pointed at him.

"Well, isn't this a pickle?" Dante asked.

"I don't understand this expression," Romanov said. "I also don't know if what you say is true about Stearns, but I do know that whether you're right or wrong, I cannot let the viruses be taken from this place."

"I don't want to take them anywhere!" Dante kneeled. He rested his gun on the floor and raised his hands. Slowly, he stood, keeping his hands where Romanov could see them. "We have to destroy them. Even now, many interested parties are enlisting their best operatives to procure samples by any means necessary. They've already infiltrated your operation. Do you think Stearns is it? That he'll be the last? He's only the first."

"Who are you?" Romanov waved his pistol, signaling for Dante to step away from the door. "How could you possibly know all this?"

"You wouldn't believe me if I told you."

The hallway door latched shut, and the sterilization process began. "Step back," Romanov said. Dante had to smile. The guard was right to think Dante would try something once the sterilization gases filled the chamber and blurred their view of one another. Romanov put enough distance between the two of them to severely lessen Dante's odds of success despite the closet-like confines of the room. Plus, the ASAP lackey seemed to be one of the good ones, placing his life at risk to stop someone he must have thought a madman.

It wouldn't have been the first time someone thought that of Dante.

He studied the guard's stance, searching for a weak point to attack. Romanov may not have been his equal when it came to hand-to-hand combat techniques, but the man was no pushover. And he had a gun.

After a sweat-inducing blast of UV light, a soft bell rang, indicating the end of the sterilization process. The scanner warned them of the presence of unknown biological organisms inside the clean room. "Proceed with caution," it droned.

Dante snickered. The gun pointed at him seemed the more pressing danger.

The door to the lab opened.

A wet, sucking-squishing sound came from inside the room, like broken waves squeezing through crags. Romanov's stare remained trained on Dante. Dante chanced a peek to his left.

"My God!" His mouth dropped open as he realized Romanov no longer mattered.

The guard, however, must have thought it some trick. He was slow to turn. When he finally did, he screamed. But his screaming was cut off by something Dante lacked the words to describe.

He didn't waste time trying to think of them. Instead, he dove for Romanov's gun.

CHAPTER TEN

Clara was sure of it. *Those were definitely gunshots. Is someone else trying to get in?*

Her first clear thought was to grab the remaining samples of the viruses in the refrigerator and toss them into the incinerator. She raised herself up onto her forearms and shimmied her way toward the samples. She had no real plan as to how she might accomplish the great feat she'd set for herself without the ability to stand or whether she could even bring herself to destroy such a monumental find, but her second clear thought made all her worries moot. *Why can't I move?*

She looked behind her and screamed. Sergei was alive, seizing on the floor near her feet, except it wasn't quite Sergei. His face oozed with boils and blisters. Things beneath his flesh wriggled and moved like acorn-sized parasites burrowing tunnels through the meat. His eyes were bloodshot, the zigzagging lines therein purple, not red. The whites turned a sickly pink. His pupils dilated so much that she might have guessed him high if not for his more distressing features. His skin had taken on the color of a bruise.

His teeth looked sharper. No, they *were* sharper. So were his fingernails. They dug into her calf and drew blood.

Clara stretched her arms out in front of her and pressed her palms against the floor, trying desperately to pull herself away though she had nowhere to go. She yelped as Sergei's nails slid down her leg, each one digging a trench, deeper and deeper until they buried themselves in tissue. She couldn't move her legs, but they sure had chosen a fine time to feel pain.

Sergei – or the thing that had been Sergei – dragged her closer. Her arms flailed wildly, and she whacked her wrist hard enough against the corner of a lab station to make her cry out in agony.

Inch by inch, the Sergei-thing clawed its way up her leg, further shredding her jeans and lab coat in a dozen places. Her fists her only weapons, she batted at Sergei's head. Blisters popped under her blows and gushed fluids that looked disgusting and smelled worse.

Sergei didn't seem to notice. He just crawled closer to her face, his shark-toothed grin drooling with a sick sort of lust.

Warm spittle dripped onto Clara's face as Sergei mounted her. A huge black tongue lolled out of his mouth and slid up her cheek like a slug, leaving a mucus trail. She cringed. Her stomach muscles cramped when nauseating hot breath blasted her face, but she was too frightened to put up much of a fight.

"This one belongs to me," the humanoid hissed. "Yet this one is not mine. Why is this one not mine? I must know."

Sergei's fingers grew longer, almost long enough to encircle Clara's neck with one hand. He lifted her and held her up as easily as if he'd been holding a rag doll. She batted at his arm repeatedly, her strikes slowing and weakening with every second she lacked oxygen. Sergei's grip continued to tighten.

"Why does this one struggle? Why does this one fight? I am inside her. I am her, and she is me. Yet she is not me."

Clara heard the mutated scientist speaking, but in her rapidly deteriorating state, she was in no condition to consider his words. Her air was nearly depleted. She raked at the fingers around her neck, begging for them to let go. They would not budge.

As the sounds around her dulled, Clara thought she heard a familiar bell. *The sterilization chamber?* Someone was coming in. God help her for thinking it, but she prayed whoever it was would hurry, even if it meant another's infection.

Sergei turned toward the sound. He let out a low growl as his razor-blade teeth sawed through his cheeks, widening his mouth into a grotesque clown grin. He raised his right arm, pointing an elongated finger at someone Clara could almost make out in her peripheral vision.

Then, Sergei's arm began to change. The transformation was slight at first, something off about the appendage that Clara couldn't quite place. The strands of hair on his arms began to stir. They broke away from their roots and stitched in and out of fresh holes they bored through his skin or inchwormed across his pallid-purple epidermis.

Large lumps formed beneath his skin. They ran like termites under bark, all in the same direction, toward his fingertips. Sergei's skin itself unraveled next, tearing itself free from the muscle and sinews beneath it. The muscle followed. Huge swaths of raw, bacon-like meat slithered like snakes toward Sergei's fingertips, where a bundle of organic materials were congregating. The strips narrowed as they moved, gained speed, and weaved their own fibers into long tendrils. His tricep looked like a beef rib with a chunk chewed out of it, bits of tendon and gristle clinging to what remained. Blood seeped out of his wounds, but no drop hit the ground. Instead, the blood formed a horizontal stream that followed in the path of the living, squirming tissue.

That organic clay formed five long, spaghetti-thin tentacles, one for each finger, that whipped and snapped at the air like live wires. All the while, Sergei smiled his wicked, animal grin. That smile widened when he thrust his hand and skin tentacles at uncanny speed in the direction of the incoming someone.

Clara heard a man scream. The wailing sent chills through her bones, reinvigorating her drifting mind. She pulled with everything she had at the hand around her throat but barely succeeded in getting the mutant scientist's attention. Her own attention waned. Her chin once again began to nod. Her eyelids closed even as the eyes under them bulged.

She was running out of chances to save herself. She summoned whatever strength she had left.

Into her leg.

And kicked.

Sergei howled as her knee drove into his chin. His gnashing bottom teeth stabbed into their upper counterparts, breaking and chipping like a picket fence caught in an avalanche. His bloated black tongue was caught in the middle. It was severed, spurting deep-purple blood. The toe of her flat dug into Sergei's stomach and shoved him back.

Clara fell free – a minor victory, she knew, but a start. She landed on her buttocks and scrambled away from Sergei and his flopping-fish severed tongue.

I kicked him. However, any wonder that realization induced was quickly quashed when she turned to see the source of the screams. Already gasping for air, Clara choked as she took in air too quickly. She swallowed a scream of her own then keeled over and coughed out vomit.

The tentacles had embedded themselves in a security guard's face and neck, tenting the skin where they didn't shred it. They pulsated like the prongs of a stun gun, but the prongs she saw were made of flesh and muscle. The guard jerked as though electrocuted. Dark red-purple clumps of plasma resembling clotted blood ran in one direction like cable cars down organic wire, each one tunneling into the guard's face and scurrying beneath the skin. She could see them mounding the flesh of his neck as they moved down it, only to disappear under his shirt collar.

The guard was seizing, much in the same manner that Sergei had. He collapsed onto the floor.

Clara tried to rationalize what she'd just seen, quivering and hugging herself close. *There's no goddamn science that'll explain that. No fucking science at all.*

Her head spun. With his free hand, the forearm elongating at the elbow, the abomination that had been Sergei swiped at her. Clara's arms ached as she scuffled out of reach on her palms and buttocks, her legs dragging along for the ride.

But the Sergei-thing hadn't been swiping at her after all. It picked up its tongue, which was somehow still animated, opened a freakishly wide maw, and gobbled down the thick muscle as if it were a gummy worm. When finished, Sergei grinned wide, flashing red-lined teeth at Clara.

Then he reached for her. Clara froze. The room blurred. Sounds dulled, as if she'd been immersed in water. Everything began to spin, faster and faster. She wanted off the ride.

A loud blast stopped the man-creature's forward momentum. What was left of its head tilted sideways. Sergei's scalp had been blown clean off. It slid down the wall to her right.

Or slithered.

Still, the man-creature came, a chicken *sans* head.

Darkness. For how long, Clara couldn't be sure. Two more gunshots – at least two that she had heard. She hadn't seen Sergei fall, but one moment, he was standing in front of her, and the next, he was lying prone. The gunshots had seemed kilometers away. Any alertness inspired by the sudden noise faded as quickly as it had come. It had lasted just long enough for Clara to see a stranger rushing to her side.

My savior. She had no time to consider whether his actions or the black cross on his forehead made her see the man in such a way before she drifted into sleep.

CHAPTER ELEVEN

Dante had never once tried to trick himself into thinking he was some kind of hero. Like everyone else at the research center, he'd been hired to do a job, plain and simple. Unlike everyone else, Dante was authorized to use any means necessary to complete his work. He'd been given a directive, nothing more, nothing special, and certainly nothing worthy of role-model material.

Still, he chose only the jobs that suited his conscience. And he insisted on the leeway to accomplish them how he saw fit. Both he and his employer preferred it that way: he liked having the control, and his employer.... Something about willful, blissful ignorance and plausible deniability.

The less contact, the better, Dante always thought when he considered his employer. Its representatives, with their silly pointy hats and upturned noses, were quick to wash their hands of the likes of Dante when his services were no longer required. *Holier than thou.* He smirked at the irony in their condescension. That condescension ran deep. He often wondered how many crimes they'd secretly orchestrated or had otherwise been complicit in, how many commandments they'd chosen to ignore, all to keep their hands clean, their souls sanctified, and believe it or not, the world safe.

He wondered: Did that make him a sin eater? Dante didn't care for the comparison. His conscience was clean even if theirs weren't. *The problem is in the people, not the principles.*

But those people always paid, half when the job was started and half when it was completed, and they paid well. *Money for Judas.* Another comparison that made Dante's skin crawl. No, Dante lacked any delusions about what he was: a specialized hired gun, a man who got things done, a killer when he needed to be, a philosopher when he could afford to be.

When that man-thing shot marionette strings from its fingers and began to play with its puppet, Romanov, Dante became the man he was hired to be. He dove for his gun purely on instinct, and he fired it for one reason only.

To kill.

So why am I helping this woman? The scientist was passed out on the floor beside a slithering mound of gore, blood-filled bubbles popping like adolescent pimples. His mission came first, self-preservation came second, catching a string quartet at some hole in the wall later that evening came third, and finding a decent stromboli in all of Siberia came fourth. She never should have made the list.

Despite that, he crouched and scooped her into his arms. He looked at her gaunt facial features, her chiseled jaw with teeth grinding even in her sleep as if fighting some demon of her mind through a nightmarish playground – a restless subconscious, something Dante could empathize with. She seemed deserving of his pity, and though he doubted she would want it, he gave it freely. And when the lines of her troubles gave way to a smooth, placid face, Dante saw her in a new light.

He placed her gently in a wheelchair he assumed belonged to her and delicately swiped her hair from her face. She was beautiful, he thought, but not at peace. She mumbled something incoherent then began to snore. He wondered what sins she kept locked away in secret.

Dante chuckled, but his smirk soon vanished. Only then did he consider that the woman may have just infected him.

"Relax," he told himself. Easier said than done, but if he was infected, he could do little about it. *At least she hasn't grown jellyfish stingers like that headless* porca vacca. *Besides, I don't feel any different…for now.* Dante knew little about biology. He knew nothing of incubation or gestation periods or any other period between contracting a disease and the time its symptoms first showed, but he was smart enough to know that just because the woman hadn't turned into a body-contorting freak didn't mean she wouldn't, particularly since she was still unconscious.

His gut told him she wouldn't, and his gut had gotten him that far. He had faith in it. Again, Dante had to laugh at the irony – he was showing faith in his hunch and in that woman though he showed his employer's people none. The woman seemed content in the brief time he held her. He was not so far gone to be lost to humanity. That made him content.

He stared at the woman, hoping she would find peace from what disturbed her mind, the trials of her day seemingly over. Then the click-clack of tapping stilettos sounded against the clean room's heat-welded vinyl flooring. Dante looked in the direction from which the sound had come and realized his trials were only beginning.

"*Madonna!*" he cried. What he saw could not be real. Maybe he was sick, starting to hallucinate. He blinked and rubbed his eyes, but the scalp of the scientist whose head he'd blown to bits was still crawling toward him. Eight jagged bone appendages made of sculpted cranium, four to each side of the pulpy-haired membrane, carried the hide of flesh and matted hair with increasing speed toward Dante. It was eyeless, earless, noseless, yet somehow alive and somehow knowing exactly where he was. The scalp crab clacked closer.

Dante had seen a lifetime's worth of atrocities and didn't lack for imagination. But that scientist's mutation and the thing scuttling toward him strained the boundaries of his sanity. He wondered if he was experiencing the beginnings of disease.

He set his jaw and decided that whether or not he was going insane, he would not let that thing get any nearer. He raised his pistol, and with the accuracy of a professional, he blew the ugly abomination to hell. He watched with uneasy pleasure as the scalp crab blasted apart. *Even imaginary fuckers can be killed with real bullets.*

One mound had become three smaller segments. He stared at them, half expecting the revelation of a punch line, like some old hidden-camera-show host making his presence known or a random pie jammed into his face. The scraps of head and hair weren't moving. He grimaced as he scrutinized one particularly bloody fragment, upturned so that its red, stringy underbelly was exposed. Dante was beginning to think he had imagined the whole ordeal and had wasted a bullet on dead flesh.

I'm losing it. This belief became so ingrained that when the upturned human morsel sprouted new crab legs, he howled with laughter. The appendages thrashed in the air, unable to correct themselves, like the legs of an upside-down turtle unable to right itself. Still laughing, he watched the newly formed scalp crab pop off its back, land on its feet, and rush him. Its two new friends also rose on crab legs and joined the assault.

"Motherfucker!" He raised his gun and took aim, then lowered it and slid it into his waistband. The weapon had only succeeded in tripling his hallucinations the first go-around, so he figured he would need to think of a different way to destroy them. His gun ineffective, Dante was weaponless.

The clean room, he hoped, could offer him a new weapon, but the scalp crabs were closing in fast. Whatever those godforsaken sons of bitches were, they were as good as dead. Dante just had to figure out a way to kill them, and since killing had always been his forte, he wasn't about to give it up then. Those creatures were an affront to nature and an insult to his mighty-fine shooting.

"Okay, you little shits. You want some of me?"

The living flesh continued its charge. Dante charged back and raised his boot high. The smallest of the three scalp crabs was in the lead, but Dante's aim was true. His heel mashed the critter into grape jelly that looked as though a cat had vomited a hairball into it then partially buried it in its white kitty litter, crunchy bone that Dante ground into pebbles.

The other two crab-things stopped, seeming to regard him with caution after what had just happened to their compadre.

Dante laughed, not with madness but with the satisfaction of victory over a hated enemy. "Did you like that?" he asked Crab Number Two. "I know I did."

The closer scalp crab's legs bent. Then it exploded off the floor, leaping into the air with amazing speed and careering right at Dante's head.

"Whoa!" He ducked just in time to see the nasty fucker sail over him.

The other one landed on his jacket, over his heart.

The crab's front legs sliced through the material of his thick vest like scalpels. White stuffing shot over the little monster like debris from a wood chipper. Dante gasped. He grabbed his lapel and pulled it down and out as fast as he could. The material went taut and acted like a trampoline beneath the crab's feet, propelling the monstrosity upward. The crab spun midair and latched on to the ceiling, where it remained stationary, as if considering its next move.

"*Merda!* The other one." A gut feeling told him to duck, and he heeded it. He jerked out of the way just as Crab Number Two leaped.

It flew past him and landed on the laboratory table, where it skidded across the polished surface and almost fell off the other side. It teetered over the edge, hanging by one scalpel pincer.

Dante caught movement above and returned his attention to Crab Number Three. It was moving away from him, toward its disgusting ally. The latter pulled itself up onto the table. The crab above dropped down on top of it and melted over Crab Number Two like hot pitch poured over ice cream, liquefying both, the resulting blob re-forming, reshaping. The two became one.

Dante had never had to fight off severed, transforming body bits before, but the novelty was beginning to wear thin. Hallucinating or not, he was in control of all his other faculties, and panicking solved nothing. He had only his gun and his training with which to defend himself. Dante laid down for no monster, human or otherwise.

Except, what he was seeing was real. It had to be. More than one person had seen the weirdness that had come out of the scientist who'd invaded the clean room. True, one witness was unconscious, the other dead, but that was not at his hands. Couldn't have been. *Could it?*

No, losing his shit was a luxury he couldn't afford. No matter how crazy things became around him, he had to assume that he was dealing with a new form of biological weapon and his worst fears had come true: someone had released it. He also had to assume that, at the moment, it was contained within the research center. He would have to do whatever was in his power to make sure it stayed that way.

I've got a job to do. He summoned his resolve. *Scalp crabs just make it a tad more difficult.*

The mound of gelatinous flesh once belonging to a human being was a scalp crab no longer. Like bad stock footage from an old Claymation Christmas special, the mass oozed and stretched into a long, oval-shaped creature that sort of looked like a deep-sea tube worm Dante had seen on some nature show.

The new organism was even more featureless than its preceding incarnations. Pink skin stretched so thin that it was translucent. Purple veins bulged out like those on a muscle head's biceps after a particularly intense workout. The flesh was swathed with patches of hair that ran along its entire length, which culminated in an orifice at its top. The hole was opening wider and wider. It looked like a mouth.

A slender blood-red strand, no more than half a centimeter thick, rose from the orifice, growing taller until Dante had to tilt his head back to see it. It swayed side to side like a cobra entranced by a snake charmer's pungi music. Dante spent a few seconds waiting for the creature to make its move before the worm-thing reeled.

He recognized the action for what it was: preparation before a strike. When it leaned back, the creature formed an S. Then it whiplashed forward and launched itself at Dante with speed that might have overwhelmed him had he not been ready. Even despite his quick response, the creature almost caught Dante off guard.

Almost.

He dropped to one knee as the creature bulleted over his head and splattered like putty on the wall behind him. It instantly began to re-form, the long, thin worm once again swaying to music only it could hear.

Dante averted his eyes with quick furtive glances around the room, searching for a means to battle the creature. Everything he'd seen up to that point suggested that he could not let the infernal thing touch him, and so far, he'd been lucky to avoid contact. But luck always ran out, sooner or later.

The biohazardous-waste-disposal unit he spied gave him an idea. The unit was built into the wall, closed unless manually held open. He would have to time things just right, and even then, he would need to rely on continued good fortune. With no better ideas coming to mind, he ran over to the unit and pulled its heavy drawer out. Opening like a post-office box, it swung down with a heavy creak. Carefully, he turned around again and faced the creature, keeping his body against the door to hold it open. Its hard edge rested under his shoulder blades.

He waited.

With no room to recoil as it had before, the snake-worm retracted into itself like a Slinky then shot forward. Dante was ready for it. He sidestepped out of the creature's path, and it flew by him, but not into the waste-disposal unit, as he'd hoped. The monstrosity collided with the wall just above the unit, splatting as it had before and already re-forming. The waste-disposal unit's door retracted.

Dante reached for the first thing he could find, a fancy-looking microscope that looked as though it had cost somebody a lot of money – not his problem. It sat on a nearby lab station. Without a second thought, he slammed its base into the creature with one hand while simultaneously pulling open the door to the disposal unit with the other.

Nothing happened. Dante went apeshit. He slammed the microscope over and over again into the creature until it oozed and simmered like soup on a stove top. The microscope broke apart in his hands, but not before the bludgeoned creature flattened back into pancake form. Its top portion curled back from the wall as it rolled into a burrito. With a *slurp*, the biomass fell into the drawer.

Dante slammed the door to the unit shut. He didn't know how to work the device, but fortunately, the buttons were clearly labeled. He gritted his teeth and turned a dial that read 'Incinerator'. He liked the sound of that.

"Waste analyzed. No danger of deleterious chemical release," a computerized female voice said, which Dante found strangely arousing. "Incineration shall begin momentarily."

He heard a *whoosh* as gas ignited. Warmth radiated from the unit.

He let out a breath and slumped against the lab station, staring at the drawer as if it were the best thing since the invention of the wheel. His mind, always slower in times of peace, tried to make sense of all that he'd just experienced.

His relief was short lived. Screaming followed by machine-gun fire came from the hallway. Dante staggered, biting his tongue in his surprise. He'd let his guard down for a second, only to learn the madness was still far from over. Suddenly short of breath, his ordeal finally catching up to him, he rested a moment, and his hand slipped across the lab table, pushing aside various scientific apparatuses he didn't recognize and knocking over a flask that broke into pieces as it shattered against the floor.

He quickly recovered. He drew his gun and checked his ammo count then turned toward the commotion, ready to battle anew.

On the other side of the door was an ASAP security guard twitching and seizing much as Romanov had been. He didn't recognize the guard, and the twinge of disappointment he felt when he realized it wasn't Stearns dispersed quickly in the face of urgency. Thin worm tentacles like those that had spread from Patient Zero into Romanov's face crept like vines up that unknown guard's neck. Somehow, they'd broken through the plastic polymer seal that prevented the spread of all known contaminants outside the clean room. The guard's eyes rolled back in their sockets, and foam surged from his mouth.

How? Dante wondered, but the answer became obvious. Through the window, he saw the tentacles and traced them back into the clean room. The tentacles writhed through a narrow crack. The seal was missing entirely. Following the lengths of the tentacles closer still, he saw their point of origin.

"He's gone," Dante muttered, though only Romanov's head and torso were truly missing.

'Gone' might not have been the best word, either. 'Stretched and liquefied' described the sight. All that was left of the man was a pair of legs and a bundle of twisting, coiling strands that ran from those legs in a pool of viscous snot to freedom.

And if they could breach one secure doorway.... Dante shuddered.

Again, he was left searching for a means to fight the biohellspawn. He knew how to fight men – all kinds of men – fat men, skinny men, tall men, short men, strong men, trained men...and women, too. He even knew how to fight off trained dogs and had some experience in altercations with other wild and domesticated mammals.

But mutating piles of human flesh had never been on his need-to-know-how-to-kill checklist. Apparently, his training regimen had had a gaping hole in it. And presently, between him and the only way out, a mass of mutating flesh in need of killing awaited Dante.

"Acid, maybe?" he muttered, checking over his shoulder for the unconscious scientist sprawled in her wheelchair. He could have used her help, picked her brain. He envied her unconscious state, as reality was looking bleak, but he wished she'd wake her ass up and share some sage advice – anything that might give him an edge in his fight against what was nothing less than a child of Satan.

He'd heard nothing more from the creature he'd roasted in the waste-disposal unit, so perhaps fire would do the trick. If movies told it true, every lab had to be equipped with Prometheus's bane. He just had to find its source.

"You're going to burn, you disgusting pile of shit." He examined several pieces of equipment, the functions of which he did not know. He stepped toward another lab station and heard a squish from underfoot.

He looked down to see the remains of the first scalp crab he'd crushed sliding up the sides of his boot toward his laces. "*Merda!* You've got to be fucking kidding me!"

With his uncontaminated foot, he kicked off his infested boot by its heel. He grabbed it by its top and raced over to the waste-disposal unit. "*Arrivederci!*" Dante said and dropped the boot into the drawer. He cranked on the fire.

A red button flashed. "Several hazardous dioxins and furans likely to be released through incineration," the computerized voice said. "However, a temperature increase to" – a pause followed by a series of beeps – "nine hundred eighty degrees Celsius will eliminate dangers to humans and environment. Do you wish to proceed with temperature increase?"

"Yes," Dante said before realizing the machine was not voice activated. He tapped a flashing red button as soon as he noticed it.

"Incineration shall begin momentarily."

Dante sighed. "Now that that's done, back to Romanov."

Outside the clean room, the screaming and twitching had stopped. Two guards were standing at the far end of the corridor, their faces ashen and mouths agape.

I know how you feel, boys. Dante found no humor in their horrified expressions.

One of them, a man as tall as an NBA center with long, lanky arms, stared through the horror, through Dante, as if what he'd seen had short-circuited his brain.

Fucking useless.

The other guard, who looked like a child beside his partner, fixed his gaze on something on the floor in front of the door. Since Dante had a good chunk of that something on his side of the door as well, he didn't have to be one of the center's overpaid, criminally reckless nerds to know that the ASAP fellow was staring at his fallen comrade, no doubt at a loss for what to do with him.

"Keep your distance!" Dante yelled. "Whatever you do, don't touch him. Burn him if you can."

He watched the two guards' faces for recognition and understanding. They definitely heard him, as the shorter guard looked his way when he spoke. Neither guard seemed to register his words, though. Their faces remained as blank as fresh pieces of paper.

Dante would have to take it upon himself to purify the area. He fumbled under his testicles for a matchbook he'd hidden there, not seeing in the lab what he needed to produce a bigger, fiercer flame. *It'll have to do.* But that didn't mean he had to like it. Using a match would mean that he would have to get close.

Unless.... He scratched his head. Dried dirt snowflaked to the ground. *Maybe I'm going about this the wrong way.* He looked at the bottles lining a shelf along the back wall. "Benzene, silver nitrate, potassium chloride, isopropyl alcohol, toluene, ethyl ether, ethyl alcohol...." All, any, or none of those chemicals might've been flammable. He didn't know what any of them were. But he knew alcohol. Molotov was his favorite cocktail.

Damn, I could use a drink. He grabbed the ethyl alcohol. The flame symbol printed low on the label reinforced his decision. As if that wasn't enough, beneath the symbol, the bottle read 'Caution: Highly Flammable'.

Jackpot. Dante ran with the bottle back to Romanov's disembodied legs. When he got there, he saw that what were once legs were legs no longer. At least, not human legs.

Romanov's boots were off. His pants were still on, but jutting out of the fabric, the organic material had mutated. The change wasn't as drastic as the complete reconfiguration of the guard's upper torso. His legs lacked any contour or bone or muscle makeup, bumped peg legs stretching beyond his hemline like the legs of a starfish.

As Dante neared, the appendages stood erect as if sensing danger. They swiped at the air between them but weren't long enough to reach him – not yet, but they were still stretching.

The starfish legs flopped and thudded against the ground more rapidly when Dante doused them with the chemical he'd grabbed. They flopped more frantically, which caused Dante to smile. With hatred in his heart and defiance in his eyes, Dante lit a match and flicked it at Romanov's warped form.

The flame blew out before it hit the abomination. Dante groaned, rolled his eyes, and lit a second match. When he flicked that one, the creature burst into flames.

A high-pitched chorus of whines erupted from the mouthless mass. It was shrill enough to set every dog east of the Prime Meridian barking. Still, the creature burned and bubbled and blistered. The flame quickly spread across the creature's entire form, as if its own living tissue were highly flammable. To Dante's wondrous joy, the portion connecting torso A to hell-of-a-mess B ignited also, and the flame surged along the tentacles and under the door. Its warm glow climbed up the hallway walls outside.

An alarm sounded, and a sprinkler system sprouted from the ceiling inside the clean room. Dante cursed as he and the creature were doused by a torrent of water. Still, the fire raged, both inside the room and out. One of the guards disappeared and came back with a fire extinguisher.

"No!" Dante shouted. "Not until there's nothing left of it but ash!"

At last, recognition registered on the guard's face. He lowered the extinguisher and stepped away from the conflagration. Dante nodded his appreciation. He warmed himself by the fire, but not too close by it, trying to counteract the chill from the icy water. Streaks of mud ran into his eyes, and he blinked out the irritation.

Behind him came a clang then a rattle of metal against the floor. He turned to check on the unconscious scientist, hoping she was awake and alert, but she had not stirred.

The body that had lain beside her was gone. Out of the corner of his eye, Dante caught something wiggling into the now-coverless air vent before it, too, was gone.

CHAPTER TWELVE

You used me, Sergei said. His voice sounded as if he were standing in the middle of a giant amphitheater buried deep beneath the earth, empty and otherwise soundless. The reality was far more terrifying. He was trapped, alone and desperate, inside a mind that was no longer his to control.

But in that mind, he was seeing wondrous, albeit horrifying, things. He saw what that sentient creature, older than the Earth itself, saw and some of what it had already seen through a million-plus eyes spread across time and space. He heard voices that were and voices that had been, yet all the same voice, through a million-plus ears. But he tasted nothing, smelled nothing, *felt* absolutely nothing, never doubting that that last part was for the better.

He knew he was lost – a mind without a brain, a soul without a body – yet that knowledge was not discomforting. Instead, it was...*freeing?* After the last few weeks of torment at the whims of an unrelenting malevolence – *what had the researchers called it? Molli?* – it had finally succeeded in its plan to become him and, in doing so, had released Sergei from the responsibilities of life and the struggles of living with the deepest heartache and an irreplaceable loss. In a way, perhaps he owed the creature a thank you. He snickered. The creature was shouldering all his burdens.

But he couldn't forgive the creature for the cruel deception it had employed to gain its own freedom. Nor could he allow it to breed, to spread, at least not if he could help it.

Sergei had tried hard in life to be a good man, a good husband, a good father, and a good scientist. He had failed in all respects. A passenger in his own body, he was stuck watching a television program featuring a character bent on global annihilation. He had no way to stop watching, to turn off the program when it came to the rough parts and move on to an afterlife where he could possibly be reunited with his daughter, with the *real* Natalya, not that hateful creature's decoy.

But since he couldn't have that, Sergei figured he had the next best thing: an eternity to torture and torment his body's new captain the same way it had tortured and tormented him. If he'd had a mouth, he would have smirked. He was never, ever, going to shut up.

Never.

You used me, he said again. *And you used her to get to me.*

"How does this one still speak?" the creature hissed, its form now more snake than man as it slithered through the air vent. "The other, the female...that one resists. How could that one resist? And I become this one, and this one is me. This one is no more, yet some part remains. No part must remain."

Well, you best get used to it, shithead. I'm not going anywhere.

"This one must go! I am this one. This one is no more!"

This one is staying right where he is. Sergei said the words to provoke the creature, but the sad reality was that he had no way of leaving, no legs to carry him away. His fate seemed inextricably tied to the creature's. His body wasn't only no longer his, but it was no longer human. The process that had altered him seemed irreversible. The best he could hope for was a satisfying and excruciatingly painful demise, for the creature anyway.

"This one is infinitesimal. I am the ender of all things and the bringer of rebirth. I am the conqueror of species mighty and fierce, the instrument of an age of ice and nothingness. I bring oblivion. It is my time anew. This one's kind is frail and inconsequential. This one's kind will end like all planetary parasites that came before it."

So what are you saying? You're like some goddamn reset button for the whole planet Earth?

"Reset? Yessss! I like this one's word! The planet will flourish. Life will flourish, free of vermin! This one is vermin."

Yeah, well, good luck with that, asshole. In the meantime, let me ask you this: If you take over other humans, aren't you going to have a lot more than just this one's consciousness to manage? I have a feeling it will be getting awfully crowded in here really soon.

"This one must go! This one must go! I will destroy this one's part that remains. I will twist and tear and render this one's body into morsels, which I will then consume until I have found this one and eradicated him."

I will never leave.

The creature stopped beside an adjoining air vent, where a fan blew into its animal face. It worked its way through the grating and the fan, getting lopped into pieces through the long process, only to reconstruct itself on the other side. Sergei wondered if the whole ordeal had hurt the creature at all. He hadn't felt a thing.

The creature had worked its way from the clean room's vent into the center's main air ducts. It slithered along until it found itself over a grate, looking down upon humans through cheese-grater-sized slits. The creature stared, and Sergei stared with it. His defiance shriveled when he saw an ASAP security guard lying on a gurney, his eye bandaged, the same eye Sergei had impaled with a fork. He wished he could take back what he'd done or at least apologize to the man. He wished even more for a means to stop what the creature was about to do to the guard.

The creature began to push itself through the trellis, a process that closely resembled meat going through a grinder, segmenting it into an immeasurable number of component parts.

The guard below stirred. Sergei tried to close his eyes, but they were no longer his to shut. He saw whatever the creature saw.

And all he could do was watch.

CHAPTER THIRTEEN

Dante shifted his weight off his left butt cheek and onto his right. He'd been handcuffed and ordered to sit on something called a Hitachi S-12480, a clean-room apparatus of unknown function. To his right was what appeared to be a centrifuge. To his left was a sink with dual nozzles that shot streams of water directly into one's eyes.

Beyond the sink stood the man who'd cuffed him on Stearns's orders, a slope-headed Neanderthal named Johnson. He looked three parts MMA heavyweight and one part gorilla, with fists as big and solid as sledgehammers. When he and the other guard – a square-jawed Russian named Belgrade – showed up to assist Stearns, Dante had enough sense not to resist their taking him into custody. He'd hoped that maybe, after what they had witnessed, he could reason with them about destroying the viruses. He'd underestimated Stearns's dominion over the crisis and the guard's willingness to neglect his need for medical attention in order to see Dante dealt with properly.

Ahead of him was the real concern, which ASAP did at least seem to be taking seriously and handling somewhat competently: an uncovered vent with little maggot-sized squirming things wriggling all over the opening and the grate below it. He'd told the ASAP guards in the room to torch it. Again to their credit, they seemed to be listening. Under a controlled fire, the leftovers of Romanov and the guard he'd infected were burned until they were nothing but piles of ash and bone, swept up, and tossed into the incinerator, where they were torched again as an insurance policy.

A big fellow with a milky-white complexion, rolled-up sleeves, and a black cowboy hat hanging low over his brow stepped into the room. He was smiling big and goofy, as if enjoying the excitement. A flamethrower hung over his back.

Another guard followed at his heels, the NBA center Dante had seen in the hallway, completely useless after one of his coworkers had been attacked by Romanov. His arms hung low from the weight of a giant lantern-thing he carried. He was sweating profusely, and his eyes kept shifting their focus, scanning the area for only he knew what. When his eyes met Dante's, they passed over him without a second glance. But when they landed on the maggoty things on the wall and floor, he squealed and backed away, clearly terrified.

Stearns appeared at the doorway, propped up by Belgrade. A younger woman – Indian and in her late twenties, Dante guessed – scooted past them and crouched near the guard Dante deemed most likely to wet his pants.

"Sampson," Stearns called.

The guard with the lantern set it down and looked Stearns's way.

"This woman works for the doctor we contacted about the potential release of the viruses into the center. They cleared the woman who was out cold when we got in here and that asshole over yonder as noncontagious" – he pointed at Dante – "though I say we shoot the asshole anyway."

"If you'll just permit me…." The woman who had followed Stearns in pushed her way past him and headed toward the machine Sampson had carried.

Stearns cleared his throat. "Yes, of course." Addressing Sampson, he said, "Your job is to give this woman whatever assistance she needs. Her name is Anju Duvale—"

"Denali," Anju corrected.

"Whatever," Stearns said, sneering. "Ms. *Denali* thinks she can tweak that scanner so that we can search out and clear the building of any infectious agents."

Anju sat cross-legged in front of the giant lantern-thing and tinkered with it. "I will need to reconfigure a few things and—"

"Do what you need to do, ma'am. Sampson, if she doesn't need you, send a video feed up the air vent after Kelly torches it and those… things…crawling all over it. Scan the room to make sure it's clear once the good lady here has it up and running. Incinerate everything you can."

Sampson, nervous and fidgeting, nevertheless nodded.

"Good," Stearns said. "Kelly, try not to burn the whole damn place down, will you?"

Kelly smiled and laughed. "I can't make any promises, partner."

Stearns didn't smile back. He looked at Dante, who would have given Stearns the finger if his hands weren't chained behind his back.

"Johnson," ASAP's fearless leader said without taking his eyes off Dante, "bring this dickhead with us. After my wounds are taken care of, I plan on giving him some of his own."

CHAPTER FOURTEEN

What the fuck? She blinked repeatedly until a film over her eyes began to dissipate. *Where am I?*

Clara closed her eyes and had almost drifted back to sleep when she snapped herself up straight. *My room? How'd I get here?*

She was sitting in her wheelchair, staring at the cold, blank wall of her room. Raising her hands before her eyes, she stared at them and trembled. *Am I infected? What happened to that man?*

The more awake she became, the more she filled with fear. "Hello?" Her room was empty. She wasn't sure why she had called out. A vague memory of someone talking to her.

My mother?

"Are you all right in there, Ms. St. Pierre?" a deep voice called from the hallway. Clara didn't know who the voice belonged to, but she knew the flat, robotic tone of an ASAP man when she heard it.

"You've been cleared for visitors, but you must remain confined to your quarters until the extent of your infection can be determined."

Infection? Clara's breath caught in her throat. "If I'm infected, what am I doing back in my room?"

"Doc says you're not contagious."

Clara frowned. "What doc?"

The man in the hall didn't answer. She rolled quietly toward the door, hoping he'd left so she could leave and figure out what the hell had happened. As she neared, she saw the shadow his boots cast through the crack at the bottom of the door.

She sighed. *So…now what?*

Clara gasped, remembering. She had been standing. She had *kicked* that man. And she had felt pain when he'd clawed up her leg. Narrow tears ran through the denim at her calf and above her the back of her knee, but she could see no wounds beneath. In fact, her legs felt strong, as they once had so long before. Slapping them, she felt a lively sting.

She wondered if – *no, I can…I can stand up right now. Maybe.*

She dug her nails into the arms of her chair, squeezing until all the pink vanished from her cuticles. She closed her eyes and took a deep breath. *One foot at a time.* She grabbed her pants just over her left knee and lifted her leg, removing her foot from its footrest and lowering it slowly to the floor. Her motions were controlled, unlike her breathing or her heart's rapid beating.

She smiled, but her confidence was fleeting. The idea that the sensations she'd been feeling were somehow real, not some vile false-positive side effect of her newly acquired disease or some cruel, phantom limb-like deception, gave her pause. But there it was, the ground beneath her sole, her foot firmly planted. She wondered, though, if it could support her weight.

She lifted her right foot and lowered it to the floor.

A knock came at the door.

Clara sighed, long and cleansing, simultaneously disappointed and relieved. She hadn't been ready to try, not really. She doubted whether she would ever be. *What if I fall? What if I fail?*

The knock came again, and she huffed then lifted her feet back onto the rests. *False hope is worse than no hope.*

She pushed her chair closer to the door. "Who is it?"

"Um, hi Clara. It's, um, Jordan…Jordan Phillips. You know, the dork who showed you his flower garden?" A high tittering laugh resonated through the door, followed by silence then incoherent mumbling. "Anyway…I just wanted to check in on you and see if you might need anything."

"Just a second," Clara said, immediately regretting it. She didn't want to see anyone at the moment, least of all that peculiar American ball of clumsy handsomeness, Dr. Jordan Phillips. And how could she? *What if I'm infectious?* She couldn't let him in, not when there was so much left to learn about Molli.

Stop making excuses, she scolded herself. *You know damn well you're not going to infect anyone.* And she did know, was quite sure of it actually, though she had no idea what had led her to such a summary conclusion – not science, that was certain. But the fact that she was outside the clean room at all suggested someone else had agreed.

You're just…you're just a damn chicken.

She set her jaw and grabbed the cloth over her knees, yelping as she pinched her skin in the process. The sound escaping her lips had been one of surprise, not pain, or rather surprise at the sensation of pain. It *hurt*. She could still feel it. A smart, stabbing sensation tingled in her leg, where no feeling of any kind had been present for months.

And the feet themselves came off the floor easily, too easily, as if they'd come up on their own volition. Clara didn't trust them.

Without further hesitation, she covered the remaining distance to the door, unlocked it, and swung it open. Outside, a tall man in a pressed green cardigan under a wrinkled and soiled lab coat shuffled his brown-loafered feet. He pushed his wire-rimmed glasses up his nose as he slowly raised his head. The last time she'd seen him, he'd been wearing only a Speedo and had double the machismo, triple the confidence, and quadruple the easy charm. Now, he looked lanky and awkward, uncomfortable in his own skin. She half expected him to pull out his collar in some cartoonish exaggeration of anxiety.

Still, his discomfort did wonders for her own nerves. *Funny, that.* She laughed, covering her mouth.

At the sound of her giddiness, Jordan's easy smile returned. His hands were hidden behind his back, and he brought them forward and revealed a dozen flowers.

"For you," he said, bowing graciously as he extended his arm toward Clara. He maintained eye contact almost the entire time, only looking away when Clara's eyes grew big.

She couldn't keep looking into his eyes for long either, blushing as she turned away. The way he'd been looking at her, his eyes smiling yet burning with intensity, the way a man looked at a woman – he was so unlike most men, those who saw her as a cripple first, a woman second. *Cripple.* She grunted. How she hated the word. But despite all the politically correct bullshit force-fed her via education since day one of grammar school, 'cripple' was the only word she would use to describe herself.

She rolled her shoulders, letting the weight of the word roll off, then accepted the flowers into her arms. "They're beautiful," she said, thinking that was what she was supposed to say. She knew little about flowers and was fairly certain that was the first time anyone had given them to her since she'd been diagnosed with MS. Then, it had been a boyfriend, who didn't stick around. *Showed his true colors. Did me a favor.* Telling herself that never made it hurt less.

The memory made her think little for the perfumed plants. At best, they were little more than a way of saying, "I pity you." At worst, they were an empty gesture entirely. She wondered what they were for Jordan. He didn't look at her with pity. But maybe he just hid it well.

"What's your angle, Dr. Phillips?"

Jordan upturned his palms, revealing empty hands. "No angle, Clara. I saw a beautiful woman with a brilliant mind undergo a rather awful day, and I thought to myself, 'Jordan, if you can bring a smile to her face on a day like today, maybe, just maybe, she'll give you the honor of being your dinner guest some evening.' Now, maybe I was fooling myself, but…I know this great place two corridors north and about seventeen east. They have the best microwaved burritos this side of a frozen tundra."

"Fantastic day-old doughnuts, too, I hear." Clara rolled her eyes and smirked. "Where are my manners? I've kept you in the doorway long enough. Come in, come in!" She rolled backward, giving him plenty of room to get by. "Have a seat anywhere you'd like. We have a desk chair and a bed…."

Clara gasped and covered her mouth as heat rose in her cheeks. She hadn't meant the comment the way it sounded. At least, she didn't think she had.

Jordan laughed it off, but she thought his face reddened, too. He took a seat at the desk.

She buried her nose in the flowers. The buttery-sweet smell tickled her nose hairs while the silky white petals tickled her cheek. Four purple-tipped stalk-things, the name for which she couldn't remember, sprouted from each flower's center. Clara really didn't like anything about flowers, but the gesture…. Maybe that had been beautiful.

"What do you call them?"

"Clara."

She stared at him blankly, speechless.

"No," he said, erupting with laughter. "I'm just teasing. We haven't given them a scientific name yet. They are a new species of *erythronium*, though they grow much larger than the largest of previously known species. They're from the seeds we found in the dig. Their growth rate is exponentially faster than other members of the lily order, but that seems to have no effect on their longevity. It's almost as if these flowers are made up of some Superman hormone that spurs growth and maintains health even under harsh conditions."

"Or maybe they have a talented botanist tending to their every need."

Jordan smiled. "You flatter me. But these babies are low maintenance. They did all this growing mostly on their own. And wait until you see them tomorrow."

Clara laid the flowers across her lap. "Thank you. I mean it, but I'm afraid I have nothing to put them in."

"I thought of that." Jordan pulled a cylindrical beaker from his lab-coat pocket. "It's not much to look at, but it should do the trick. Tiger Lily isn't going to die on my watch."

"Tiger Lily? So you have named it? Not very original."

"It's only temporary. It's not too late to call it Clara, if you'd prefer." He laughed.

She didn't. "You'd better not." She stared at the beaker in his hand. "But I have no wa—"

"I thought of that, too." Jordan pulled a bottle of water from his other coat pocket. He shook it, and the water became cloudy. "My own special blend. This stuff's like spinach to Popeye."

"Who?"

"He's an old American cartoon character who…. Never mind, it's silly." Jordan twisted off the bottle's cap and poured the liquid into the beaker. He pointed at the flowers. "May I?"

"Oh, sure." Clara handed the flowers back to Jordan. He placed them in the beaker then arranged them with care until they conformed to some secret standard he wasn't sharing with the rest of the world. He placed the makeshift vase on her nightstand and wiped his hands on his coat.

"There. Perfect," Jordan said, not looking at the flowers.

"Thank you." Clara felt the blood rise in her cheeks yet again and fidgeted. She crossed her arms over her legs and bit into her lip, trying to think of what to say next. Despite her awkwardness, she craved contact, a sort of desire budding in her that she hadn't felt in many years. *God, I hope he can't tell.*

But maybe a part of her hoped he could. Just a little. She bit into her lower lip, the pain having the opposite effect of what she had intended.

"So…." Jordan rubbed his palms into his thighs. "How are you holding up?"

"Well, you know, almost murdered...exposed to an unknown and potentially lethal microorganism.... Does it get any better than this?"

"I suspect, in your line of work, it's just another day at the Shakhova-Mendelsen Siberian Research Center."

"Truly, my job isn't all that glamorous or dangerous. Usually. But for a high-security, top-of-the-line outpost, this facility is proving to be fairly easy for maniacs to penetrate. I mean, two security breaches in one day?"

"Well, they're treating you with caution. Round-the-clock guard posted outside your door, ready to shoot you if you try to leave. I'm surprised he let me back in."

"Back in?"

"I agreed to stay with you and warn them if anything strange started happening. I figured you'd want to wake up to a friendly face over one of those trigger-happy morons."

A sheen covered his eyes as they filled with something wild. His stare lingered just a little longer than it should have. He took a deep breath. "Well, after the morning you've had, the important thing is that you're safe, relatively speaking, that is. If there is anything I can do—"

"I'm fine." Clara wasn't sure why she had blurted that. *Defense mechanisms,* she supposed. A good-looking, thoughtful, intelligent man was there trying to be her white knight, but she couldn't let him. If it wasn't bad enough that she couldn't accept help from anyone, the fact that he showed interest in her must have been evidence of something wrong with him. *I'm my own goddamn knight, the only one I've ever had.* She sighed. *And my worst enemy.*

Jordan cleared his throat. "Any theories why you're...um...."

"Not like Sergei Kobozev? Not murderously insane? Not boiling over like a medieval serf with syphilis? Not dripping skin faster than a leper?"

Jordan's nose crinkled as if the odor of rotten fish had just wafted by. He frowned. "Something like that."

She shrugged. "I'm not even sure how I got out of the lab."

"How much do you remember?"

"Most, I think. I remember...being attacked, Sergei trying to get at the sample. *Mon Dieu! Il l'a bu! Mais pourquoi?*"

Jordan squinted then blinked. He said nothing.

Clara shook her head. An eyebrow rose. *Oops.* "I lapsed into French, didn't I?"

"Yup."

"Sorry. That happens sometimes when I get excited."

"And are you?" The corner of his mouth curled. "Excited?"

Clara pouted. The question tasted sour. She looked away as she felt heat again flashing in her cheeks, wondering what experiences or lack thereof had caused her to grow into such a prude. Then again, it hardly seemed the right moment for such blatant flirtation. Then again, no time ever seemed right for her. Her social skills and the interactions they invited ranged from socially awkward to the functional equivalent of a loud fart in a quiet elevator.

She pretended as if she hadn't heard him or, at the least, didn't understand his meaning. "I'm anxious, and if I'm being honest, a little afraid."

"A little?"

Since she'd woken, she had been ignoring the elephant in the room as best she could. She could ignore it no longer. "I'm fucking terrified! But I only have two choices: sit here and lament my fate while I nurse my wounds or get back in the lab and see what makes me so different. If Molli's running rampant through the research center, I shouldn't be wasting any time and should be looking for the cure. I am in a unique position where I may be carrying the answer somewhere in my genetic code."

"It's okay to be scared, Clara. You were just attacked by a coworker without reason or provocation. I'm no psychiatrist, but I have to imagine that would rattle the strongest of us."

"He drank Molli, Jordan! He grabbed the petri dish and poured her down his throat, never so much as taking a moment to consider that doing so might be detrimental to his health, never mind everyone else's. Where's the reason in that? The man was a scientist, like you and me. Logic, rationality, sensibility...hell, good ol' common sense are supposed to be tools of the trade. A clear, systematic approach, step-by-step cause-and-effect analysis, the scientific method – these are what govern our research and our actions. We don't go slurping amoebas out of petri dishes."

Jordan grunted. "Um, silly question: Who or what is Molli?"

"The virus, damn it! He drank the fucking virus!"

Jordan hung his head. "I'm sorry." He waved a hand dismissively. "I didn't realize you had pet names for viruses."

Clara groaned and grabbed the arms of her chair a little tighter. If that devilishly handsome buffoon continued to get under her skin, she was as apt to tear him apart as she was to tear off his clothes. She took in a longer breath and released a longer sigh. *Logic,* she told herself. *Only animals allow their emotions to triumph.*

"You have scientific names for your flowers, correct?"

"Yes. Of course."

"And you also have nicknames or common names for them, right?"

"Yes. But plants are—"

"I am sure it is not hard for you to imagine what a pain in the ass it would be to have to constantly refer to my examination subject as *Mollivirus sibericum.* The time spent saying and writing that elongated name is time wasted. So, we have simply resorted to calling her Molli."

Jordan stroked the salt-and-pepper stubble that rounded out his prominent chin. "Okay. That makes sense, I suppose…even if you did just call it a 'her'."

Infuriating man. Clara huffed. She bet he had a pet name for his penis. Was naming Molli really so different? *Mon Dieu, I just equated a microorganism to a penis.* She huffed some more. "Look, we are getting a bit far afield here. The facts, as I understand them, are such: One, I've been exposed to a virus – well, it's not a virus, actually – to a single-celled organism with what appears to have hundreds of genes, where the common virus causing the flu has only eleven and some far deadlier diseases have less. The potential for Molli to be a cold-blooded killer was better than hitting it big on a slot machine, the risk of it causing other harm better than hitting on a red or black bet at the roulette table. We've already seen the monstrous impact Molli has had on one human body."

"Two, actually."

"What?" Clara's heart leaped off starting blocks and took off at a sprint in her chest. *Stay calm, rational.* She tried to soothe her nerves. *You're a scientist, damn it.* She met Jordan's stare. "When I blacked out, Sergei Kobozev and I were trapped inside a clean room." As frightening as that was, she forced her mind back into that clean room and analyzed the data, trying to see what she might have been missing.

And she did remember. A strange man had helped her.

She rubbed her forehead. "The man with the black cross," she mumbled. Her mind struggled to recall the other details of his face.

"No, not him." Jordan's voice reeled her back into the here and now. "That man was, however, responsible for the explosion—"

"What explosion?"

"He set off several bombs in the parking garage. Thankfully, no one was hurt. Whatever that crazy bastard was after, I'm just thankful he didn't harm you either, which is more than I can say for those assholes from ASAP." Jordan flexed his fingers and scowled.

He was by no means an imposing figure, more apt to sew up his own cardigan than to rip it off. *His pants are permanently pleated, for fuck's sake.* Beneath his clothes, he had muscle mass only slightly greater than that of a prepubescent boy, despite how her daydreams had portrayed him.

Still, she had to admit that his anger at her apparent mistreatment was touching. "It seems I missed much when I was out cold. Maybe you should start from the beginning."

Jordan began to fidget. "D-D-Doc...er...D-Doctor Werniewski could explain all that much better than I could," he stuttered. "He should be back any minute now, and—"

"Jordan," she said softly. "Please. Just tell me."

He cracked his knuckles one at a time while he considered her request. His shoulders drooped. "Please understand, Clara. This sort of scientific analysis falls way outside my area of expertise. Dr. Werniewski's the clinical microbiologist, Dr. Thomas an excellent pathologist. And then there's yourself. All of you are far more qualified to discuss your...condition. I'm just a botanist, and if I'm being honest, more lucky than good at that."

She went to pat his hand but he recoiled and straightened. "It's okay, Jordan. I know I was exposed. If I weren't in my room and in complete control of my molecules, I would have assumed I was infected. Given your hesitancy to discuss it with me, I assume I must be." She paused, thought long and hard about her next question and whether or not she truly wanted an answer to it, then asked it before she could come to a conclusion on the matter. "Why did ASAP want to harm me?"

"You're.... I'm sorry, Clara, but you're.... How can I say this?"

"Easy. Just say it."

"I'm not qualified to—"

"*Mon Dieu*, Jordan. Just say it already. I'm infected?"

"Your...your assumption is correct." He looked everywhere around the room, focusing on everything except her, as his finger rapped on the desk. "Wait.... 'Infected' might be the wrong word. The virus—"

"It's not a virus."

"The vir…. *Molli* is inside you." He leaned closer to her and placed his hands over hers.

She snapped her hands away.

"It-It-It's not what you think," he stammered. "Molli is inside you, but according to Dr. Werniewski, you're not contagious. The entity is a blood-borne pathogen. I think that's what he called it. While you were out, he took skin, mucus, and…*other* samples and found absolutely no abnormalities. He said that other than your blood, you are completely germ free, like freakishly so, as if your body had eradicated every trace of harmful bacteria."

"But my blood—"

"He hasn't actually tested your blood yet, felt it a bit too intrusive without your consent. But initial biometric readings from his scanner show evidence of infection and a white blood cell count that was through the roof. But everything seems normal, even your white blood cell count, now."

"That doesn't sound right. I have MS, a disease that attacks the autoimmune system. My white blood cell count, even at its most consistent rate, has never been normal. The scan must be wrong."

"I'm sorry, Clara. I wish I knew more. You've been on near-constant surveillance since the clean room was compromised except when I snuck out to bring you some flowers. I'm sorry I wasn't here when you woke. The ASAP assholes wanted to shoot you and incinerate your body. If it wasn't for the quick action of Dr. Werniewski's assistant, they just might have. Werniewski was called in to assess the breach. His assistant literally threw herself in front of your chair, I'm told. Like you, she's a very brave woman. I think she said her name is—"

"Anju." Clara smiled. "I will have to thank her when I see her next."

"She fell on top of you. Can you believe that? She's the reason why we know you're safe to touch. All her biometrics came back negative." Jordan shuddered. "Not like the others."

"What others? Kobozev is dead – I saw his head explode – and I thought you said the terrorist jerk wasn't infected?"

"The others have been incinerated," said Dr. Oleg Werniewski as he pushed open the door to Clara's room without knocking. "Sergei Kobozev, unfortunately, remains unaccounted for."

Jordan must not have closed the door properly. Clara wondered how long her colleague had been standing outside, listening.

Dr. Werniewski was an abrasive man. Though they were colleagues working the same project, Clara avoided him whenever possible lest she be entrapped by one of his self-gratifying tales of his own opulent grandeur. Physically, he was equally repugnant, the type of man who always stood a few inches closer than he should, whose eyes had a tendency to wander. Clara wondered if she disliked him more for being lecherous around her associates or for never being so toward her. Not that she wanted him to be. It simply reinforced her low self-esteem to know that a standardless pervert like Werniewski wouldn't even give her so much as a second glance.

She wondered how Anju put up with what must have been constant sexual harassment. Just imagining his potbelly rubbing up against Anju's back, sweat pouring off his bald head as he grunted and wheezed through stained teeth, made Clara want to gag. Yet every time she saw Anju, the young assistant was smiling.

Thoughts like that are how rumors start, she warned herself, preventing the line of thought from continuing into the realm of pure, unwarranted speculation. As if summoned by the thought of her name, Anju pushed past the doctor and entered the room.

"Excuse me, Dr. Werniewski," she said, short of breath. "This is heavy." She was lugging some sort of mechanical device that Clara found vaguely familiar but had a difficult time placing. Anju plopped it on Clara's desk.

"Is that—" Clara began.

"From the clean room, yes," Anju replied. Her warm smile was contagious as she greeted Jordan and Clara. "I just made two of these for ASAP, and I figured it could not hurt to have one of our own."

Clara nodded. "I heard I have you to thank for saving my life."

Anju blushed and looked away. "It was nothing."

Dr. Werniewski cleared his throat then spoke louder than was necessary. "That's not all you have to thank Anju for. My little lab-assistant genius was able to reconfigure the clean-room scanner into a portable version."

"It was not hard, really," Anju said. "I just disconnected it from its wall mount then modified its directional scanning capabilities from a stationary, cone-shaped scan radius to a three-hundred-sixty-degree rotating scan—"

"Bottom line," Dr. Werniewski interrupted, "she made the scanner travel ready. In addition to having learned invaluable laboratory skills and knowledge of the biological sciences from yours truly, she also acquired some technical savvy along the way." He stroked his assistant's arm.

Anju stiffened, but her body relaxed as soon as the microbiologist removed his stubby fingers.

"It's as I always say: the most brilliant minds deserve the most brilliant assistants," Dr. Werniewski said.

Clara rolled her eyes and set her jaw. "We are all familiar with just how brilliant you are, Dr. Werniewski, but if you'd be so kind, I'd really like to know what you've learned from your unconsented-to tests of my body."

"Desperate times call for—"

"Just," she started sharply then held herself in check, "give it to me straight."

"Anju," he said, "would you do the honors?"

Anju returned to the device on Clara's desk. It resembled a battery-powered camping lantern without a handle, though Clara knew its lighting and power sources were much more complex. It looked as though it might weigh a ton, and apparently Jordan thought so too since he offered his assistance as Anju pushed the scanner to the center of the desk.

"In a moment," Dr. Werniewski began, "Anju will begin a biometrical scan of this room, though the reach of the scan will probably go well beyond the confines of these four walls. The brightness of the scan may cause temporary to permanent injury to your eyes. Everyone, please close your eyes and keep them closed until I say to open them. Anju?"

Clara did not close her eyes. She watched as Anju slid a thumb drive into a USB port on the scanner then typed in something at its base. The large canister illuminated at its center. The light quickly grew in strength, and Anju closed her eyes. Then Clara did the same.

"Initiating scan for biological contamination," said the voice of a familiar computerized woman. It was the same voice from the sterilization chamber and the clean-room safety protocols. It spoke without inflection and always reminded her of a GPS her parents had purchased when she was a kid.

She wondered if computerized voices were reused across electronic platforms as the inside of her eyelids went from black to pink. A wave of light and heat spread over the room with a muffled boom followed by a static-like crackle.

"Scan completed," the computer said. Clara opened her eyes, not waiting for Dr. Werniewski's permission.

"You may now open…" he started then realized everyone already had, ending his sentence with, "Oh."

A screen above the scanner's light source displayed an image resembling an x-ray of the entire room. Everything and everyone inside it was cast in black, white, and silver. "Unknown organism detected." The machine beeped and whirred. "Unknown organism detected."

"Twice?" Dr. Werniewski asked, his voice squeaking. His mouth hung open, and the blood drained from his face.

Clara held her breath, knowing something was wrong even if she didn't fully understand what.

"No," Anju said. "That should not have happened twice."

The machine fell silent. So did the room. After a few seconds that passed like minutes, the machine said, "Locations of organism contained and identified in red."

"Locations?" Anju asked. "As in more than one?"

Everyone's eyes fixed upon the screen. The image of Clara sitting in her wheelchair turned red. A smaller image, sitting at the far end of her desk, also turned red.

"The flowers?" she asked.

"Air quality normal," the scanner chirped. "No other contaminants detected."

All heads turned simultaneously toward Jordan. Anju shrugged. Dr. Werniewski was glowering.

"Relax!" Jordan's face flushed, with a combination of anger and embarrassment, Clara assumed.

"You introduced an unknown, untested organism into a nonlaboratory environment, potentially endangering the lives of everyone in this facility, for what?" Dr. Werniewski's tone was low and quiet, as if he were reining in a verbal assault. "To impress a lady?"

Jordan's fists rolled into balls as his face darkened to a color just shy of purple. "You heard the scanner. The organism is contained, *and* it has been fully tested. We're not incompetent. That 'unknown organism' has already undergone a multitude of tests and research among the six members of my team. All results have proven it to be completely harmless to humans. The 'organism' your scanner is picking up primarily consists of chlorophyll bonded with some kind of enzyme we suspect is responsible for the flower's spectacular growth and survival rate. It's not like anything we've ever seen before, granted, but I don't think I can overstate its importance to science. If we can just extract the enzyme from the chlorophyll—"

"I don't think you want to do that," Clara said.

His scowl softened, but his hands remained fists. "What? Do you think this enzyme is somehow related to your released biological agent, which, let me remind you, had nothing to do with my team?"

"We know too little—" Dr. Werniewski began.

"Oh, come on!" Jordan blurted. "We are dealing with two different things here, and you all know it. What chemical or biological entity, organism, enzyme, et cetera, can any of you point to that can stimulate plant growth and cause mutations in human DNA in the manner in which we have been exposed to here?"

Clara shrugged. "With over five thousand known viruses—"

"It's insane, and you have no research to support any of your conclusions. If, for the sake of argument, there were some connection to your organism, it has bonded with normal plant cells and evolved in such a way that has rendered it absolutely harmless."

Anju grinned. "Maybe it likes plants just fine. Maybe it just does not like humans."

Jordan's eyes lit up with what some would call passion, others madness. Clara wondered if her eyes had lit up the same way when she had seen Molli under her scope. "Well again, for the sake of argument, if your Molli is in my plants, it certainly is a boon to their existence. If we could extract it and introduce it into other plants, the world would be healthy and green, lush as a jungle. The way this enzyme works with the chlorophyll, takes in sunlight, absorbs carbon dioxide, and produces oxygen…. We're talking about a potential fast-growing food source with established air-purification capabilities, not to mention a potential Nobel Prize. This enzyme's penchant for cleaning air is exponentially compounded by its rapid growth." He pointed at the lilies. "Just look at those beauties. They've probably grown an inch or two since they've been in that vase, with little water and no sunlight."

Clara stared at the flowers. *They do seem bigger.*

"Back in the lab," Jordan continued, "some are as big as sunflowers. Can you believe that? The implications for our inner cities, counteracting the effects of exhaust, smog, other forms of air pollution…." Jordan trailed off. He stared at his audience, his eyes pleading.

When no one said anything, he sighed deeply, apparently giving up. He turned to Clara. "Anyway, when they have grown to twice their current size tomorrow, I thought maybe you might see them and smile despite all that you're going through."

That did make Clara smile. That might just have been the stupidest, nicest thing anyone had ever done for her. *Excepting Anju's saving my life.* She wondered what she'd done to deserve this sudden appearance of people who cared for her, people she hardly knew.

Dr. Werniewski coughed, immediately extinguishing any tenderness Jordan's thoughtfulness might have brought to their circumstances. "With the exception of Dr. Phillips's flowers," he said with no hint of being impressed, "using her original creation, Anju and I conducted this scan of your room, the clean room, and everywhere between four times with consistent results. In the clean room, biological agents were found in the air vent and on the, uh, the remains of the infected ASAP personnel, all of which were collected and incinerated. The rooms have been cleared. However, whatever remains of Mr. Kobozev—"

"I remember!" Clara shouted. "Sergei Kobozev...he...he mutated somehow, and...he did something to that guard. I'm not sure what, but I saw his skin, his *entire body*, transform and...*qu'est que c'est*...insert? Yes, his fingers stretched thin, and he inserted them into the ASAP guard like—"

"Yes." Dr. Werniewski nodded, his lips pressed flat. "And in doing so, Kobozev transmuted his condition to that guard, whose remains have since been destroyed. All contaminated personnel and inventory have been carefully confiscated and incinerated, and no remnants of Molli remain except for vault-protected samples and—"

"Those inside me," Clara said. Jordan reached out for her hand again. She let him take it.

Dr. Werniewski shook his head. "If only that were true."

Jordan sprang to his feet. "You insensitive prick. I should—"

Dr. Werniewski held up a hand toward Jordan, who quieted like an obedient dog. "I only meant that we have a more serious problem than Dr. St. Pierre's medical abnormality. I don't mean to downplay your infection, Clara, but your vitals are aboveboard, and barring intravenous or other intrusive forms of contact" – he eyeballed Jordan, who looked away, face apple red – "you appear to be no more of a threat to human safety than a carrier of HIV. You don't have any plans to mutate on us, do you?"

"I feel fine," Clara said and meant it. "Better than fine, even. The aches from sitting in this chair so long are gone."

"Anju did a great service in protecting you," Dr. Werniewski said. "Thus far, though this organism lives inside you as it did the infected, you seem to be experiencing no ill effects from its presence. At this stage, we have no data to calculate how many people this organism could infect or how quickly it could spread. We have no idea what segment of the population may be immune or resistant. Your body's apparent ability to ward off the symptoms of your infection is more than just a blessing. We will need to find its root cause, isolate it, and begin work on an inhibiter if not a cure."

"I agree," Clara said.

"Easier said than done," Jordan added.

Dr. Werniewski ignored him. "On the other hand, Sergei Kobozev, or more accurately, the life-form that once was Sergei Kobozev, remains a vital source of contamination. Anju has provided two teams of ASAP guards with scanners retrofitted in the same manner as that one. With any luck, they will destroy the organism before it can spread and, hopefully, without burning this place down."

Clara frowned. "So Jordan mentioned that you took a closer look at my biometrics and discovered an increased level of white blood cells. That's not uncommon for sufferers of MS."

"'Increased' hardly begins to cover it."

"Okay, how much are we talking? And what do you suppose it means?"

Dr. Werniewski shrugged. "You were somewhere in the range of twenty thousand cells per microliter but have since reverted to a healthy human range. I would like to begin testing on you, as you say, *tout suite*. We've been asked to stay put, but given the immediate interest we all have in working toward a cure for this...affliction.... I am not so sure ASAP security rules trump our moral obligations." He paused, scratching white lines into his bald head. "As for your resistance to a full-body takeover of this parasite – and let's not split hairs, this organism is clearly feeding off its hosts – my guess would be that your body is producing massive amounts of antibodies to fight off the foreign invaders. This is just a guess, but there seems to be something different about your immune system that is kicking it into fourth gear. It's astounding, really. I could probably inject you with measles, shingles, Ebola, and bubonic plague right now, and with or without proper vaccinations, your immune system would give each some serious resistance. I doubt you'd experience so much as a cough or runny nose."

"When I contracted the organism," Clara said, "I stood up soon after. I mean, I can stand up on rare occasions, so this alone may not be too surprising. But as Sergei held me up in the air...." She choked up then settled herself and continued. "While he was strangling me, I kicked him. And not just some feeble leg jerk. I kicked him so hard underneath his chin that his teeth clenched down on his tongue and severed it. I felt the muscles in my legs working, felt the pain when he clawed them up."

With all eyes on her shredded jeans, Clara pulled up her cuff to expose her calf. She twisted her leg inward, but could see no injuries to her skin. If she could just lift her leg, she could show them all.

She gripped the arms of her wheelchair until they screeched from the pressure. "Do you understand what I'm saying? I felt my legs like I haven't felt them in years! I used them!"

"Can you feel them now?" Anju asked.

"I...I don't know."

Clara did know. She could feel the muscles in her legs, full of energy and life. But she shuddered at the thought that the feeling might be a mirage. Trying to stand meant risking a fall. When it came to falling down with respect to her career, Clara always bounced back up, used it to rise higher. But when it came to her disease, falling down meant down and out. There was no getting back up.

She shifted everyone's attention elsewhere. "When I was in the clean room, I had an opportunity to study the organism. Molli is an invasive species, no doubt about that, but as it interacted with the amoebas in the petri dish, it penetrated them but did not consume them. As you say, Dr. Werniewski, Molli acted like a parasite. And no good parasite kills the host that feeds it."

Clara pictured the infected amoebas as they'd appeared after Molli invaded them. "In fact, the amoebas were noticeably larger and appeared stronger, healthier, still retaining their typical features. What if...."

Clara knew her stream of thought was leaving science and wandering dangerously close to science fiction, but all science had begun once as science fiction. Still, her theory was so far outside the box, it had left the damn thing's orbit.

She shook her head. "Never mind."

"Please," Jordan said, his smile inviting. "Go on."

"Well, the organism was discovered in the same squirrel nest as the seeds that spawned your super flowers. Certain bacteria can withstand extreme elemental conditions, live inside vastly different terrains and climates, some even inside a vacuum. Molli may not be a bacterium, but she's more bacterium than virus. Is it really so hard to believe that Molli...."

Jordan stiffened and looked as if he were about to object but then simply said, "Yes?"

Clara nodded. "Isn't it reasonable to believe that Molli was or has become part of everything found in that nest? That we've been concentrating on the so-called pandoravirus in the abstract, in an extracted sample pulled from its environment when maybe we should be looking at the organism as part of its environment and maybe as an essential component to it."

"The seeds we found in the nest, in all respects, were normal seeds, albeit of some very old flowers," Jordan said.

"But that's exactly my point!" Clara couldn't help her excitement. "The seeds retained their shape and form much like the amoebas did, and much like...I do. And what those seeds produce are bigger, stronger, and better in all ways. I think that whatever Molli is, in the right conditions...."

"I think I see where you're going with this," Jordan said. "You think Molli, for lack of a better term, acts like some kind of growth stimulator and has boosted the amoebas' structural integrity, the flowers' ability to convert sunlight and carbon dioxide into energy and oxygen, and your own autoimmune system." He looked away. "That sounds...all well and good, Clara, but I just think that maybe you are looking for a miracle where maybe only a horror exists."

"I'd say," Dr. Werniewski snorted. "What sort of organism would have such an ameliorative cross-species impact in both the plant and animal kingdoms? It's outright preposterous."

Clara's face flushed with her embarrassment, which only made her defensive. "Is it? All life, be it plant or animal, contains proteins, enzymes, amino acids...maybe we've discovered an organism that excretes reparative enzymes or reconstructive proteins or-or-or...or a goddamn god gene! Can you really turn your heads to the idea that maybe we've stumbled on the reason for the existence of life itself?"

No one said a word. They didn't have to. Clara could read their disbelief in their gaping mouths, furrowed brows, and open glares.

At last, Dr. Werniewski spoke. "Dr. St. Pierre, you've had a long, difficult day, and—"

"I am happy to help prove or disprove your hypothesis," Anju interrupted. Her tone was strained as she chose her words carefully.

Clara wondered if the grad student had realized how close Clara had been to exploding.

"Maybe in your personal time," Dr. Werniewski said.

Anju ignored him. "Who knows what secrets hide in this thing's DNA? I, for one, am excited to find out. At the least, we may discover an inhibiter to the symptoms of MS, or" – she smiled – "an evolutionary building block or two."

"Tell that to Sergei Kobozev," Dr. Werniewski said.

Jordan frowned. But before he could say what had entered his mind, Clara touched his arm.

"No, he's right." *Even if he is downright infuriating.* She sighed. "My passion makes me stupid sometimes."

"No need to be so hard on yourself, my dear," Dr. Werniewski said. "Intelligent persons with debilitating conditions such as yours have always looked for cures wherever a suggestion of hope could be extracted, grasping at proverbial straws where the wealth of evidence points to the contrary. It's human nature, I suppose."

Clara ignored the comment as best she could. She said, "Here's what I do know: the organism, as I said, more closely resembles a bacterium than any other known form of life. It can reconfigure human biology in the most extreme ways—"

"That," Dr. Werniewski said, "has not been confirmed."

"What?" Clara wanted to strangle that thick-headed snot. She had seen what she had seen, and she hadn't been the only one to see it.

"You were unconscious when ASAP found you. Your recollection cannot be trusted."

"What about the other witnesses?" Anju asked.

"A criminal and two ASAP guards, likely of low intellect?" Dr. Werniewski stroked his chin. "I'm not sure what their game is, but if they are telling the truth, then it seems far more likely that the sample released some sort of toxin, possibly hallucinogenic."

"I have to admit," Jordan said. "That is a lot easier to swallow."

"What about me, then?" Clara asked. "Am I not living proof of the organism's ability to repair, if not reconfigure, its host? If it is symbiotic, as I suspected when I tested it in the lab, isn't it possible that my high T-cell count was indicative of my body's...or Molli's attempts to fix me?"

"It seems more likely that the high white-blood-cell count reflected your body's attempts to fight off Molli," Dr. Werniewski countered.

"MS is an autoimmune disease. We've seen a little of what Molli can do. Maybe the reason I still feel the same, the reason I am not like Sergei Kobozev or the guard he infected, is because Molli supercharged my immune system so well that it is defending against any of the organism's negative side effects. It healed me to make me a better host but did its job so well that it damned itself."

Clara shrugged. Listening to her theory spoken aloud, even she couldn't believe it. She sighed. "Or maybe I'm just speculating, based on the obvious difference between myself and the other infected individuals. For all we know, maybe it was the oatmeal I had for breakfast this morning that saved me from Sergei's fate."

"I hope so," Dr. Werniewski said flatly. "I had the oatmeal, too."

The room fell silent, lapsing into awkwardness.

"Well," Jordan said, alleviating the maddening noiselessness, "until ASAP clears the facility, we're supposed to be confined to our rooms."

Anju snickered and raised her arms. "And how is that working out for everyone?"

Jordan smiled. "Anyway, we have a pretty good collection of minds right here. So if anyone has any other ideas that might help ASAP make this place safe a little quicker, let's hear it." He leaned in close to Clara. "What about you? Were you able to learn anything else about this organism?"

She rubbed her hands together. She'd been holding back the weirdest part of the encounter, at least before Sergei decided to shoot barbed tendrils out of his fingertips. And she really didn't want to tell them then, but....

"There is...one more thing, but you're not going to believe me."

Jordan and Anju leaned so close they were almost sitting on her lap. Dr. Werniewski huffed impatiently.

Clara took a breath. "Molli spoke to me."

"That's imbecilic!" Dr. Werniewski threw his arms up and walked toward the door. "Absolutely absurd. Clearly a hallucination." He turned and faced Clara. "That's…Dr. St. Pierre, do I really need to tell you how insane that sounds? It's ludicrous." He shook his head, waved a hand dismissively, then headed back toward the door. "I'm not even going to entertain that line of inquiry. You can't truly believe that a single-celled organism, after having been buried in ice for thirty thousand years, invaded a Russian astrobiologist and used his mouth to…to what, exactly? To speak to you? In what language? This sounds like some kind of first-contact nonsense. Did Molli ask you to take it to your leader?"

Anju put a hand on Dr. Werniewski's shoulder, and his excitement dwindled.

"Ridiculous," he muttered for good measure under his breath. He raised his head and met the others' stares. "This organism is just a virus or bacterium perhaps. It is not sentient! Do you know how complex the human brain is? To suggest a single-celled organism could have the capacity to think and communicate, in our tongues no less, is heretical to the gospel of evolution. What you saw was a man, a sick man, plain and simple. Whatever he said was the result of his sickness, ailments caused by a new disease we are tasked with curing."

Clara had to concede that it sounded implausible, but she'd heard what she'd heard. Either Sergei, for whatever reason, thought he was under another's influence, wanted everyone to believe he was under another's influence, or actually was under another's influence. She opened her mouth to push the issue but shut it again, realizing her comments would only cause more friction. All her theories and all their proposed research came secondary to the matter of containment.

"All right, Dr. Werniewski," Clara said. "What do you suggest we do next?"

"We sit tight, let ASAP destroy the specimen. The samples too, if they're of a mind. We can always extract Molli from you if we need it."

"And that criminal who helped rescue me?" Clara asked.

Dr. Werniewski didn't miss a beat. "Also ASAP's problem now."

CHAPTER FIFTEEN

Monty felt pretty good for a guy who'd been stabbed in the eye with a fork.

I mean, who does that? Who stabs a bloke in the eye with fucking silverware?

He was taking it rather well, all things considered. The question, he decided, was of little consequence. The fact was: someone had stabbed him in the eye with a fork. He saw no use in crying about it then, even if the tear duct was still functional.

What's done is done, mate, he told himself. *What's done is done. Of course, I'll kill the fucker once I get out of here if he ain't already dead.*

He sighed and collapsed back onto his examination table, allowing himself a short-lived and well-earned reprieve from active duty. He supposed getting stabbed in the eye had that as a necessary and unavoidable consequence. What he really wanted was a fucking cigarette. But the self-righteous whackers who ran the joint didn't allow smokes anywhere on the property, not even out in the parking garage.

Every man needs a vice. Who are they to stifle mine?

His nicotine addiction had put him on edge, so he reached into his pocket and pulled out a tar-colored gum that was supposed to stave off his cravings. He popped the small, square morsel through its plastic sheath and tossed it into his mouth.

"Mmm," he muttered, grimacing at the taste and the pointlessness. He still wanted a smoke.

He folded his hands behind his head and stared up at the ceiling through his one good eye. Replaying the attack in his mind, Monty thought about all the ways he might have prevented it. He could have ducked. He could have drawn his gun sooner. He could have done a lot of things differently. Instead, he got stabbed in the eye.

"Who the fuck stabs a bloke in the eye with a motherfucking fork?" he asked again, this time aloud.

"You okay in there?" Ms. Valentina, his attending nurse and a blond Russian bombshell to boot, called through his curtain separator.

"Right as rain, beautiful," Monty answered.

Still, as much as he wanted to move on from the topic of his now multi-pupiled eye, he couldn't let it go. Alone with his thoughts, he had nothing better to do. *Things could have been worse. I could have been stabbed with a steak knife, for example, or maybe a fondue skewer. Hell, I might even have been stabbed with a pencil or a safety pin.* Any one of those, he figured, might have broken all the way through his eye and damaged his optic nerve, causing instant blindness.

As his condition stood, Monty did not know if he'd ever be able to see out of his damaged eye again, but uncertainty left him with at least a little hope. Nobody had ruled sight out yet. The cover of bandages pressed tightly over his socket rendered his left eye useless for the time being. The retina had detached, but hell, he still had one good one.

One beautiful, perfect eye. He smiled, but without mirth.

As he rested his head on his hands, he used his good eye to map the cracks in the stucco ceiling. The ceiling was nothing special to look at – just a flat white, for the most part an even and totally noncaptivating surface, as boring to watch as the PGA Tour.

Perhaps I'm being too hard on the ceiling. He laughed.

Then the ceiling moved.

At least, he thought the ceiling had moved. *Or is the paint…melting?* The infirmary was kind of warm – not Earth's-core warm or solar-flare warm, but toasty fireplace warm. Definitely not ceiling-starting-to-melt warm. He wondered if perhaps he were just feeling the residual effects of Nurse Valentina's plump, fine ass from when she'd sashayed through his temporary quarters fifteen minutes before. And it was fine, no doubt about that. *What I wouldn't do, given fifteen minutes with that.*

Envisioning the nurse's round, fat-apple bottom almost made him forget about the ceiling. Then it moved again, and his attention was once again redirected.

Or is something moving on it?

He sat up and squinted. "What is that?" Something tiny was squirming around above him. He strained to see it better. The squirming thing came in clearer as it fell from the ceiling toward him.

It landed on his chest.

"Ngahh!" Monty gasped and stared at the tiny, peachy-pink maggot that landed over his breast pocket. He tried to blow it off, not wanting to touch it, but the critter had a good grip. It lifted one end of itself, what Monty assumed was its head. It was featureless except for a mucous liquid glistening on its skin. He studied it with equal parts amazement and revulsion as it danced its worm dance. And as he watched it, it seemed to watch him.

The maggot-worm's head stretched. A point formed on top, angling outward like a spade. Monty had seen enough. He was just about to flick the boogery thing away when its head dove tip first into his shirt.

"Jesus!" Monty yelped as he instinctively tugged his shirt away from his skin. The fleshy maggot-worm flew off his shirt and fell to the floor beside his examination table.

He stood up and stomped it, smiling with sadistic gratification. Then he looked up, and his smile vanished. Maggot-worms, easily thousands of the disgusting buggers, wiggled and writhed between miniscule stucco stalactites.

Monty's feelings of disgust grew into a throat-tightening unease. Unease morphed into dread when he heard the screams. One, then another, then another: all around him were people screaming, people banging and falling and flapping just outside his privacy curtain – people whose silhouettes told tales of pain and confusion.

Those people stood between Monty and the exit. He slipped silently from beside the table, never taking his eyes off the ceiling.

Thump.

Something heavier than a maggot-worm and a lot squishier landed near his foot. He looked down to see a slightly longer maggot-worm tethered to what looked like a wrinkled, fleshy walnut. *A testicle?* Monty dry heaved, but even as he did, he couldn't take his eye off the flopping ball and chain. The nutshell cracked in a long, vertical slit, which widened, revealing the eye beneath. Iris and pupil shifted to look up at Monty.

He held back the vomit in his throat. Nurse Valentina busted through his curtain, shouting and pirouetting and nearly taking Monty down with an elbow. One of those maggot-things had landed on the voluptuous nurse's cheek. It tunneled into her skin like a drill boring through wood. Nurse Valentina tried to yank it free. She had a firm grasp on the wretched critter between her thumb and forefinger, but when she tried to pull it out of her face, it broke in half. The portion between her fingers disappeared into her thumb. The other half disappeared into her face.

The nurse fell to the ground. Foam sputtered from her mouth, making a sound akin to gargling mouthwash. Her eyelids fluttered like moth wings, and her head jerked to one side. Every muscle flexed. Every vein protruded.

Then she stopped gurgling. Her body went limp.

"Fuck this!" Monty shouted.

He threw back his curtain and jumped back just as another nurse fell onto the floor directly in front of him, convulsing like Nurse Valentina had before going limp. Another staff member did the same closer to the exit.

He heard the sound first, the pitter-patter of raindrops splatting on a hard surface. Everywhere, maggot-worms poured down.

Monty decided that was his cue. He sprinted toward the infirmary door as the nurse who'd fallen beside it slowly rose. The wriggling critters were spotting the woman's scrubs. He kept a wide berth as he passed.

He was beginning to think his day couldn't get any worse when something landed in his hair. He didn't know much about the strange animals, but he attributed the seizures and potential death to the appearance of maggot-worms on the ceiling. He grabbed a clump of his sandy-brown hair and ripped it from his scalp, dropping it as soon as he did. He wasted no time checking whether he'd torn the worm out of his hair or if it had even been a worm at all, instead choosing to keep on running. If it had burrowed into his noggin, he would know it soon enough.

He blasted through the infirmary's double doors and collided with a man with a black cross painted on his forehead. As their shoulders butted, Monty spun sideways but did not fall. "You don't want to go in there," he said, gasping for air.

He slowed and slid against the corridor wall, stopping to catch his breath and check himself for maggot-worms. When he looked up, he recognized several people standing behind the fruitcake with the Crayola paint-by-number cross on his head.

"Stearns!" Monty sprinted toward the friendly face, with three more standing behind the first, all ASAP guards he knew to varying degrees.

Johnson, Kelly, and…that other guy, the Russian…Belgrade. But when he saw the rest of Stearns, he slowed.

The guard's foot was wrapped in gauze. Blood had soaked through the bandages. The foot's shape was all wrong. "What the hell happened to you?" Monty asked. "Your foot looks like ground sausage."

"This guy happened," Stearns said, jabbing the butt of his assault rifle into the small of the dirty stranger's back, but it was Stearns who grunted. "The fucker blew a good chunk of my foot off."

Monty gave the stranger a once-over, for the first time noticing that he was handcuffed. But whoever the man was, he wasn't the fucker with the fork.

"Well, it looks like you got this one's shoe," he said, noticing the man's filthy woolen sock. "A fair trade for part of your foot?" He looked the man up and down. "Wait a second…. Do I know you? Fuck, I do know you! That cross is a dead giveaway!"

"You know this guy?" Stearns asked.

"Well, no," Monty said. "Not really. He blocked my car on the way in today. Fucker just stood there, trying to stare me down or something. I knew the bastard was going to be nothing but trouble."

Stearns smiled wickedly. "Not anymore, he won't."

"And that other asshole?" Monty scanned the group, shaking and talking quickly. "The one who did this to my eye?"

"Dead," Stearns said. He grimaced.

"I wouldn't be so sure," the strange man said.

"You shut up!" Stearns shouted, wincing. He took a step toward the prisoner, his face going beet red. He looked as though he wanted to kill the stranger, and if Monty knew his coworker as well as he thought he did, Stearns would have done just that if given a clear shot and a room empty of witnesses.

"Guys, can we talk about this later?" Monty asked. "Something very weird and very frightening is going on behind those doors." He pointed at the infirmary's entrance. "And I don't want to be around when what's in there comes out here."

"Why?" Kelly asked. He was a burly man, as Texan as Texans come, from his black cowboy hat down to his black boots. The flamethrower strapped to his back, however, Monty found not convincingly Texan. "What's behind those doors?"

"I don't hear nothin'," Johnson added.

Monty listened. He didn't hear anything either. The screams had stopped. So had the raindrops and the seizures, apparently. "Don't ask me how or why, mates, but that room right there is crawling with creepy crawlies: nasty, snot-covered maggot-worms."

"Worms?" Johnson asked, the corners of his mouth twitching. He shook his head and walked toward the infirmary doors. "And I thought you's a man, Monty. Been in the thick of it and all that, right?" He laughed, pushing open the door with his back as he egged on his partner. "You hear this shit, Kelly? Monty here's afraid of—"

Johnson froze midturn, propping the door open with his boot. "Worms?" His face paled. The floor of the infirmary looked like the bottom of a grain silo before harvest, except the grains were moving, little squiggly lines writhing all over it. Nurse Valentina stood in the center of a large mass of night crawlers. Bigger worms dropped off her body like wet noodles, plopping on the ground and squirming their way toward Johnson.

Monty gagged, fear and vomit rendering him speechless. The worms weren't dropping *off* her body. They were dropping *from* her body. And they were getting closer to Johnson, who seemed caught in a stupor. One worm mounted the toe of his boot.

Monty finally found his voice. "Get back! Don't let them touch you!"

Johnson seemed mesmerized by the undulating nastiness on his boot. When it tunneled into his boot, straight through a steel toe, Johnson was too late in his efforts to shake it off.

The others watched, aghast, as the maggot-worm disappeared into the guard's shoe. They did nothing as Johnson screamed and tried to pry his boot off. Whether consciously or unconsciously, they all stepped back.

Sampson, an ASAP guard who had started at the research center at the same time as Monty, came waddling up the hallway, a lantern-shaped device swinging between his legs. "That scientist who breached the clean room, whatever he is now, he broke through the wall of the clean room's air vent and got into the central air-circulation system! The probe I sent in couldn't trace him as far as he moved. He could be anywhere!"

"I think we found him." Stearns aimed his rifle at the nurse. "Belgrade, keep an eye on the prisoner."

Sampson yelped, stopped short, and almost stumbled. He dropped the scanner, pulled his AK-47 off his shoulder, and aimed it at Johnson. "What's wrong with Johnson? Oh geez, oh geez. Not another Romanov." Sampson turned to run.

"Stand your ground, soldier," Stearns ordered.

Monty stepped back as Stearns turned his weapon on Sampson. Stearns was the CO on shift. Disobedience meant termination, and with Stearns, one never knew if that meant just one's job.

Sampson took another step then froze. He turned around. Monty heard his coworker's stomach turning and saw the sweat pouring down his forehead. His whole body shook worse than Johnson, who was presently in full-seizure mode.

Sampson had been there when Romanov attacked Kleinhoffer, another guard who'd been called in to assist at Bio-Lab 347. Monty had heard some of the madness over his portable radio but hadn't been able to separate facts from hysterics. Apparently, someone had torched Kleinhoffer. Romanov, too. That might have been Sampson himself, or that sorry-ass bloke in handcuffs. He wondered if it was connected to those worms and figured it had to be. *What did you see, Sampson? What did you do?*

Sampson's lips trembled. His voice shook as he said, "Johnson's not human anymore." He stepped closer to Kelly. "You have to light him up," he said softly. He lunged for the nozzle. "We have to burn him!"

Kelly tried to push Sampson back, but the latter had hold of the torch before Kelly could pull it away. Sampson pressed down on Kelly's forefinger, already bent over the trigger. Flame spurted along the floor, up in the air, everywhere in sporadic clouds. Stearns hobbled out of range, assisted by Belgrade. Their CO left his prisoner in peril, though the man with the black cross was quick to get himself out of it. The prisoner started down the hallway, trying to seize an opportunity for escape, but Belgrade tripped him. He crashed down to the floor, twisting sideways to let his shoulder break his fall with a dull thump.

While Kelly and Sampson wrestled with the nozzle, a random burst blasted toward the seizing Johnson. He ignited with a *whoosh* and immediately bubbled and crackled. That seemed to ease Sampson's nerves a bit. He threw his hands up and stepped away from Kelly.

"What the hell are you doing?" Monty snapped as he cracked

Sampson in the jaw. Sampson rocked on his feet, but Monty grabbed him before he could fall into the funeral pyre. Even as he held Sampson up with his left hand, he reeled back for another haymaker with his right. Belgrade grabbed his arm and prevented a second blow.

"He was infected," the square-jawed Russian said in a tone that sounded as angry as a bulldog's growl but really was just the way he talked. "Sampson did what he had to do. He did what we should have wasted no time doing."

"Agreed," Stearns said from where he was sitting atop the fallen prisoner.

"Have you all gone mad?" Monty got right up into Belgrade's face. "Johnson was still Johnson. He didn't look any different to me until that asshole scorched him with a bloody flamethrower."

"They're right," the stranger said, his voice strained beneath Stearns's heavy frame.

"Oh, hell, even the fucking dero has an opinion on the matter. Well, that's just fucking great! Not a single one of you has any fucking clue what you're—"

Nurse Valentina burst through the infirmary's double doors and latched her fingers into Sampson's cheeks – not on his cheeks or around his cheeks but *into* them. Monty blinked then blinked some more, hoping his eye was playing tricks on him. Human fingers didn't just pass through human cheeks.

Nope, that's what I'm seeing.

Sampson screamed as the nurse's milky hands melded with his dark skin, swirling like the froth atop a cappuccino. The pigments blended so quickly, Monty could no longer tell where Valentina's hands ended and Sampson's face began. Everything melted together like Harlequin ice cream left out on a hot summer day.

Whatever process caused the flesh to appear to be melting turned to actual melting when Kelly sprayed them with fire. He held down the trigger long and hard, his teeth gnashing, and the conjoined infected went up like cherries jubilee.

"Jesus fucking Christ, mate! You're going to burn the whole goddamn facility down!" With no one holding him back, Monty rushed Kelly.

Sampson and his forever-entwined lover were sizzling like bacon on a stove top, though they smelled more like roast pork. Monty kept his distance from the blaze and managed to refrain from throwing another haymaker.

"Look," he said, "I'll be the first to admit that that was some seriously fucked-up shit, but has everyone here gone completely homicidal? There are doctors here. We're supposed to help sick people, not charbroil them."

Someone grabbed Monty's shoulder. He turned around to find Stearns back on his feet, with Belgrade babysitting the prisoner, who was now standing behind him.

"You saw what was happening," Stearns said. "It's some kind of mutation, and damn us all to hell, it's loose in this facility. We've got to destroy it before it infects us. Are you with me?"

The hall went silent, and for the first time, Monty noticed his teeth were chattering. If he was terrified, the adrenaline pumping through him kept him on his game. He'd seen the worms. He'd seen the seizures they caused. He'd even seen Nurse Valentina, a bloody waste as that was, melt over Sampson as if she were cheese on chicken parmigiana. It didn't make sense. None of what he'd seen made any damn sense. Viruses, even those the world's governments tried to claim were dead and buried, didn't do the type of shit he just witnessed to ordinary blokes. Leprosy or Ebola might make one's flesh fall off, maybe even get a little melty for all Monty knew, but he was sure as shit that neither disease acted that quickly or that freakishly.

He looked from Stearns to Kelly to the stranger they had in custody. They all had stepped away from the infirmary doors and the human bonfires. Monty's teeth still chattered, though a little less, and his body was trembling, but he felt no shame for being afraid. After taking a cleansing breath, he asked as calmly as he could, "What the fuck is happening here? Does anyone know? I mean, does anyone *really* know?"

Stearns shook his head. "We don't know."

"Sure you do," the stranger said. "You had to go meddling where your stupid, meddling noses didn't belong."

"Belgrade," Stearns said.

Belgrade slugged the dirty vagrant in the stomach. The man grunted then grinned through obvious pain.

Stearns continued. "That scientist, the one who attacked you, he infected himself with some sort of...hell, I don't know. You've seen what it does as much as I have. Some sort of biological weapon, if I had to guess."

"Certainly," the stranger said, "in hands like yours—"

At a look from Stearns, Belgrade punched the man again, knocking the wind from his lungs.

"All we know," Stearns said as though he'd never been interrupted, "is that it's a nasty motherfucker, can spread through contact, and seems to be susceptible to fire. At least, fire's done the trick so far. Belgrade, run the scanner."

"I'm not really sure how," Belgrade said, "but I'll try."

Monty watched as Belgrade played with the device Sampson had brought down the hall. He hit the same button five times on the keypad at its base. "Everyone, close your eyes," he said. "The girl who made this said it might blind you if you don't."

The machine sparked a light at its center, which rapidly grew in intensity as if it were a star imploding. "Initiating scan for biological contamination," a robotic female voice said.

Monty pressed his eyes shut though he was tempted to open them as a wave of heat permeated his body. A soft *boom* and an electric sizzle sent vibrations through him.

"Scan completed," the robot female said. An image of the hallway and everyone in it, as well as the inside of the infirmary, normal as could be, appeared at the top of the scanner. For almost a minute, it remained silent. Monty assumed it could not find what it was designed to look for.

That has to be a good sign. He allowed himself a glimmer of hope. *But what about the worms?*

"Unknown organism detected," the machine announced in a loud, clear voice. "Location contained." The image of the burning mound of humans turned red. The scanner beeped in rapid staccato. "Unknown organism detected – unknown organism detected – unknown organism detected – unknown organism detected – unknown organism detected...."

"Will someone shut that thing up?" Stearns said, glancing back and forth from the scanner to the infirmary and back again. His rifle shook in his hands as he backpedaled on his heels.

"Is it broken?" Monty asked.

Belgrade played with the keyboard. "I...I don't know. I have no idea how to work this thing and am just following the prompts."

All the while, the robot voice said again and again, "Unknown organism detected – unknown organism detected – unknown organism detected...."

Monty stared at the image at the top of the scanner. "Is it...turning red?" They all stared at the image. Dot by tiny dot, the scanned image of the infirmary ran red.

The infirmary's double doors swung open quickly, as if they'd been kicked. They crashed against the hallway wall and swung shut again, then back open, rocking back and forth and creaking on their hinges. Monty watched those doors with increasing panic. The scanner wouldn't quiet, its toneless voice drilling into his skull with its monotonous repetition. As he stared without blinking into the infirmary through the opening left by the swaying doors, he saw nothing. At least, nothing alive. No worms, no melting people, no nothing – just the infirmary as it should have been, same as it had always been. The doors creaked in a final sway before closing.

"Unknown organism detected – unknown organism detected – unknown organism detected...."

Monty howled. He charged at the stranger and grabbed him by his tattered vest. "Did you do this, you son of a bitch? Did you make this all happen?"

With a sinister slowness, the man's head lowered as if to examine the hands latched to his coat then raised just as slowly, revealing a scowl and eyes that burned with an intensity Monty didn't quite understand. The man spoke. "If I had known something like this existed within these walls, I would have brought this whole building down on top of everyone in it. I still may, if given the—"

The scanner fell silent except for the low hum of some fan or gear spinning inside it. Monty held his breath, waiting for it to do or say something, not knowing what it was supposed to do or say.

At last, the scanner broke its silence. "Locations of organism uncontained. Identified in red."

Monty looked at the image at the top of the machine. "I don't understand," he muttered. Judging by the masks of terror worn by everyone else, he wasn't the only one who didn't.

The entire screen was red.

"Air quality normal," the robotic female said, almost mocking. "No other contaminants detected."

"Are we infected?" Kelly asked.

"Shh!" Stearns said. His ears perked up as he stared at the ceiling.

Monty listened too, for what, he couldn't be sure. He wondered if maggot-worms made sounds. All he heard were the occasional squeaks of a door hinge in desperate need of oil and the crackling fire toasting a coworker he'd known fairly well and a nurse with a booty that could have duped him into falling in love.

His gaze fell upon the burning mound, and he thought it strange that he could no longer distinguish male parts from female parts. A transformation had completed while he hadn't been looking. Their bodies had become one.

He grabbed a fire extinguisher from the wall, amazed the fire had yet to set off the alarms and sprinkler system. No one said a word, their focus not on him but on the double doors and whatever lay unseen behind them. Kelly held his flamethrower high, ready to ignite anything that moved.

As Monty raised the extinguisher and pointed its nozzle at the still-raging heap, the vagrant criminal said, "I wouldn't do that. Not just yet."

Monty didn't listen. In fact, he considered dousing the flames just to spite that stinking son of a bitch. A cloud of cold white partially obscured his view of the infirmary.

The doors exploded open again.

Monty saw nothing at first, but he did hear something he couldn't quite place, like a handful of dice – no, something lighter, softer than dice – like a handful of teeth skipped over a wooden floor. However, the noise sounded like a hell of a lot more than a handful of teeth. He imagined a giant cauldron like those filled with burning pitch that castles poured onto invaders in medieval movies, but that cauldron poured out millions and millions of teeth. The sound didn't only come from the floor but the ceiling and walls, too.

The maggot-worms' larval stage was over. A metamorphosis had begun.

"Oh, shit!" Kelly shouted. He floored the gas on his new ride, shooting fire in wide horizontal arcs across the floor one way, the ceiling back the other. Fire alarms blared, seemingly from everywhere in the facility. The corridors flashed with blinking red light.

The smoke in front of Monty cleared. His mouth opened to scream, but he stifled it by biting down on his knuckles. Hordes, goddamn infinite legions, of nickel-sized bugs swarmed into the hallway, their tiny needle feet carrying them speedily across the floor or clinging them to the walls and ceiling.

In the center of a skittering mass inside the infirmary, one of the nurses stood, whole and unfazed. He raised his arms out to his sides as if the creatures were his gifts to the ASAP team, then he fell apart into thousands of the ugly pinkish-purple flesh-bugs. All that remained was his clothes and ID badge, crumpled in a heap from which an army of insects scuttled.

Monty screamed but held his ground. Wave after wave scoured new paths beneath their burning brethren. Many were unable to dodge Kelly's skilled aim. The bugs exploded like engorged mosquitoes against a match, the blood inside them boiling. They burst everywhere on the walls and floor, leaving little red-and-purple paintball-type splatters where not dissolved entirely in flame.

Kelly was doing a fantastic job of holding them off, considering he was one against millions, but they were too many and too small not to miss a few hundred here or there. Monty couldn't comprehend their numbers. At least four or five staff members had been inside the infirmary and maybe another patient or two. *Did all these...these things... come from so few people?*

Monty couldn't wrap his head around it, and he didn't want to. The scene was like something out of a horror movie, not real. *It can't be real.* His chin quivered. *Can it?*

Can I take the chance that it isn't?

"Everyone, get back," he said. "There's too many of them."

Belgrade shook off his stupor. He nodded, grabbed Stearns's arm, slid it over his shoulder, and began walking him at a snail's pace down the corridor, away from the conflagration.

"Let me help," their forgotten captive said. His hands were still cuffed though somehow in front of him — how the criminal had managed to shimmy the cuffs under his butt and slip his legs through without being quadruple jointed and anyone noticing, Monty had no time to consider

— but the captured man was nevertheless able to grab Stearns's other arm and sling it over his shoulders.

Stearns pulled back at first but then gave in. The three of them scurried away like participants in a three-legged race, in their case four-legged.

Monty stood as close to Kelly as he dared. "I'll stay with you and make sure the path behind you is clear, but we need to get the fuck out of here. Keep suppression fire on them but keep moving back—"

Kelly shrieked as a dart shot into his neck. A purple tube jutted from the charred mound that had been Sampson and Nurse Valentina. It reminded Monty of a stint he had done in Brazil and those crazy rainforest tribes and their fucking blowguns. He stared at the mound as blackened skin flaked off from one spot, then another. New tubes surfaced in the clearings.

Turning to run, he glanced once more at Kelly, who'd begun to seize, his flamethrower spurting erratically. Monty made one half-hearted attempted to take it, but he doubted he could pull it off Kelly's back before either the bugs or Kelly got him.

The dart in Kelly's neck was mostly gone, having wriggled its way inside its new host. Monty walked backward, his legs weakening as if they might refuse to support him in his hour of need, while the critters climbed up Kelly's legs and burrowed under his skin, moving inside Monty's former coworker.

And the bugs were inches from his own feet.

Running, Monty looked around for the others. He wondered how they could have gotten so far so quickly, how they could have just left him behind. *Where the hell are they?*

Another question mattered more: *How close are those motherfuckers?* He dared not turn around to look. He wondered if the bugs could jump. He wondered if the bugs were already on him.

But as Monty ran, he wasn't alone for long. A young woman stumbled out of a doorway and stopped almost directly in his path. She wore a bathrobe and slippers, and she rubbed sleep from her eyes.

"What's going on?" she asked, halfway through a yawn. "Is there a fire?"

"Christ!" Monty shouted, managing to jerk sideways enough to avoid collision. As he passed by her, he grabbed her sleeve, trying to pull her along with him.

The woman yanked her arm free. "Jerk!" she yelled. Then she started to scream.

Again, Monty wasted no time looking back. He'd seen too much of that horror show already. The woman's screams were quickly snuffed out. The bugs were too close.

Keep running, he pleaded with himself. And run he did. More doors appeared ahead of him. They lined the main hallway and the offshoots, too.

Living quarters. Monty's good eye blurred with tears. *Where ASAP confined everyone when the explosion occurred.*

"No," he mouthed when another door opened. The fire alarm would have everyone coming out into the halls. Monty kept running. He could do nothing for them now.

CHAPTER SIXTEEN

The incessant clamor of the fire alarm was beating a migraine into Clara's skull. "Do you still think we should sit tight?" She massaged her temples. "The entire building sounds like it's on fire. Anyone remember our assigned evacuation route?"

Dr. Werniewski looked to his assistant. "Anju, grab the scanner. We'll just check out the hallway and make sure it's safe, see if we can't find someone from ASAP and get an update." He peeked out into the hallway. Flashing red light cascaded into the room. "Where are those jerks from ASAP when you actually need them?"

Anju strained as she lifted the cumbersome apparatus of her own making. Jordan moved to help her, but Anju smiled and nodded him off. Still, Clara thought it nice to see at least one man who hadn't given up on chivalry in the face of feminism, or worse, who used feminism as an excuse to be lazy.

Dr. Werniewski and his grad-student accomplice disappeared into the corridor. They left Jordan and Clara in awkward silence, notwithstanding the unrelenting fire alarm.

"Initiating scan for biological contamination," the scanner announced from somewhere outside her room. She didn't say a word or even move until she heard, "Scan completed. No biological contaminants detected."

"What do you suppose they would have done had the scanner picked up something?" Jordan asked, chuckling. "Can you picture ol' Dr. W. taking on anything bigger than a hamster?"

"Hopefully, we'll never have to." Clara's severity wiped the grin from Jordan's face. She knew she was being unfair to him, but the time wasn't right for levity. The fire alarm was driving her insane, and people were infected with an organism that could alter their genetic makeup, herself included. She had no way of telling if the organism was contained or if it even could be contained.

The thing that made her heart sink lowest was that Monty had been right all along. She'd been blind to his observations, deaf to his warnings. She doubted he was waiting somewhere out in the halls for her to pass just so he could say he told her so. *That's not Monty. The poor, poor man....* She did hope he was somewhere out there, still Monty, still alive and well.

She hadn't realized that Jordan had risen and was standing by the door until she heard it click open. The sharp sound snapped her from her reverie. Jordan poked his neck out into the corridor.

"That's funny," he muttered. "The guard's gone."

"What are you doing?" Clara asked.

"They're not back yet. It's making me restless."

"They've only been gone for a few minutes."

"I know. It's just.... I don't know." Jordan slapped his sides. "This whole thing's kind of crazy, huh?" He laughed, but his eyes didn't. A shaky edge underlined his tone. "We never have these sorts of issues back at Stanford. Our idea of excitement is a clogged toilet or an extra umbrella in our umbrella drinks."

Clara tried on a comforting smile. It didn't feel right on her face, but it seemed to settle Jordan. He stepped inside the room and let the door swing back into place. He blocked it from fully closing with his foot. They heard someone running down the hall, coming fast.

Jordan stepped out into the hall. "Hey," he called out, but Clara couldn't see to whom he was speaking.

A blur passed by the open door, then another. The blurs kept coming.

"Stop!" Jordan shouted. "Where's the fire? How bad is it? Can someone please tell us what's going on?"

Clara rolled up to the door and pulled it all the way open. She saw the back of an ASAP uniform as its owner raced by, huffing and wheezing. The guard had gauze wound around his head. *Monty?*

"Where do you suppose he's going in such a hurry?" she asked. "If this is a fire, shouldn't we be instructed along our evacuation routes in an orderly fashion? Announcements over the intercom? Why's everyone running, even the people charged with keeping us safe?" She frowned. "I don't like this."

"I don't think it's where they're going that we should be worried about."

"What do you mean?"

"Listen."

Clara did. She hadn't heard it sooner, with that obnoxious fire alarm drowning out most other sounds and banging a beat into the bass drum of her brain. Someone was screaming.

No, not someone. Someones. A whole bunch of them.

"Clara," Jordan said, eyes widening with fear. "I think we should go."

"Please." Clara reached out to a frenzied passerby who paid her no heed. "What's happening?" she asked another whom she didn't recognize as the woman sped by.

The woman's eyes were wide-open orbs, her mouth spraying spittle as she bounded down the hall.

"Run!" another woman shouted at them. She turned a corner and disappeared.

Bouncing on his toes, Jordan looked down the hall, then back at Clara. He hurried toward her, stepping in front of a short, round rock of a man.

The man didn't brake. Instead, he dropped a shoulder and drove it into Jordan's gut. The botanist keeled over with a loud grunt then fell on his side.

Clara was pushing her chair over to help Jordan up when a goliath of a man ran past her, scooped Jordan up, and planted the scientist on his feet with what looked like no effort at all. The man was built like an Olympic power lifter. His hair was black and slick, combed back tightly against his scalp. His nose was prominent, his jaw was prominent, and his pecs, his glutes, his bis and tris were all prominent. Only his eyes were soft, the softest sky blue. He grabbed Jordan by his arms and held him straight.

"I'm good." Though coughing, Jordan waved him off even as the gentle giant tried to hurry him along. "Thank you."

The big guy's brow crinkled. He started toward Clara, who was just about to thank him for stopping when her chair lurched forward.

"I got her, Alfie," a man said with a heavy Bostonian accent from over her shoulder. "We need to keep moving."

"*Mon Dieu.* It's loose, isn't it?" Clara's stomach panged hollow, and her mouth went desert dry. She suddenly wanted to be anywhere but right there, in that hallway, waiting for whatever the men were running from to show itself.

"If by 'it'," the man pushing her wheelchair said, "you mean whatever the fuck is turning people into human skin puppets, then yeah, I'd say *it* has definitely gotten out of its cage."

As if to demonstrate the American's point, a woman in a white lab coat and fuzzy rabbit slippers had gained on Clara's wheelchair and was about to pass her when five long strands of stringy living tissue shot into her spine and neck and yanked her back down the hall in the direction she'd come. Her cries for help ended abruptly, replaced by what sounded like a padded hammer repeatedly whacking into a concrete slab.

Clara wondered if the woman was seizing, if her head was pounding against the floor and making the sound. She didn't look back to check.

"Faster, Sebastian!" the one called Alfie shouted.

The man behind her answered the call, popping the chair into a wheelie and driving them forward, faster and faster. Jordan ran a few meters ahead, Alfie between Jordan and them.

Jordan glanced back, did a double take, turned sideways, and stared back. The color left his face and hands until they went bleached white. The hair over his ears went just as white, unless it had always been that way and she was just noticing it for the first time. She couldn't fathom terror so powerful that it could alter hair pigmentation, even on a day she'd seen an astrobiologist mutate and attack her and an ASAP guard, using his skin like silly putty to impregnate the latter with an infectious organism. She had a feeling Jordan was seeing something much, much worse.

"Wh-Wh-Where d-do we go?" he managed to ask.

Alfie took a glance behind them and gasped. "I don't know. Not back that way" – he threw a thumb over his shoulder – "that's for sure. We need to get out."

"The organism and its host have already breached a sealed clean room," Clara said. "I doubt there's a door in here that can hold it back."

"Then we get the fuck out of here, plain and simple," Sebastian said between heavy breaths.

"We can't," Clara answered. "This place is on lockdown. If I remember correctly from orientation, that means no one gets in and no one gets out. Heavy metallic shutters have seen to that."

"There's always a way out," Jordan said. "There has to be. Or at least a way to override the shutters."

"I doubt it," Clara said. "Our best chance of getting out of here is to destroy the organism and anyone who has been infected."

"But doesn't that mean—" Jordan began.

"Everyone's been infected!" Alfie shouted.

"Everyone, then," Clara said firmly. "ASAP used fire to destroy Molli...uh, the organism...when it first took a human host. We could set a controlled fire to keep it back while we figure a way out of the mess. Of course, we may be able to hold the organism back, but we might bring the whole research center down on ourselves in the process."

"How do you suppose we start these fires?" Jordan asked. "Where?"

"We may not need to go to such extremes," Alfie said. "Follow me. I have a better idea."

CHAPTER SEVENTEEN

Even as he helped carry Stearns down the corridor away from the conflagration, Dante had no difficulty sliding Stearns's key ring off the chain latching it to his belt and using it to remove his handcuffs undetected. He slid the light metal clasps into his back pocket then reached around Stearns's waist to offer stronger support.

They had managed to put some breathing room between themselves and the skittering horde of human-flesh insects, but they'd lost their flamethrower, not to mention half their security team. And from what Dante knew of Stearns, they'd lost their better half.

"How did you—" Stearns blurted, his spectacular powers of observation finally alerting him to the fact that Dante had shed his cuffs like a snake its skin. He shoved Dante away from him, shrugged Belgrade off, and grimaced when he placed weight on his injured foot and drew his sidearm, leaving his rifle hanging from his back.

Dante raised his hands. *Only one witness, and he appears to be Stearns's bitch. This does not bode well.*

"What's gotten into you?" Belgrade asked as he shoved his coworker back.

Dante smirked. *Surprise, surprise.*

Stearns shook but kept his pistol trained on Dante. He shifted more weight onto his good foot, beginning to look a bit like a crane. "Back off," he said gruffly, low and menacing. "This guy's the reason we're in this mess."

"In case you've already forgotten, he and I just carried your sorry ass halfway across this building. He helped save your miserable life." Belgrade scowled. "And we don't have time for this bullshit. We – no, *you* – need his help if you expect to get anywhere on that foot—"

"*He's* the reason my foot is like this in the first place!" Stearns snapped through teeth gritted due to either pain or anger. His finger tightened against the trigger but didn't squeeze it.

"It's no use," Dante said to his more reasonable companion. "Belgrade, is it? Stearns won't, Stearns *can't*, let me live. Do you want to know why? Well, you know I got into the clean room, but did you ever ask yourself *how* I got in there?"

Stearns growled. He squirmed under his collar. "Shut up," he said, sweat rolling off his forehead.

Dante had no intention of shutting up. "He can't let me live, not knowing what I know about him, what your late associate Romanov learned about him. Stearns, here…. Well, he's not playing for team ASAP. Oh, no." Dante laughed. "He's playing for a different team altogether."

Stearns's growling grew fiercer. He was more rabid dog than crane. "I said shut up!" The gun shook in his hand. With it held high, he hobbled closer to Dante, who remained perfectly still. "Shut up! Shut up! SHUT UP!"

Another guard barreled around the corner, the Australian guy with the injured eye. He skidded to a halt, inches from Belgrade's AK-47, which was raised and aimed at the Aussie's good eye.

"Whoa!" the man shouted. "It's me. Monty. They didn't touch me! They didn't touch me!"

No one moved. Stearns never took his eyes off Dante as the guard squinted down the barrel of his FN 5.7 tactical-grade semiautomatic pistol. His finger twitched over the trigger. The hammer slowly drew back.

"Hey, mates," Monty said, giggling awkwardly. "We don't have to fight each other. There's a whole army of—"

A vent cover crashed onto the floor at Stearns's feet, barely missing his wound. His gaze shot toward the ceiling, his hands and gun following. He screamed and got off one shot before what looked like a swollen human arm, fingers curled to form a hand-shadow snake, dropped down from a square opening. The warped appendage descended on Stearns with the speed of a cobra's strike. Also like a snake, the monstrosity had fangs. They buried into Stearns's head, snatched him off the ground, and lifted him into the vent.

But only Stearns's head could fit in the opening. Whatever had a hold of him pulled and thrashed so fiercely that the vent buckled on one side. On the other side, Stearns's shoulder gave way first. The vent's edge sawed its way through from clavicle to armpit, severing the arm and cramming Stearns's twitching, kicking body like garbage into an overfilled receptacle. A trickle of urine ran down one of his legs. From the smell, Dante was sure Stearns had also shat his pants.

Belgrade opened fire, sending as many bullets into the ceiling as he did Stearns. The AK-47's barrel ran red hot.

When the ASAP man had emptied his clip, Monty nudged him forward. "Come on, mate. We have to keep moving."

But Belgrade didn't move. He looked shell-shocked, staring up at the ceiling with wide-eyed wonder and jaw-dropping disbelief. Dante was taking a step toward him to help escort him away when Monty bitch-slapped his coworker hard enough to leave a print.

Belgrade snorted then shook his face and body loose. "I'm good. Let's move."

Dante ran over to Stearns's severed arm, watching it and the convulsing body above closely as he did. The severed arm still had its hand. That hand, to Dante's great fortune, still held Stearns's gun.

He grabbed the barrel and whacked the arm against the floor until the hand fell away from the grip. As a precaution, he avoided touching anything that had once been part of Stearns. When the arm began to flop on the floor, he commended himself for his decision.

He slowly backed away from the arm. Looking at the remaining two ASAP guards, neither of whom was pointing a weapon at him though they watched him with clear suspicion, he said, "I agree. Let's move."

"We heard gunfire, and..." a man in his fifties or early sixties said before trailing off as he took in the remains of Stearns. Given the lab coat the man was wearing, Dante figured him for one of the douchebag scientists he blamed for their current predicament. He eased his finger off the trigger.

The Indian woman he'd seen in the clean room bumped into the man's back when he stopped in front of her. She looked up, screamed, and dropped the heavy device she'd been carrying – Dante recognized it as another scanner – on the ground with a clang. The man in front of her covered his ears.

"Anju!" Dr. Lab Coat shouted as he turned around and shook the woman, whom Dante found absolutely stunning even in her duress. "Run the scan!"

"No, just run!" Monty shouted. He tried to usher them away, but no one moved. Belgrade stared blankly, still a little shell-shocked, offering no support.

"Is there a point?" Dante muttered. He wondered if he could trust the newcomers. Perhaps *that* was the point. The newcomers were suspicious of *him*.

"Close your eyes or look away." The woman, Anju, came to her senses, knelt beside the scanner as if she'd never lost them, and hit some buttons on a keyboard at the machine's base while Dante and the two ASAP guards moved cautiously toward them with weapons drawn.

"Initiating scan for biological contamination," the machine said as if it hadn't the least bit interest in doing so.

"Are you infected?" Belgrade asked as he, Monty, and Dante fanned out around the two newcomers.

Dante confirmed the point of the scan then. It wasn't for what was *behind* them. It was for *them*. The Russian reloaded his assault rifle and aimed as he took one step, then another, drawing a little closer with each.

"No," the older gentleman said, raising his hands as Anju stayed on her knees beside the machine. "Of course not. Are you?"

A flash brightened the hall, and Dante was momentarily blinded. He blinked his eyes clear.

"Scan completed," the scanner said. "Unknown organism detected." It made a series of beeps, chirps, and whirrs. "Unknown organism detected, stationary, approximately nineteen meters south-southwest. Elevation: five meters above scanner location."

"Stearns." Dante glanced back over his shoulder.

"And whatever ate him," Monty added. "Stay away from the vents."

"Unknown organism detected, seventy-four meters south-southwest… unknown organism approaching, now seventy meters south-southwest… sixty-seven meters south-southwest…sixty-two meters south-southwest. Estimated time of encounter: less than forty seconds."

"Well, it's not us your gadget detects," Dante said. "And it's not you either. By the sound of it, we need to leave, right now. Something's coming, and I don't want to be here when it arrives."

"Unknown organism detected, forty-four meters south-southwest…"

"I second that," Belgrade said.

"Anju," Dr. Lab Coat said, "grab the scanner."

"Leave it," Monty said. "It'll only slow you down, and you don't want to be slowed down. Trust me on this."

"…thirty-six meters south-southwest…"

"Nonsense," the scientist said. "We may need it."

"Your call," Monty said. "I'm out of here." He started off down the hall.

Belgrade followed. So did Anju.

"Anju?" The older scientist reached out a hand.

"Respectfully, Dr. Werniewski," the Indian woman said, jerking back to face him and glaring, "if you want it so badly, you carry it."

"...thirty meters south-southwest..."

Dante shrugged at the doctor and jogged past him. Anju joined him. He didn't look back to see if Dr. Werniewski was following and didn't have to. The *clap-tap* of his fancy dress shoes against the floor gave away his presence just fine.

"Twenty-five meters south-southwest," the machine said behind them, left all on its own to experience the encounter it was forewarning.

The party jogged briskly but without a spoken destination, the goal merely to be anywhere but out in those halls with god knew what chasing them. Dante chanced a look back. Whatever was drawing near had yet to show itself, but a headless Stearns dropped from the ceiling and hit the ground with a bone-snapping crack. The remains arched backward until neck stump and feet formed a tripod on which the creature pursued them.

The sound drew the others attention. Anju gulped through a hand over her mouth. Dr. Werniewski's skin blanched. The others stood gaping in revolted awe.

"We need to run," Dante said, snapping them out of their stupors. He grabbed Anju by the arm and dragged her along with him as he ran. After running the length of the hall and turning a corner, and hearing the others at his heels, he shouted, "Any ideas?"

"The control room!" Monty yelled through heaving breaths. "We'll be able to see the whole base and be able to tell how badly the infection has spread. Maybe seal it off or at least slow it down."

"Fourteen meters south-southwest," the machine said, a soft voice in the distance, mostly drowned out by the alarms.

Dante didn't look back again. He didn't want to know how close that Stearns-thing was. It was enough to know that it was coming. "Lead the way," was all he said.

Monty did, taking off in a full sprint. The others followed, all of them running as fast as they could.

CHAPTER EIGHTEEN

Screams came from every direction. As Sebastian pushed her past the front entrance, Clara saw a mob scrambling and fighting, its participants piling upon the backs of the fallen and broken. The security booth was empty, the metal detectors knocked over. Heavy shutters blocked the doors out. Humans were hurting humans, hurting themselves, as they tried to break through the unbreakable. They'd given up on society, looking out only for self, as she'd done for so very long.

Clara almost cried, but the moment passed. *Well, there's no escape that way.* Their time was short. The infected were closing in.

No escape any way.

Molli was loose, and based on the sounds of panic and chaos echoing down every hall, the battle had been lost as soon as it had begun. Instead of saving lives, the security measures had damned many uninfected humans who might have found safety, might have escaped death, had it not been for the research center's contamination protocols.

No one in. No one out.

However, Clara knew that once Molli had finished her meal inside her new petri dish, she would find a way out.

I caused this. Her eyes blurred with tears. *Everyone dead...or worse, because of me.*

She buried her chin against her bosom, wallowing in shame, despair, hopelessness, allowing herself to be pushed by a man she didn't know, wherever he chose to take her. It didn't matter. There was no way out.

The big, dumb ox doesn't think so. She cast a glance at Alfie, a brawny mammoth who probably thought his strength would protect him. *He's a fool,* she thought, sickened by his set-back shoulders and head held high. *So full of confidence. So full of hope.*

Dumb, naïve hope.

Jordan hung at Alfie's heels like a loyal Labrador. He peppered the brawny man with questions, causing more noise than their group needed to be making. "Where are we going? What are we doing? How can we stop them? How do we get away?" Clara couldn't make out the answers over the barking alarms and the pulsing of blood beating in her skull.

For his part, Sebastian remained quiet. Clara assumed he was conserving his energy for a fight for survival she had no doubt would come. Her mind darkened with shame even as her heart filled for the man who had slowed his own escape in a futile effort to help with hers, a woman he'd never met and, at most, had seen only in passing.

Every now and then, a droplet of his sweat would hit her cheek or neck. The contact, his selfless exertion, renewed her faith in humanity, even if only a little.

"Guys," Sebastian said, "I need a second to catch my breath."

Alfie stopped and turned around. "You okay?" He frowned and took a step toward Clara. "Here, let me take over."

Jordan grabbed him by the elbow. "Alfie—"

"The name is Alfonse," their fearless leader said matter-of-factly. He pointed back at Sebastian. "Only he gets to call me Alfie."

"Okay, then. Alfonse," Jordan said. "Tell me again how this plan is supposed to work? How are you supposedly going to get us past the goddamn dome that now covers us? Goddamn it! I feel like I'm in a goddamn Stephen King novel."

"As I told you," Alfonse said, "Sebastian and I are astrobiologists."

Clara stiffened. *Hadn't Sergei Kobozev been an astrobiologist?* The thought scared her even if it was crazy to think that insanity promulgated within certain professions. *Dictators, maybe.*

"What does that have to do with anything?" Jordan asked. "You're not going to turn psychopath on us like that other guy, are you?"

Clara raised an eyebrow. She had thought it a fair question, but when she heard him say it aloud, she realized just how absurd it was. "Calm down, Jordan," she said softly, trying to keep the peace without being condescending.

"Calm down?" Jordan paced, turning on his foot in an exaggerated about-face every time he'd gone about two meters. "Calm down?" Finally, he stopped pacing. "We're trapped in a quarantine zone with a truly horrific life-form that's turning people into Play-Doh, and you want me to calm down? We may very well be the only people not yet infected in this goddamn facility, and who knows? Maybe we're already infected, and it's just taking longer for it to affect us. We already know *you're* infected."

"What does he mean by that?" Sebastian asked.

"It's..." Clara began. She shot Jordan a sharp glance that was meant to wound. "Nothing. Relax, Jordan." The sharpness in her eyes fell upon her tongue. "Your panicking will get us nowhere."

Jordan's chest swelled. He looked as though he was going to explode, but after a moment, he began to deflate. "I'm sorry." His sincerity glimmered behind his eyes a moment then was gone. "Our lives are at stake here. I'd just like to know that the plan I'm following is a solid one."

"Do you have a better plan?" Sebastian asked.

"Our cell phones!" Jordan blurted as he fumbled in his pocket.

Clara frowned. "Wasn't yours confiscated?"

Away from the clean room, she rarely encountered security staff on campus. But when a rule was broken, the excessively macho brutes would swarm in like the Foreign Legion. She'd only seen that twice, but those times taught her not to violate so much as a quiet-time policy. The first had been a grad student who'd tried to e-mail his professor's research notes outside the facility. The second had been an office worker who'd kicked a vending machine when his candy bar got snagged on a lower shelf. Clara had not seen either delinquent again.

After those instances, no new policies were instituted with respect to the vending machines, but sending e-mails to anyone not located within the facility was prohibited and, Clara assumed, blocked entirely. She wasn't brave enough to try it and find out. Soon after that, their cell phones had been taken away. Outgoing calls were prohibited unless they were chaperoned by men with very large guns. Internet use was permitted, but only as it related to scientific research, and Clara guessed it was highly monitored.

"I have two phones," Jordan said proudly. "Surely, they must go back online in a crisis."

No one said a word. Clara let Jordan figure it out for himself as he mashed the buttons on his phone.

After a minute, he growled and whipped his cell phone against a wall. He turned to Alfonse. "I'm guessing there has to be some kind of vent, maintenance hatch, rooftop exit, bulkhead...something that will get us out of the building and past the gate."

"Even if that were so," Clara said, "we don't know where that is or where to look. We'd be dead before we found it."

"So we find someone who does know," Jordan said, waving his arms like a drunken composer as he spoke. "I bet those ASAP pricks know half a dozen ways out." He took a deep breath then pointed a finger inches from Alfonse's face. "Should we just put our faith blindly in this guy? We don't even know who he is."

"As I was trying to explain" – Alfonse folded his fingers and squeezed them tightly – "Sebastian and I are astrobiologists assigned to the Mars Big Dig Mission—"

"Again," Jordan interrupted, "I fail to see the relevance—"

"That's because you won't shut the fuck up long enough for him to explain it, asshole," Sebastian snapped.

"He's just scared," Clara said meekly.

"We all are," Sebastian said. "It doesn't give him the right to act like an asshole." He grumbled more curses under his breath. "Anyway, what my more patient friend is trying to tell you is that we have a way off this rock. Or, at least, out of this godforsaken research center."

"Exactly," Alfonse said. "You see, NASA would never let one of its multibillion-dollar pieces of equipment blow up without first trying to extract it—"

"Wait," Jordan said. "What do you mean, 'blow up'?"

"For the last time—" Sebastian began.

"Now hold on." Clara turned in her seat to face him. "That's a legitimate question."

"Don't tell me you don't know about this center's self-destruct capabilities?" Sebastian asked, rolling his eyes. "They put that in because of all the deadly viruses and bacteria being studied here. If one were to ever get loose...." Sebastian slowly extended his arms up and out, making the sound of an explosion.

Then Jordan gave Clara a look that could kill.

She shook her head. *Not a word, Jordan. Not a word*. He got the message and kept his mouth shut.

"We know about that," Clara said. "But no one's triggered it."

"No one has to," Alfonse said. "Rumor has it that it can be detonated remotely."

"So what you're saying is, we not only have to worry about being killed by human puppets inside, but by those *outside*, too?" Jordan asked.

"Don't worry," Sebastian said. "By the time they go through all the red tape needed to blow up this place, we'll be long dead – if we're still in here, anyway."

"That's…comforting," Jordan said.

"And that's why we are taking the rover and getting the hell out of here, *capisce*?" Alfonse asked.

"Rover?" Jordan asked. "As in a Mars rover?"

"Top of the line, baby!" Sebastian said. "She's a real beauty. Not only is she equipped with all the fixings for all-terrain travel, but a self-propulsion system that can shoot us all the way into the Earth's orbit if we so choose." He beamed with pride as if he'd had a hand in building it. "We call her Edna."

Clara realized that, as a group, they'd begun moving again, and she wondered when that decision had been reached. Sebastian had resumed his guardianship of her wheelchair and was already building to a moderate pace.

She didn't know much about space exploration and knew even less about Martian vehicles, but Jordan seemed interested in the topic beyond whether or not it could save their lives. "I remember the *Curiosity* and the *Opportunity* rovers from my childhood. I even had the toys. But if I remember correctly, those things were unmanned. I don't remember any of them since ever being manned."

"Next gens were designed to seat one person, and there were plenty of us willing to volunteer for such a mission," Sebastian said, his words coming out excited, as if spewed from a turret, "but human psychology just isn't designed for that length and duration of solo space travel. The *Endeavor* and the *Pioneer* were both disasters, the extra unused equipment just getting in the way of their more practical functions. But Edna, better known as the *Herald*, is the first of its class." He exchanged a glance with Alfonse. "She should be able to get all of us out of here safely."

"But what about the shutters?" Jordan asked.

"A good question." Alfonse gave Sebastian a wink. "I think he's finally paying attention, Sebastian." He smiled at Jordan. "There is no shutter over the landing platform. Like the faraway finger on the trigger, NASA can and will operate the rover remotely if or when it feels its property is in jeopardy, or we can manually commence launch ourselves any time Sebastian or I see fit to do so. NASA will intend to launch it unmanned. But regardless of whether NASA launches it or we do, we need to be onboard. It will seat the four of us comfortably, but...that's about it."

"And if we can't get out," Sebastian said as he gave Clara a pat on the shoulder, "there's enough rocket fuel in the rover to blow us and this place to kingdom come."

"Again," Jordan said, "not comforting." He shuddered. "So what are we waiting for?"

"This whole place is like a giant wheel with the rover and launch pad at its hub," Sebastian said. "Unfortunately, this wheel's spokes make up a rat-race lattice filled with dead-end corridors and blind turns that look exactly like the real ones until you try them and find your nose pressing against a wall."

"There are two entrances to the hub," Alfonse added. "A north and a south entrance. We've been weaving our way toward the southern entrance. Both entrances require a keycard and passcode like every high-security area here, and both Sebastian and I know those passcodes and have those keycards. The problem is: we don't know if the path to either entrance is clear."

"Well, we certainly can't go back the way we came," Clara said. "And I doubt we can hide from—"

"But maybe that's exactly what we should do!" Jordan shouted. "Hide. Lay low. Stay safe. Hole up until the cavalry arrives."

"Like talking to a fucking wall." Sebastian groaned.

Clara rolled her eyes. "Who do you think is coming, Jordan? Who out there would you call who isn't automatically informed of our situation as soon as those shutters fall? We are in full-system lockdown. No one is coming inside here until either this entire facility is deemed safe and germ-free or everyone in the facility is dead alongside the organism."

"Look," Jordan said. "I've never had to deal with anything like this before. I'm a botanist, for Christ's sake. I'm just trying to help."

"That explains it," Sebastian muttered, but only Clara seemed to have caught it. Louder, he said, "Easy. Just keep your shit together."

Jordan raised his voice in response. "I think my shit's together pretty well, all things considered, thank you."

"Everyone, relax!" Alfonse shouted. "You Americans – always bickering. We're making too much noise!" Perhaps realizing the irony of his remark, he added in a lower voice, "Listen. I don't know what attracts these infected freaks, but it seems foolish to assume they can't see, smell, or hear us. So let's keep moving," he turned the corner, "and pray to whichever god you worship that we don't run into any of those – gyahh!"

Alfonse dove out of the way of something plump and slithery that seemed to swim along the floor. Human skin, part resembling the wrinkled, spotted flesh on and around a kneecap, made up most of its body, but the rest was unidentifiable, particularly when it was oozing and sliding its way toward them like snot sneezed onto a mirror.

The bulbous mound was heading straight for Clara, who dug her nails so far into the padding on the arms of her chair that she broke more than half of them. *I'm going to die.*

She shrieked and jerked sideways. Her chair tipped over and dumped her onto the cold, unsympathetic tile.

"Sebastian!" Alfonse ran to his friend, reaching out toward the tail of the whipping eel creature that had buried its head in Sebastian's chest.

It wiggled into Sebastian like sperm penetrating an egg and having much success, already deep into the astrobiologist's muscle.

"No!" Clara shouted. "Don't touch him!"

Alfonse ignored her. But even as he reached for the wriggling tail, Sebastian sidestepped his advance. "R-Run," he said hoarsely, his voice hardly recognizable as human. His eyes rolled back, revealing the blank whites. As he began to seize, he bit down on his tongue so hard that blood squirted from his mouth.

"I'm so sorry," Alfonse said through tears. He roared in pain and anger and dropped to a knee. Clara thought he was lost to them and she, in turn, was lost as well.

But Alfonse rose and looked down at Clara with deep sadness but also sheer strength of will shining in his tear-filled eyes. "Jordan, help me get her.... Jordan!"

Clara followed Alfonse's raving-mad glare to see Jordan dashing toward the end of the hall and disappearing around a bend. He was running away from them, from *her*, leaving her to fend for herself. *Some man he turned out to be.*

Alfonse said it best. "Coward!"

More wriggling limb eels oozed into the corridor up ahead. Screams followed closely behind. Alfonse kicked her wheelchair aside, scooped Clara up, and carried her toward their only hope of a way out, a room in the middle of the hall, labeled Radiology.

Alfonse flung Clara over his shoulder and held her up with one hand as he tried the doorknob with the other. The door was locked.

"I have access." Clara's voice quivered as the flesh monsters bore down on them in a grotesque wave of slurping, sliding, and even crunching – on what, only God knew. "My keycard – it's on my belt!"

If Alfonse was even a quarter as terrified as she was, he wasn't showing it. He grabbed the card and tore it from her waist. With a steady hand, he slid it through the card reader.

"Please," Clara begged. "Hurry." As she spoke, she heard the sound of the locking mechanism retracting. "*Vite!* They're coming!"

Alfonse tore open the door and burst into the room behind it. He spun and slammed the door shut.

Wham! Wham! Wham!

Bang after bang after bang came from the door as it rattled in its frame. Alfonse braced it with his free shoulder. The lock reactivated, and the bolt sealed the door shut. Only then did Alfonse back away.

The banging didn't stop. *It's not going to stop.* "We have no time to waste," Clara said. "If we're going to do something, it has to be quick. They'll be under that door soon enough."

"Any ideas?" Alfonse said, sobbing quietly.

"Not a one, friend," she said. "Not a one."

CHAPTER NINETEEN

Though a death-metal dirge of confusion and fear filled the passageways, the path to the security control room had thus far been clear. As Dante trotted down one hall then another, he was no longer guided by instinct or experience. He simply allowed himself to follow the ASAP guards in what seemed like a rational plan, at least until he saw a way to affect a plan of his own making.

Get to the control room. Assess the scope of infection. Seal off as many of the infected as we can. But the control room itself was proving harder to get into than Mother Teresa's underwear.

The fire alarm continued its unremitting wail, reminding him of another alarm that wouldn't quit when he'd escaped an off-the-grid Cambodian prison, which in turn, reminded him of the great number and deadly extent of dangers to which his work had exposed him.

Human evil was a fact of life, probably far more so in his life than in most others', granted. Dante had seen so much of it that he could take one look at a man and know the depths of his depravity, the sins he would commit without second thought if given the right provocation, and the blackness that pumped viscous sludge through his heart. Women were trickier, not so much due to any particular guile on their part, but more because of Dante's own semichivalrous, semichauvinistic failings. Even then, he always read them right before it was too late.

The infected were another ballgame. He'd already seen enough of them to know that trying to read them, trying to predict their movements, was an exercise in futility, like pissing into a hurricane. Their faces were expressionless, perfect poker faces, and their methods of combat thus far completely erratic. *Am I afraid?* The sensation seemed strange since death had been breathing down his neck since long before he'd taken up assignment with the Pointy Hats. He assumed his fear found its roots in the fact that, before that day, he'd always understood the evil he'd been up against: Stearns's kind of evil, motivated by malice or money or revenge – the human kind.

Dante didn't understand that other form of evil, as alien as anything born from outer space. He didn't understand it, and he hadn't signed up for it. He wondered if his employer had understood it and had sent him in anyway.

His mind drifted back to his last meeting with the Pointy Hats, which Dante had taken to calling them since they had no official name – at least not one they'd told him. They weren't wearing their hats then, though – just black hoodies and scowling mouths as they converged in that back alley of the Vatican. And Dante had been scowling right back.

He'd never liked the Pointy Hats. They'd consistently shown him contempt, acting as if they were so special, so much better than he was because of what he did *for them*. They found him repugnant, and the feeling was mutual. Dante couldn't count how many times he'd had to remind himself that the Pointy Hats were the good guys. That was the truth, he knew. Despite all their arrogant assholishness, they were trying to save the world in their own way, one crisis at a time. Behind the scenes, the Pointy Hats did what governments and global peacekeepers couldn't because their bureaucratic heads were so far up the asses of politics and nepotism and, oddly enough, moral constraints.

The Pointy Hats often reminded him of that famous philosophical question: If you could go back in time and kill Hitler before his rise to power, before his adulthood even, would you? Most people in his experience, Dante included, answered affirmatively. The Pointy Hats would've built a time machine just for that purpose. They would've traveled back in time to cut little Adolf's throat while he was still in the womb if they'd had the power to.

Well, they wouldn't have gone back themselves. Dante grimaced. *They would have sent me.*

And there he was at the Shakhova-Mendelsen Siberian Research Center at the Pointy Hats' command. They'd sent him to save the world from a potential virus or disease that, according to his well-informed benefactors, had already been the impetus for many backroom deals and behind-the-scenes governmental maneuvers. The research center itself was the brainchild of a conglomeration of United Nations member countries, each trying to get a leg up on the other while nonmember factions tried to get a foot in the door.

Like most divorcing parents, each country wanted more than joint custody of the child. Each wanted *sole* custody, though none would openly admit it. Each was willing to tear its child apart before letting another parent take that child away.

The worst offender in Dante's quagmire was the presumably neutral court officer, ASAP, hired to keep the peace and enforce joint-custody privileges. Ostensibly, the security company served as a high-functioning babysitter, but in reality, the private corporation was little more than a facilitator for the greedy without a soul to sell to the highest bidder.

Instead, it had the viruses to sell.

Fortunately, not every country wanted the potentially deadly biological weaponry for themselves, and some had strong claims or good reasons for wanting what they wanted from the facility. Nevertheless, the Pointy Hats had declared the viruses off-limits. They gave Dante a dossier filled with blueprints; personnel files for both the center and for ASAP; photographs; equipment specifications; laboratory and cold-storage locations; detailed insight into top-secret projects; the names and identities of stooges, plants, spies, and double agents; and the same for those with top-level facility access and knowledge of the forever-changing passcodes – the best information money and influence could gather.

Beyond that, the Pointy Hats had given Dante a briefcase with two million incentives for a job well done and the promise of another two million once the job was completed. They'd sent him on his way, leaving in his capable hands the details of how he would get inside the building and bring their plan to fruition.

Getting inside places had always been Dante's forte. A child without a family, at least one that gave a damn, he'd grown up sneaking and thieving and conning, mostly in Rome, where he'd learned every escape route. He'd gotten by for a long time lifting wallets before he realized he could do far better. As he got older, the game got riskier and the scores bigger. He rarely got caught, and he never got caught with the goods. The few that caught him would always turn him loose with the hope that he'd lead them to where he'd stashed his prize, but Dante would always give them the slip.

Until the last time he was caught. That time, his captors offered him training in lock picking and safecracking, advanced burglary techniques, martial arts of various disciplines, marksmanship and weaponry, hacking and languages…even a full education in the humanities. They asked nothing but commitment in return, but even then, Dante wondered what the true cost of acceptance would be.

It didn't stop him from accepting. And after all his training was done, they – the Pointy Hats – still asked nothing from him. Instead, they offered him a job, and a high-paying one at that, never seeking reimbursement for services rendered.

That had been a lot of jobs before, and Dante had amassed quite a fortune. Still, he kept taking the jobs offered, getting himself into all sorts of needless trouble. Yeah, getting into it was his forte. Getting back out…not so much.

He'd drawn the conclusion that getting out of the research center was going to be a steep, uphill battle. Obtaining that second briefcase seemed about as likely as the Pearly Gates spreading wide for him when the infected claimed his body.

He hoped the devil needed someone with his skills. *Better to rule in hell, yadda yadda yadda*…. But Dante couldn't shake the feeling that he'd already met the devil that day, hiding behind the still, dead eyes of Sergei Kobozev.

"We're here." Belgrade threw out an arm to block Dante, who was coming in hot.

Monty punched a code into a keypad adjacent to a heavy-looking bomb-shelter blast shield of a door. In its center was a placard that read in small white letters on a black background, 'Control Room'.

No hiding the ball there. Dante didn't expect a hidden war room filled with men in uniform pushing pawns over maps, but he did expect a bit more…. *Pizzazz? No*…. Je ne sais quoi.

Monty cursed. He slid his badge through the ID reader and punched in a code once more. Again, nothing happened. He looked at Belgrade. "Have they changed the codes since this morning?"

Belgrade frowned. "Step aside," he said, already muscling his way past Monty and grabbing his own badge. "Let's try mine." He repeated the process Monty had just gone through, but when he swiped his card, the door unlocked and swung open.

Monty grunted. He stood beside Belgrade, who held the door open as Dr. Werniewski pushed his way into the dimly lit entrance. Anju, Monty, and finally Dante made their way inside.

"Wait! Please! Wait!" a man's voice shouted up the hall. "Hold the door! Please!"

Only a few steps past the entrance, Dante's curiosity got the better of him. He slunk back to the door. Anju followed, clinging to him like a newborn possum. Her breath was hot on his neck, her fingers gently tugging on his vest.

Her proximity might have made him nervous had he not been so intent on the incoming traffic. The man begging for help wasn't much to look at: one of those lean, compact guys who appeared strong until you stood him next to a soldier or a weightlifter. Strength was absent from his gaunt face. His complexion had taken on a more sickly hue than his ugly, preppy green sweater.

Dante instantly hated that sweater. By extension, he didn't care for the man, another lab coat-wearing scientist. But compared to the swelling formation of human body parts following the scientist closely – too damn big and with far too many appendages to be made up of just one human – Dante liked the man just fine.

He scrambled into the control room. His dossier had spent a great number of paragraphs on that room – what exactly it could control and what goodies hid within. With two swift kicks to a wooden door marked 'Armory', he entered a treasure trove of weapons, enough to make any arms dealer proud.

He didn't waste time picking and choosing but went for the weapon he'd already seen work best.

"That is Jordan Phillips," Anju said from the entranceway.

The sound of loafers pounding against floor tiles mixed with a more unsettling sound, like rusted-over pruners forced open and closed. Those last sounds grew louder.

"Do not shoot," Anju said.

"How can you be sure?" Belgrade asked.

"Because he is being chased by that…that…giant purple people eater!" Anju answered.

Banging and crashing came from outside the control-room door as Dante hoisted the tank onto his back. Armed like Prometheus, ready to share fire with the whole damn world if he had to, he stormed out the armory door. From inside the control room, a five-foot-nothing ASAP lackey sprinted past him as he hurried toward the entrance.

The guard never looked Dante's way. He bounded toward Anju and Belgrade, clearing the distance in a second, yelling at the top of his lungs for them to close the door.

Dante doubted Belgrade had heard the man, for he had opened fire, aiming high. Though Dante couldn't see Belgrade's target, he could tell from the guard's shifting feet and blazing-wide glare that he was hardly managing to keep it back, whatever it was. Anju and the newly arriving guard do-si-doed, each going opposite directions. She passed Dante on her way deeper into the control room, her face whiter than bleached sheets.

She was followed by another, on hands and knees, the man with the puke-green sweater. The scientist met his stare and even gave Dante a polite nod before continuing his frantic crawl away from the chaos outside.

"It's not stopping!" Belgrade shouted from the entrance. His shoulder was propping the door open as he fired into the hall.

"Close the door!" The short guard kept shouting. He maneuvered skillfully past Anju and the crawling scientist, but his momentum carried him forward as he reached past a gun-blazing Belgrade to yank the door shut.

Belgrade had enough presence of mind to pull up his gun as his coworker lunged over him, but he didn't have time to pull back his leg.

The guard crashed face-first into the door, pushing it open. He spilled into the hall, falling onto a long spear-like tail constructed from two or more spinal columns and a sharpened pelvis. It pierced through the guard's back and emerged from his stomach. The spearhead caught on his large intestines. What it didn't pull out began to spill out of the exit wound like cooked spaghetti drenched in sauce, what non-motherland Italians tried to pass off as Sicilian gravy.

At that moment, Dante didn't miss home cooking. He reached Belgrade, who'd resumed firing, either too panicked to close the door and shut the thing out or too rational to know there was no shutting the tail's owner out.

When Dante moved into position, he guessed the latter. He

hesitated, too stunned to speak or move. He gaped up at the tail's tip as it carved divots into the ceiling, then followed its length down to a giant, multilegged, purple-hided scorpion of sorts. Its massive pincers were made from the cracked femurs of two no-longer-recognizable humans whose bodies had melted into the creature's sides. Instead of having anything resembling an arachnid's head, the abomination wore a human torso, nearly complete, as if it were some wicked horror version of a centaur.

Half man, half.... He chuckled despite his terror, familiar with the song inspiring Anju's choice of words. 'Giant purple people eater' sufficed.

The shish-kebabbed guard had died instantly, yet he was seizing on the creature's tail. His fervent shaking jostled the vertebral blades up through his chest then out the base of his neck. He was like turkey breast pushed through a meat slicer. After sliding down the tail and onto the creature's back, he acid-melted into the purple hide.

Fucking red shirt, Dante thought, recalling a joke someone had made about an American show that constantly went in and out of syndication back in Naples. The show was only slightly less ridiculous than its follow-ups, which as far as he could tell, starred a different individual playing the same character each time he'd seen it. He whistled the show's catchy tune, his mind unusually off his game, no longer afraid unless fear made him retreat inward.

"Light him up already!" Belgrade yelled.

Dante jumped, but he hit the trigger, sending out a gush of fire that engulfed the flesh scorpion as if it were a match head. Bubbles boiled and popped on its skin before oozing fluids formed larger blisters. When those too popped, fist-sized miniatures of the creature tried to extend their short lives by jumping and fleeing, but all were caught in flame, popping like corn kernels. The human mouths stretching from the centaur head and those stretching from shallow graves in the beast's sides opened in silent screams.

Dante kept the fire burning strong and hot as the purple people eater skittered left and right, slicing and scissoring the air with vicious but blind attacks. Whatever smarts the organism had, no one had ever taught it to stop, drop, and roll. Instead, it collapsed onto its folding-chair legs and burned as brightly and as pungently as a compost heap.

The monster's movements slowed then stopped. Dante turned to say something about campfires to Belgrade, but the guard had abandoned him sometime during his firefight. He shrugged, closed the door, and stepped inside, where the Russian waited for him in the dark.

"They must know where we are now," Dante said. "That door will only stall them. Is there another way out of here?"

"One," Belgrade said. "Follow me."

A man of action, not indecision. Dante thought he'd found a wartime ally, one who seemed to understand priorities. He followed Belgrade down a short hallway that led past the armory and into the main room, a circular central point with wall-to-wall screens and more buttons and consoles than twelve commercial airplane cockpits.

Belgrade stopped. He and the rest of the crowd fixed their gazes on a massive monitor with multiple split screens, the biggest of the displays showing the giant purple people eater still twitching but burning nicely outside the control room's door. Sprinklers were showering everything everywhere but had no noticeable effect on the burning mass. Other screens showed people running, some toward other people and some away from others. A greater portion of monitors showed people convulsing, people dying, people changing, and people becoming part of the horde.

Everywhere.

"*Cazzo!*" Dante hung his head.

"The facility is lost," Dr. Werniewski whispered.

"Is there any way to reach the outside?" Jordan asked. "You know, call for help?"

"No," Monty said. "Not during lockdown." Standing over Jordan, he rested a hand on the scientist's shoulder. "I'm sorry, mate. There's not much we can do. Even if we could get hold of them, you wouldn't like what they'd have to say. The whackers probably already have us surrounded, making sure none of us get out alive."

"So that's it?" Dr. Werniewski asked. "We're doomed?"

The room went quiet. No one broke the silence for what seemed like an eternity, until Anju muttered, "All those people…Are we able to help any of them?"

No one answered that question either. Not until—

"Most will be dead way before we could get to them," a woman said. Everyone turned to face an ASAP guard Dante hadn't noticed before, and by the startled looks on the others faces, they hadn't either. She sat at the consoles, rising from a slouch in a chair below the big screen. Her long blond hair was ponytailed and tucked through the back of her ASAP ball cap. Given her dark-as-night complexion, Dante doubted the hair came naturally. Or that it matched the—

"Well, there's that guy," she said, pointing at a screen. "He might be heading our way."

"What guy?" Belgrade asked.

The faux blonde's knee bounced, and she kept clenching and unclenching her fingers. She stared everyone down as if she were sizing them up. She seemed hesitant to look back at the screen. "Does it matter? It's too late for them. Shouldn't we gather our things and leave?"

Belgrade frowned and stared at her expectantly.

She slowly turned to the monitors. "Well, he was here, but now he's...here!" she shouted, pointing at another screen as something flashed across it then was gone. "I'll get you." She tapped on her keyboard. One by one, the monitors mapped out the facility like a puzzle pieced together.

But Dante's intrigue remained with the guard. They'd been too focused on the on-screen horror show to get caught up in their own fleeting circumstances, a mistake Dante wouldn't make twice. Since the woman had announced her presence, her smooth skin, muscular gymnast figure, and confident beauty could no longer be missed. Dante took in the sight, staring at her breasts long enough to pick up the name on her nametag in passing. *Dikembu.*

"Whew, that boy can run," she said, snapping him from his trance. She pointed at a young man, no more than twenty, running down a whitewashed hall.

He was wearing a blue jumpsuit and looked like any one of the maintenance and janitorial staff who faded into the background of the facility, just a regular guy trying to make a few euros doing regular work at a not-so-regular place. Dante hoped the boy received hazard pay. He certainly wasn't paid enough for the hell that was chasing him, close on his heels.

The freakish absurdities chasing the young man were big, clumsy looking, odd-duck monstrosities that had no business moving with the ease and speed at which they were. They kept pace with the center employee almost stride for stride. They reminded Dante of an image he'd seen many times, though the only particular place that he could then recall having seen it was his grammar-school biology textbook. He saw that image clearly in his mind: a fish emerging from water, its fins having evolved into front legs, while its tailfin remained unsuited to life ashore. Lungs on the outside of its body stood in for the gills they covered. The image was supposed to represent evolution, but Dante found it anything but natural, the hateful mutant looking like the inbred child of newt siblings that had spent their lives drinking and swimming in toxic waste.

But if the toxic newt thing was disgusting, those grizzly-bear-sized mudskippers were downright grotesque, aberrations of nature and biology that, if truly representative of evolution, were at the same time God's cruel joke. Their fat, wide heads seemed too big for their bodies, their toothless mouths too big for their heads. Their lack of pointed incisors made them no less terrifying, and their worm-purple lips secreted a mayonnaise-like substance. They half crawled on human arms and elbows – the only parts of them that appeared human – and half glided sidewinder-like toward their fleeing prey: a single man, terrified out of his mind, running for his life.

As he left one camera view, and thus one monitor, Dikembu pounced on him with the camera tied to the next screen. She targeted him down one hall then the next, amazingly so far avoiding a dead end. Dante couldn't help but feel that, though the young man shouldn't have made his list of priorities, much less rule it, if they could save the maintenance guy, maybe there was hope. Maybe they could even save themselves.

Belgrade had the same idea. "Kill the alarm," he said to Dikembu. "And the sprinklers." He picked up a rather anachronistic microphone connected to an intercom system that all the other equipment made look ancient. The lights everywhere finally stopped flashing red. The blare of the alarm died.

"You, in the maintenance uniform," Belgrade said. "We have you on video. Keep running."

If the young man heard him, he made no effort to acknowledge Belgrade. Not that Belgrade had given him sagely advice.

Keep running? Dante shook his head and frowned. *You think?*

Belgrade placed a hand over the microphone, an unnecessary

precaution since the speaker was button-activated. "On my mark, seal off Corridor 492," he said softly to Dikembu.

Dante raised an eyebrow. *Sealing off corridors? Now* this *is something.*

"Take a right at the next intersection," Belgrade said. "Your other right! Good."

The young man was listening. That meant he had a chance. On a close pass by one camera, the man's features came in with crystal clarity. Dante could see he'd been generous in the years he'd afforded the youngster. He was just a boy!

Run, kid, he barely had time to think before toothless, crescent-moon smiles trampled his spark of hope.

"We're going to seal off your next hallway," Belgrade said. "If we time it right, a barrier will separate you from…them." Belgrade wiped his brow. "Timing is everything, son. You may have to slide."

The boy nodded, his expression weary and strained. Dante released a breath, happy to see the boy's head move up and down. Had it moved left and right….

"Close the shutter," Belgrade said.

Dikembu hit a series of buttons, each keystroke clacking in a language all its own. Immediately following the end of her typing, Dante heard the shutter's closing mechanism roar to life, not through one of the monitors as he'd initially thought – they had no audio component, at least none that was functioning or turned on – but somewhere in the hallways nearby. The boy was close, which meant so were the things chasing him.

Dante made the sign of the cross. "Come on, kid," he said quietly. He watched as a metal gate on rollers descended from a slid-back panel in the corridor ceiling. "You can make it."

Cameras had been placed on each side of the metal shutter. On the one side, the maintenance-team member ran from toxic newt mutants with spindly human arms, but no one in the control room could see it. The camera had been angled to face the shutter. Dikembu entered in another command or two, and the camera swiveled just in time to catch the boy as he emerged from around a far corner. One of the creatures behind him hit the corner with a heavy crack and enough force to send a small tremble through the wall, shaking the camera. It missed the boy by mere inches, but it stumbled and tripped up the others following it, giving the boy a little more breathing room.

But not much.

The boy's arms swung back and forth like reaping scythes. His legs stretched into elongated, almost exaggerated strides. The shutter was closing. He was six meters away.

The massive steel gate descended like a garage door at a rate Dante estimated to be close to half a meter per second. It was still two meters above the floor. The boy's feet left the ground, and he threw his arms out in front of him. And as his eyes widened in shock, he must have figured out what everyone watching in the control room must have known: he'd started the dive too early.

Dante winced and closed his eyes for a moment when the realization hit him. The maintenance employee crashed down onto his stomach and, though he bounced once, barely slid anywhere. But he had more time than Dante had calculated. He still had a chance.

Grimacing in pain, the boy military crawl-scrambled beneath the knee-high shutter. Once on the other side, he rolled onto his back and propped himself up on his forearms, watching the gate drop.

What are you doing? Dante ran a hand down his face. *Keep moving! Get out of there!*

"Get back!" Belgrade shouted into the mic, to Dante's gratification. But the boy didn't move; he just stared with his mouth hung open and lips quivering. He lounged back on his elbows, letting the shutter determine if he lived or died.

One of the creatures tried to follow the boy under the shutter but collided with the unyielding metal with a sound resembling an aluminum garbage can being crushed. The shutter, though, seemed unaffected. The toxic newt's head smashed inward and reeled back, bringing the creature with it. It flipped over backward and flopped on the floor in an almost cartoonish display of slapstick no one found humorous. The shutter rattled on its rollers, stopped descending briefly, then resumed.

A second toxic newt monster slid head first toward the narrowing gap. Dante saw the boy gasp in fear, scuttling back on his buttocks, then smile as the creature's bulbous fat head wedged itself between shutter and linoleum. It ripped its head free a second later, so fiercely that it scalped itself. A clump of flabby meat, like the contents of a biohazardous waste bag at a liposuction clinic, plopped wetly onto the floor. It looked like a beached jellyfish.

The boy sat up, still grinning with defiance. The creature's head had been too enormous to fit through the remaining crevice. Its tongue had not.

The slimy-sticky muscle lashed forward with such speed that it was nearly undetectable. It wrapped around the boy's bent knees and jerked him toward the mutant newt's black-hole maw. All that stood between the creature and its dinner was the steel shutter. The shutter dropped shut.

The final eight inches of the shutter's descent was a free fall of floor-shattering tonnage. It rolled free from its brakes, perhaps damaged by the collision, and slammed into the floor, not letting anything stand between it and its final resting place.

Not even the creature's tongue…or the boy's legs. His shins were crushed, his legs severed below the knee. His feet and ankles disappeared into the scalped newt's mouth. Anju gasped. No one else made a sound as the rest of the boy wallowed in quiet agony.

At least quiet for Dante, who watched a soundless screen, but heard faintly the boy's frantic and tortured cries somewhere out in the hallways. The severed portion of the newt's whip tongue writhed with the boy on the less-infected side of the shutter. The tongue appeared to be forming spindly appendages up and down its length, becoming like some prehistoric centipede.

The boy curled up into a ball, trying only once to put pressure on his wounds before apparently finding it too difficult a task to bear. He stared up, as if instinctively, toward the camera, with great big eyes as blood poured between his fingers and emptied from his cheeks. Cognition set in long enough for the boy to reach out a blood-soaked hand to the camera, pleading for help that hadn't budged.

The camera went dark with interspersed speckles of light. A black cloud appeared farther away, and Dante realized the cloud had passed in front of the camera. The cloud spiraled like a tornado, ever moving closer and closer to the boy.

Dante couldn't hear it beyond a dull echo, but he knew what screaming looked like. The maintenance employee was screaming well before the black swarm descended upon him, but he was screaming even louder after it did, the echo in the hallway sounding nearer.

When the swarm lifted, the boy was gone. Whatever biting and gnawing things had attacked him seemed to double in number.

Belgrade raised his pistol to his temple and set his jaw. "I won't go out like that."

"Now, just you wait a second," Dr. Werniewski said, throwing his hands up. "We need you here. You guards are our best chance of getting out of here alive."

The others murmured. Anju put her hand delicately on Belgrade's raised forearm but didn't try to move it. "Hey," she said softly then nothing more.

"Look!" Dr. Werniewski shouted. "There!"

He pointed at other survivors, a man and a woman, trapped inside the front office of a radiology lab. They were waving at the camera.

"Is that Dr. St. Pierre?" he asked.

CHAPTER TWENTY

Clara watched, helpless, while Alfonse barricaded the door. He knocked over a filing cabinet in front of it, pushed a desk behind the cabinet, then piled every heavy transportable object he could find on top of the desk and around its legs. The door was secure. At least nothing big was getting in.

And they weren't getting out.

Alfonse, God bless him, wouldn't give up. Just watching him was making Clara tired. After scouring the square office and waiting area meter by meter for windows, vents, doors, gates, magical modes of ingress and egress – Clara didn't know what exactly he was looking for – he moved on to the adjoining room, where the DR machine, CT scanners, ultrasound machine, and other equipment were housed. The radiology lab hadn't been designed for her team's use, but Clara and Doctors Werniewski and Thomas, among others, had use of the room as a backup facility for examining symptoms of microbiological infection.

She sat in a plastic chair bolted into the floor as though its owners had been terrified someone might actually steal the uncomfortable piece of crap, maybe taking off with the nasty shit-brown carpet, too. *This is not where I envisioned my life would end.* Her depression and the fact that she really was trapped in a box, surrounded by things that wanted to kill or absorb her, was dampening her spirits.

Alfonse had only been in the back room for a minute or so before he returned, frowning, looking as frustrated as she felt. "Most of that junk is bolted down," he said, throwing a thumb over his shoulder. He began pressing his palms against the walls, testing their solidity in several areas. Clara watched him with mild curiosity, presuming he was looking for structural weaknesses, but for what purpose, she couldn't guess. The thought of him trying to bash his way through the wall, like a cartoon barbarian, might have made her chuckle at any other time, but right then, she just found it sad.

"It's no use," she said.

Alfonse turned to face her, stubborn anger flaring in his eyes. "We're alive, aren't we? If we're alive, then there's still hope."

That made Clara laugh. "That was corny."

"What?" Alfonse's shoulders heaved. "Look," he snapped, "just because you've given up, doesn't mean I will. A good friend of mine died trying to save your ungrateful life. I won't honor him by lying down like a wounded horse, waiting for death."

"I didn't ask him for help," Clara shot back and instantly regretted it. Her cheeks flushed with guilt and embarrassment. "I'm sorry, I—"

"Does it matter?" Alfonse's eyes were puffy, raw, and red. His cheeks were blotchy. Though he looked as though he would cry at any moment – her words certain to have stung him – he held back his tears. "Does anything matter right now besides surviving? He helped you because that's the kind of guy Sebastian was, all cantankerous on the outside but a heart of gold on the inside. And now he's gone, and you and I are stuck with each other."

"I'm sorry." Clara dropped her gaze and picked at a loose string hanging from a button on her lab coat.

The door banged more loudly as if in response to her voice, but whatever was outside couldn't get in, not in its current form. They seemed safe, for the time being. Relative safety didn't make the banging any less terrifying.

Alfonse walked over to Clara and dropped into the chair beside her. He sighed then tried on a smile. "We're in this mess together, you and me, like it or not. We might as well be friends. My name is Alfonse, as you know. Alfonse DiGregorio. I'm one of the seven-member international team of astronauts, cosmonauts, and astrobiologists assigned to this frozen wasteland as we prepare for a mission to Mars that none of us truly believes will occur in our lifetimes. All that ice and rock-hard earth outside is supposed to replicate conditions for Mars excavation and subterranean exploration. If you ask me, all we're succeeding in doing is getting our fingers and toes frostbitten and our asses chapped." He tried to laugh at his own joke but lacked the heart. "Sebastian," he said, his eyes going distant. He choked up.

Clara stared at her hands while he regained his composure.

"Sebastian," he said again. "He was on my team."

Instantly, Clara filled with a bitterness she tasted on her tongue. She scowled and pursed her lips as she thought of the astrobiologist who was responsible for everything that had gone wrong that day, the same individual who'd tried to squeeze the life from her neck. "I know your team," she said, letting emotion take over. "The acclaimed team that unearthed the ancient squirrel's nest and, in doing so, unleashed this goddamn plague upon us all." She clapped. "Well done. Bravo."

Alfonse scowled back, but his face softened before he spoke. When he did, his tone was weak and low. "Something tells me you have no right to judge."

Clara sighed. A tear fell before she could harden herself against it. "You're right. I don't, and what I said was completely uncalled for. I'm sorry. I really don't know what's gotten into me. I seem to be feeling everything more today. And...and Sebastian. I am grateful for his sacrifice and terribly sorry for your loss."

She sat up straighter and smoothed out the wrinkles on her pants. "I am Dr. Clara St. Pierre, professor of microbiology and genetics at University Paris Descartes and lead researcher on all projects involving the study, categorization, and examination of the pandoraviruses your team found in that nest. I was here working on the very sample responsible for this crisis when Sergei Kobozev entered my clean room and – I still can't believe I'm saying this – *ingested* the sample and growth medium containing *Mollivirus sibericum*, the fourth of the giant viruses discovered. The sample would not have been vulnerable had I not taken it from cold storage and left it exposed on the laboratory station at which I'd been working. So, in a way...maybe in the worst way...I am responsible for your friend's death."

"No," Alfonse said shakily. Then he repeated more firmly, "No, you're not." He paused and combed his hair back with his hands, watching the door as the pounding continued. Clara tried not to look that way, pretending not to notice. She thought Alfonse was trying to do the same.

"So you were studying this thing? Any idea how we might be able to stop its spread or, better yet, kill it?"

Clara shook her head slowly.

"Fuck."

"*Oui.*"

The fire alarm cut out, and the red lights in the hall stopped flashing. The pounding in Clara's temples began to lessen almost immediately. *Thank God for minor miracles.*

The banging at the door could no longer be ignored. In fact, it grew louder, more insistent, as if the creatures outside were also more clear minded and intent on getting inside since the alarm had been cut. *Maybe they are sensitive to sound?* Clara doubted she would live long enough to test that hypothesis.

Another loud thud, accompanied by splintering wood, made Clara jump. The next whack against the door rattled through the file cabinet and into the desk so hard that a lamp slid off it and smashed against the ground.

"Well," Alfonse said, "if you can think of anything, now's the time."

"What happened to the alarm?"

"No idea. Maybe it tired itself out. Can't say I'm complaining."

"You, in the maintenance uniform," a male voice echoed through an intercom. "We have you on video. Keep running."

"What was that?" Alfonse asked.

Clara gave Alfonse a once-over. His striped button-down shirt and blue jeans hardly passed for a maintenance uniform, and he wasn't running. She placed a finger over her lips and looked up at the ceiling. Alfonse's eyes followed. They froze and listened.

For a moment, Clara heard nothing but the successive, rhythmic banging against the door, now accompanied by more splintering and cracking. Then the voice came again.

"Take a right at your next intersection.... Your other right!"

"Someone must be watching through the security cameras!" The thought filled Clara with energy. She rose in her seat and may have smiled, if only for a moment. "They're trying to help someone. Maybe they can help us!"

"We'll need to get their attention—"

"Exactly!" Clara patted his knee. "Help me find a security camera."

Clara didn't need help, immediately finding what she was looking for. The camera was propped in a corner, affixed to the ceiling on a swivel mount, exactly where she'd expected it to be.

"There!" she shouted, as if the small victory was enough to win the war. As she threw out her hand, index finger extended in the direction of the camera, her body followed her hand's momentum, and she spilled out of her seat. "*Merde.*"

She fell forward. Her foot jerked forward, too. It caught her fall.

"I...." Clara glanced timidly down at her foot. It was firmly beneath her, supporting her weight, her torso resting on her thigh as if she were stretching before a race. Clara hadn't gone for a run since her college days.

With a conscious effort, no longer used to her legs being under her mind's control, she dragged her shaking back leg forward. She pulled herself into a crouch, and, with her only discomfort caused by her attempts to rise with caution, straining for balance and control, she stood.

Alfonse's expression resembled that of a scolded puppy: all big eyed and pouty lipped. He raised an eyebrow as deep grooves marred his olive-skinned forehead. "You can stand?"

Clara was conscious of her big, fat smile and how out of place it must have seemed to poor Alfonse. Still, she couldn't wipe that smile from her face no matter how hard she tried, even in spite of the death banging at their door, soon to gain entry. An overwhelming feeling of joy rose within her, a feeling of being whole for the first time since the lesions had appeared on her spinal cord. "I'm standing!"

She couldn't believe it, yet there she was, standing the same way she did in her dreams. She could feel her legs under her, holding her up, unwavering. That feeling was amazing. Even with all the death and chaos she'd witnessed so far that day, even with her own death imminent, she couldn't remember a time when she'd been happier.

How selfish that must seem. How sick does that make me?

"You are." Alfonse stared at her through squinting, suspicious eyes.

"I'm sorry. It's just...." Clara couldn't help but giggle. She took in a breath. "I haven't stood on my own for two years. And...." She lifted her right foot, held it in the air, then set it down again in front of her. "Unbelievable."

"What am I missing?"

"I can walk...Alfonse, I can walk!" Before she knew what she was doing, Clara was doing more than walking. She ran into his arms, throwing her own around his neck and pressing his firm body against hers.

He smiled awkwardly and blushed as she peppered his cheeks with kisses. "Um, would you mind telling me what's going on? And, is it really the right time for...whatever this is?"

"I'm infected!" Clara blurted as if it were the best news in the world. The man on the intercom continued his instructions, but she hardly noticed a thing he said.

"That probably isn't the best thing to tell a guy while you're kissing him." Alfonse grabbed her by the arms and pushed her away gently. "You'll have to explain that if we somehow get the hell out of here, but for now, assuming I'm not infected and you're not going to turn into one of them, we should really concentrate on how we're going to get out of this room alive."

He turned back to the security camera and waved his arms frantically. "Help!" he shouted, doing everything in his power to get the attention of the man on the intercom.

Clara joined in. She hopped up and down, shouting and waving and smiling and worrying, thinking her legs would remember what atrophy felt like, still in awe of the fact that she was hopping up and down, shouting and waving, free of frailty. She was experiencing no discomfort in her legs.

"Oh my God!" a new voice crackled over the intercom, still male but higher pitched and with an American accent. "Clara, is that you? It's Jordan. I'm so sorry, Clara. So sorry for leaving you back there. I was scared and.... Are you standing?"

"Give me that," the original voice said. "You two, you can stop jumping. We see you just fine, but we can't hear you. So stop shouting. You'll only draw more unwanted attention to yourselves."

Clara stopped jumping, but she didn't stop standing or smiling. She had reason to smile and reason to live. Help seemed a voice box away. Briefly, Jordan's betrayal had hit a sore spot, but she was already past it, too happy to give a damn and smart enough to know that whatever spark she'd been carrying for him had been extinguished. She knew why Jordan had left her. Fear made people selfish. She could forgive him for that, but she couldn't forget it. Still, she was happy to know he was alive.

Slowly, painfully slowly, the direness of their predicament stifled her excitement. But only a little. She had enough sense left in her to point at the door. The camera swiveled toward it. The door rattled, along with the barricade, with every hit from whatever demon spawn remained outside.

After a moment, the man with Jordan said, "My name is Visely Belgrade. I'm a member of the ASAP security force here at the facility. I am in the control room with several survivors. The corridor outside your current position has been compromised."

"No shit," Alfonse muttered.

"We will not be able to come to you," Belgrade continued, "but we will not abandon you either."

Clara turned to Alfonse. "What do you suppose he means to do?"

Alfonse shrugged and stared up at the camera as if he could see who was speaking to them through it. All Clara saw was a black concave glass that reflected their image with funhouse-mirror distortion.

"Lie down on the floor inside the back room and close the door. I am about to release a gas we generally use to sedate intruders, and by that, I mean *human* intruders. I am not sure what effect, if any, the gas will have on the things outside, but it is quite effective when used to incapacitate and render unconscious selected targets. Some of the gas will undoubtedly seep into the room, but it is lighter than air and should rise before it reaches you. It is designed for quick dissipation to eliminate collateral damage."

"Some plan." Clara scoffed. However, she followed Alfonse into the back room and closed the door. Before lying down on the frigid floor, she noted the medical equipment around her and thought how wonderful it would have been to have a look at her spine with them. *Perhaps some other time.... If I survive.* She pulled her coat up around her head, overlapping the material across her mouth and nose.

The banging outside grew louder and faster, frantic, as if whatever was out there no longer just wanted to get into the room but needed to get in. A *crack*, like a tree hit by lightning, came from the door, and Clara knew it had split open. Then, the banging stopped. An animalistic wail reverberated through the air.

White, billowing smoke seeped in through the crack at the top of the door. It formed a puffy cloud that blanketed the ceiling, which soon began to dissolve. After a minute, only tendrils and wispy trails remained, then nothing.

"It should be safe to stand now," Belgrade said. "The gas didn't knock the creatures out as we had hoped, but it did scare them off."

Clara and Alfonse rose. They opened the door, walked out into the waiting room, and approached the camera, where they awaited instructions.

"Now is your chance to move," Belgrade said. "In a moment, you will hear metal shutters dropping into place. We'll clear a path for you as best we can, leading from your current position to the control room, sealing off the creatures wherever possible."

Alfonse whipped his head dramatically from side to side. Clara joined him.

"We'll wait for you…. What is it?" Belgrade asked.

Clara looked at Alfonse. "How do we explain it to him without words?"

Alfonse scampered over to the desk and rummaged through it. He ripped open a drawer, pulled it off its rollers, and dumped its contents on top of the desk. Finding several writing utensils, he gathered them into his hand. A printer sat at a corner of the desk. He tore the blank sheets of paper from its tray.

Examining the writing instruments in his hand, Alfonse settled on a blue highlighter, which had the thickest pen stroke. Clara watched as he held the marker as if it was a knife and he was poking it into someone, stabbing vertically, then horizontally, then vertically again, until he had drawn the word 'HUB' in big, thick lines filling the sheet of paper. He carried it over to the camera and lifted it in front of the lens.

"The hub?" Belgrade asked. Alfonse nodded. "I don't recommend heading there. You would have much better odds of survival with us, I think."

Alfonse scrawled on another sheet of paper with a frenzy just shy of madness. When he finished, he grabbed another sheet and wrote on that one, too. The first said 'LAUNCH', the second 'MARS' above 'ROVER'. He held them consecutively in front of the security camera.

A long pause. Clara assumed whoever was on the other side of the intercom had much to debate about the merits of Alfonse's plan.

"I think we understand," Belgrade said, "but won't the shutter—"

Alfonse shook his head violently. "No shutter," he mouthed.

Another long pause. "Okay," Belgrade said. "If you're determined to go to the hub, we'll do our best to help you get there. We'll seal off as many of those bastards as we can, but doing that will only give you one route to the hub's south entrance. I don't see anything moving around in there, but these cameras have more blind spots than an eighteen-wheeler. You'll be on your own from here on out. We are going to try another way out, an underground tunnel you can access from the control room, if you can get into the control room, or via any of those service hatches that look like manhole covers in the floor. There is more than one tunnel, but they all have an outside exit, which will probably be barred shut. So if we can't get out that way, we'll be heading toward you via the north entrance."

"Thank you," Clara said to the silent black orb. Alfonse nodded his agreement.

"Good luck," Belgrade said. The intercom went silent.

A clamor arose outside in the hallways. Shutters whirred and clanged, sounding like can openers and airplane landing gear as they spurred into action and dropped into place. The rat-maze complex was a maze no longer, though Clara was certain she could still find any number of dead ends. She would have a hard time finding a place to hide.

The hairs on her arms and the back of her neck stood on end. Every day she'd spent at the research center was like being trapped in a maze. Suddenly, she felt trapped in a mausoleum. Her palms grew clammy, and the air itself seemed to be closing in on her.

As shutters fell into place with deafening rattles, her happiness at having regained her legs seemed a distant memory. *What good is having legs if you're not alive to enjoy them?* She shrugged. Her cup had been half full for a little while, and that was a pleasant change, but returning to reality had become prudent.

And reality sucked.

"I don't hear anything out there," Alfonse said, his ear pressed to the wall beside his office-fixture barricade. "I'm going to clear the way. Whether that ASAP guy was telling the truth or not, we may not get another chance." He paused, set his jaw, crossed his arms, and gave her a hard look. "Now's as good a time as any for you to tell me why I shouldn't keep you locked up in here. What did you mean, you're infected?"

Clara clapped and moved over to the desk. "Well," she said as she slid aside a box of records Alfonse had propped against it, "help me with this, and I'll give you the short version as we go."

While the two removed the makeshift blockade piece by piece, Clara relayed the events of her exposure to Molli in the clean room, her altercation with Sergei Kobozev, and her admittedly borderline yet unrefuted theory concerning her autoimmune disease and its apparent remission. When she finished her recap and the only obstacle left was the heavy filing cabinet blocking the door, she studied Alfonse for hints of what he might be thinking.

Alfonse looked more confused and distrusting than ever, back to standing with arms crossed. At last, he said, "Sergei Kobozev had been having difficulties since his daughter's death. It was absolutely tragic what happened to her – family vacation at the beach. She was caught in a riptide and drowned, Sergei and his wife nearly drowning themselves as they swam out to save her. None of us ever thought he would recover, at least not to the extent necessary to do what we do. He was sidelined for almost a year before some pencil pusher cleared him to return. Sergei had a brilliant mind and was always a welcomed member of the team, but I don't think any of us thought he was ready to come back when he did." Alfonse frowned as his shoulders drooped. "Still, Sergei was a good man. I know loss like he experienced can change someone, but I just can't believe he would do something like this."

"That's it?" Clara shied away. "After all I've told you, that's all you have to say?"

Alfonse stared at her blankly, then let a grin, which he'd obviously been holding back, creep along his cheeks. "Oh, you mean about you?" He crouched and dug his fingers where he could under the filing cabinet, then grunted as he heaved it upright.

Clara chewed on her thumbnail while she waited for Alfonse to conclude his thought. She refused to make eye contact with anything over knee level. The cabinet creaked as things inside it shifted back into place.

Their path unblocked, Alfonse dusted off his hands. "The milk has been spilled – is this a French expression? The way I see it, I've carried you, hugged you, been kissed by you…. I'm still the same Alfonse. I feel normal, or as normal as anyone can feel with people-absorbing monsters running around. I didn't know you before this outbreak happened, but you seem one hundred percent human now." He offered her a sincere smile, tinged with subtle sadness she didn't think had been caused by her. "Just…if you start to feel, uh, less than human, you'll let me know, right?"

She wondered what his strong hands might do to her if she did drop a bomb like that on him, but she dared not ask. "Will do," was all she mustered. "You, too."

"Deal." He waved a hand at the unblocked door. "Shall we?"

Clara took a deep breath. "There's no time like the present." She placed her hand in his, feeling like a child lost at the mall. The sensation of dread disappeared when he accepted her hand and squeezed.

He opened the door and soundlessly peeked out into the hall. "All's quiet," he whispered. "Looks clear. A shutter is blocking our route back."

"Then it looks like our decision has been made for us." Clara pecked him on the cheek and said, "Thank you," into his ear, then, "Let's go."

CHAPTER TWENTY-ONE

Monty watched Belgrade lift his pistol from the console where he'd left it after tearing the intercom from Dr. Phillips's hands. He waited, not saying a word, just watching as Belgrade holstered his gun as though nothing had happened.

Monty couldn't keep quiet any longer. "Are you done feeling sorry for yourself, mate?"

Belgrade glared at him through eyes of stone and fire. "I'm good."

"That's good," Monty said. "That's real good, mate. Because right now, you need to grow a fucking pair, man the fuck up, and help me get these people here someplace safe."

"There is no place safe," Dikembu said. "I've been in here the whole time, watching these screens, trying to plot a way out, and—"

"Not fucking helping," Monty interrupted.

"In the land of the blind, the one-eyed man is king," Dante mumbled, chuckling.

"What was that?" Monty asked. "You're a right funny bloke, ain't ya?" He jabbed a finger at Dante's face. "The verdict's still out on you, you fucking whacker. I mean, what the hell are you even doing here, mate? Blowing up cars in the garage like some kind of loony? If I hadn't seen firsthand the bloke t'was responsible for this shit, I'd take you down myself, right here, right now. But you've proven yourself quite a talent with that thing." He nodded toward the flamethrower. "The demand for skills such as yours exceeds the supply. But know this" – he threw back his shoulders and stepped closer – "I have my eye on you."

"Just the one?" Dante asked.

"Yep, a real fucking comedian." Monty wasn't laughing. His rather limited reserve of patience drew thin as he tried not to slug the grubby-looking dero.

Dante wiped the grin from his face. "Relax. I'm with you. I say we arm ourselves to the teeth and get the hell out of here as fast as humanly possible." He turned to Belgrade. "Where's this way out you mentioned?"

"You're practically standing on it." Belgrade pointed at Dante's feet. His face had reverted to the mix of disinterest and mild annoyance he usually wore, thin lips mashed flat, jaw squared and strong as an iron trap.

A circular hatch that looked a lot like a manhole cover lay next to Dante's right foot.

"It's an underground tunnel system built for ASAP by ASAP," Belgrade said. "We use it when we need to move something or someone unnoticed by civilians."

"A secret passageway?" Dr. Phillips asked. "Really? Who are you guys? CIA? MI6?" He glanced from one guard to the next. "I suppose I should be thankful...."

"Who cares who created it and why?" Dr. Werniewski asked. "The important question is, can it get us out of here?"

"It could," Monty answered, trying to determine how much of the truth he should tell them. He opted for all of it. "If we weren't in lockdown. This building has four camouflaged exits, one at each compass point, for sensitive extractions, political visitors...the like. The shutter does not extend underground, but during lockdown, impenetrable gates block the tunnel exits. The bars of these gates are two-inch-thick reinforced steel, spaced three inches apart, not that different from the door to a prison cell. It would take us far longer than we have to torch through or cut away those bars – many hours, days even."

"So there's no way out?" the younger male scientist asked, his voice whiny.

"You're American, right?" Dante asked.

Monty failed to see the connection.

"Yes. My name is Jordan Phillips. I'm a—"

"What did a green shirt mean on *Star Trek*?" Dante asked. "Not the same as red I hope."

"What?" Dr. Phillips asked.

Monty scratched his head. He did notice the scientist's lime-green sweater for the first time, though. *Just awful.*

"Never mind," Dante said. He gave Dr. Phillips a wink. "Why don't you let the big boys talk, okay?"

Dr. Phillips's face flashed red with anger, but the look Dante shot him said in no uncertain terms to shut the fuck up. He sat silent, stewing in his cowardice.

"So," Dante continued, "you're thinking we go around the gate somehow?"

"Ace!" Monty said.

"It's risky," Belgrade said. "We have enough explosives to blow through rock and ice, but we could cause the tunnel to collapse and bring the research center down on top of us."

"Better to die that way than to become one of those creatures," Anju said. "I am in. I may not have your training, but let me know if I can be of any help."

"Can you use a gun?" Monty asked.

"I keep a .22 in my purse." She stood taller. "I have been licensed to carry since I went to university."

Dr. Werniewski scoffed and shook his head. "Guns are for savages."

"Well, I guess we know where you stand." Monty quickly wrote off the old man as a hippie tree hugger. "And you, Dr. Phillips?"

"I've never held a real gun in my life," Dr. Phillips said. "I don't want to be in anyone's way."

"You're thinking we should give them all access to the armory?" Dikembu asked.

"You object?" Belgrade asked.

She didn't answer right away but then sighed. "I suppose not."

"Me either," Belgrade said.

"It's settled, then," Monty said. "Everyone raid the armory. Take whatever you're comfortable carrying. If you think that, if armed, you're more of a liability than an asset, take nothing. We'll need someone to help us carry the explosives."

Dante and Belgrade led the way to the armory. True to his word, Monty kept his eye on the former. He watched as Dante rummaged through locker after locker. Monty considered stopping the blatant theft but figured it didn't matter. The lockers' former users were dead.

The ragged man with the black cross on his forehead certainly made for a sight, but Monty didn't know what to make of him. He saw through the ruse, though. Dante's skills had given him away. *But why is he here, and who is he working for?* He wondered if circumstances had changed so much that none of that mattered anymore. *There are only two sides now: us against them, and by 'them', I mean anyone with the ability to melt like cheese.*

As far as Monty knew, Dante had made no attempt to retrieve the virus and abscond with it. As long as he continued to make no attempts to do so, they would get along just fine. *Regular mates.* Monty laughed as Dante tossed aside a clean, pressed ASAP uniform and pulled a pair of boots from a locker. Monty hadn't noticed before that the wannabe vagrant had been missing a shoe, not until Dante kicked off his remaining shoe and laced up his pilfered boots.

Yes, Dante was stealing ASAP property, but boots were the least of Monty's worries. He was already giving complete strangers and, in some cases, rank amateurs access to some pretty sophisticated weaponry. His stare followed Dante as he joined the others combing the shelves for the weapons that best suited them.

Surveying the crowd, he noticed that only Dr. Phillips was absent. Anju was examining a Beretta while another handgun was already tucked into her waistband and a heavy flashlight jammed into her pocket. Dr. Werniewski had selected two small rapid-fire machine guns that looked like Uzis but the make of which Monty couldn't be certain. He snorted at the doctor and his weapon of choice and thought about advising against it. But he let that slide too. *If we're all going to die anyway, what the fuck does it matter?*

"What?" Dr. Werniewski asked, meeting Monty's gaze. "I'm a quick study." He pushed past Monty and headed back toward the center of the control room.

Dante cast him a sidelong glance. Monty just shrugged.

Belgrade sneaked up behind the stranger, placed a firm hand on his shoulder, and squeezed. Dante turned to face Belgrade, the two close enough to lay each other out. Monty watched with growing amusement and excitement, wondering who was going to flinch first.

Neither man so much as blinked.

"Look," Belgrade said. "I don't know who you are or why you've come here, and to be honest, I really don't care so long as you stay out of our way when it comes to saving as many of these people as we can. You'd make a hell of an ally with that flamethrower strapped to your back, and your actions with Stearns and since have shown regard for human lives other than your own." He laughed. "I'm not even sure *I* wanted to help Stearns, and I worked with the guy. Well, that's probably *because* I worked with the guy."

He released a long breath, relieving some of the tension and machismo in his muscles. "Make no mistake – if I have to, I will end you. But I'm really hoping there's a decent person behind that black cross." He gently tapped Dante's forehead. "Anyway, all I need to know is this: Can I trust you?"

Dante put out his hand. Belgrade took it in his. They shook.

"For all intents and purposes, my name is Dante. And I'm here to destroy the viruses, not the people, to make sure nothing like what's happening in here" – he made small hand circles as if waxing the floor – "happens out there." He spread his arms wide. "I'll help you get as many survivors as we can to safety, but then I'm blowing this whole damn place straight to hell. If you try to stop me from doing that, I'll kill you." The two men met each other's stare. "Now that we have our threats out of the way, is that honest enough for you?"

Belgrade glanced at Monty, who couldn't think of any qualms with Dante's proposal that merited immediate investigation. He nodded at his coworker and at Dante. A silent pact was made.

Belgrade smiled. "Not only is all that fair enough, but it appears our interests are aligned."

"More so than you think," Monty added.

Belgrade reached into a giant duffel bag he'd placed on a bench nearby. He pulled out two cylindrical canisters and shoved one into each of Dante's vest's front pockets. "Smoke grenades."

Dante nodded.

"After the way those fuckers ran from the knockout gas we blasted them with outside the radiology lab," Monty said, "those should be useful. Keep the flamethrower, too. You're more adept with it than any of us, I think. I've never used one, anyway, and have never been trained in its use. We only have the one other one, which I'm guessing you'll take, huh, Belgrade?"

Belgrade grunted. "Sounds like a plan."

Monty hastened over to a locked cage and swiped his ID card to open it. Inside was a crate filled with canisters not unlike those Belgrade had slipped into Dante's pockets, but they were bigger, redder, and so much better. They were Monty's babies.

"Incendiary grenades." Monty beamed as he grabbed as many as he could. "These bad boys are like mini A-bombs." He dropped four into a backpack he pulled from a locker then added four more. He was about to zip up the pack when he decided it needed four more explosives. He dropped in the additional goodies, closed the zipper, and slung the pack over his shoulder. "Between these babies, my Desert Eagle, and my AK-47, I'm as good to go as I'm going to be." He pulled the two firearms from his locker and loaded them up.

He patted Dante on the shoulder. The former prisoner flinched, answering Monty's question about who would do so first. Still, Monty had a feeling he needed to trust the man. He wondered if the man would trust him in turn.

Dikembu slipped by, carrying her own backpack overfilled with whatever her weapons of choice may have been. She squinted and flared her nostrils when she passed Dante, a look that lingered as she squeezed past Monty as well.

What's that all about? He understood the stranger not trusting him, but he had worked with Dikembu long enough to develop a rapport. He let her slight slide off as the nothing it probably was.

He headed back to the control room, where he and most of the survivors waited for the stragglers. Belgrade was last to arrive, the flamethrower's heavy tank strapped to his back, goggles and nose-and-mouth shield propped atop his head. He held a duffel bag, which he bowled over to Dr. Phillips. "C-4," he said. "And other types of explosives. Enough to turn this entire place into the Grand Canyon. Don't stand too close to the flamethrowers."

Dr. Phillips's eyes widened, and he tried to speak, but all that came out was gibberish. *Blubbering vagina.* The scientist's Adam's apple wiggled as he swallowed hard. Still, Monty had to respect the man when he grabbed the bag's handle and plopped it between his legs.

Monty looked up and found his eye hadn't been the only one on the bag. Dante was watching it closely, as if he had x-ray vision and could see inside. Monty cleared his throat and Dante looked up, feigning a smile as transparent as glass.

"There's just one thing left to do," Monty said. "Dante, could you open the tunnel while we set the facility to self-destruct?"

The look that Dante shot him then, purposeful and utterly intrigued, betrayed his intentions. He was slow to mask it even as the other civilians gasped and grumbled. Monty threw him a crowbar. Dante grinned, that time for real, caught the bar, and nodded. He walked over to the hatch and began to pry it open.

"What do you mean, 'self-destruct'?" Dr. Werniewski asked. "You can't be serious."

"I told you," Dr. Phillips blurted. "These guys are straight out of a spy movie, and a bad one at that. Only evil geniuses with egos the size of planets build self-destruct mechanisms into their crazy, remote laboratories where they develop biochemical weapons in order to take over the world." He paused, irises rolling up to the corners of his eyes. "Wait—"

"Yep," Dante said. "Now you're getting it. This place may not be evil, and it's debatable whether it's run by evil geniuses, but its out-of-the-way location and work researching and experimenting with viruses whose negative capabilities range from nil to total world annihilation make this facility a prime candidate for a shiny red button."

"But a self-destruct button?" Dr. Phillips guffawed. "That's preposterous." He tittered a bit then stopped. No one was laughing with him. "Isn't it?"

"I'm afraid not, mate," Monty said.

"It actually used to be fairly standard for facilities of this kind," Dr. Werniewski said. "My work dealing with some of the nastiest microorganisms over the years has brought me in contact with a few such governmental structures, most of which were underground. They are built far enough away from civilization and rigged with a thermonuclear explosive that can quickly remedy the situation in the event of the airborne or uncontrolled, or I suppose, purposeful, release of a potential pandemic. Casualties are limited to the building's staff. It really is quite the speedy and efficient way of handling a potential outbreak at its source, before it becomes too big to manage. But I thought the practice had been done away with by the end of the twentieth century, and never, ever, have I heard of it installed in a building of this magnitude, with a staff of.... How many? Nearly a thousand on any given day?"

"Instant purification by fire," Anju said, staring off into space. Her body was trembling.

"Exactly," Monty added. "The blast radius here is barely enough to cover the research center. Whatever isn't destroyed directly in the blast will be radiated or incinerated by fiery temperatures and blazes. But you worry too much, mates!" He smiled toothily and slapped Dr. Phillips on the arm. "We'll either be long gone or long dead before this place goes kaboom."

"That's comforting," Dr. Phillips said. "Why am I getting déjà vu?"

"To begin the self-destruct procedure, three clearance codes are needed," Belgrade said. "Fortunately, we have just enough qualified ASAP team members here to initiate the countdown. We'll have two hours to escape, enough time to run fifty laps around this building—"

"Maybe for you," Dr. Phillips interrupted.

Belgrade stared him down. "As I was saying, once the countdown initiates, we'll have two hours to get outside the blast zone, which the shutters will do much to hinder. This isn't Nagasaki or even Chernobyl, but will be a controlled, cleaner blast designed to destroy the base and everything in it but not a whole lot else. Once we're outside the shutters, *if* we can get outside the shutters, we're, as you Americans say, home free."

He smiled at Dr. Phillips, probably to be comforting, but Belgrade's square jaw had not been made for smiling. It made him look like a psychotic robot.

"I'll go first." Dikembu sat at her console and punched a series of long commands into the keyboard.

"I understand the need to prevent the spread of this disease," Dr. Werniewski said. "All too well, believe me. But shouldn't we talk about this? Two hours isn't a lot of time, particularly should something go wrong. What if we can't get past the gate?"

"Then we go for the rover and pray it hasn't launched without us," Belgrade said.

"And if it has?" Dr. Werniewski asked.

"Do you really want me to spell it out for you?" Belgrade countered.

"That's it?" Dr. Phillips jumped to his feet. "That's Plan A and Plan B all rolled up into one, and if neither works, Plan C is to suck our thumbs and pray it won't hurt?"

"You won't feel a thing," Dante said, instigating the scientist's panic.

Dr. Phillips said, "Well, I vote we—"

"This isn't America, and it sure as hell ain't a democracy," Monty snapped. "Dikembu, initiate the sequence."

She rose and pushed several more prompts into another keyboard at a slightly higher console. A small silver hood retracted from a waist-high inset in the monstrous contraption that served as a base to the largest monitors. Three keys of different colors – red, green, and blue – appeared behind another keyboard. Dikembu circled the console and walked toward the keys. She typed yet another code into that keyboard, waited until she heard a *click*, then turned the unlocked red key.

"All yours," she said to Monty as she returned to her seat at the console. With most of the hard work already done by Dikembu, Monty walked over to the keyboard set in front of the keys, typed in his password, and turned the green key without hesitation.

"Can we please just talk about this?" Dr. Phillips asked.

When no one answered, Anju grabbed his hand and said, "This is the way it has to be."

Dante interrupted the process when he shifted the hatch cover over and dropped it. It wobbled like a quarter on its way to lying flat, ringing like a Tibetan singing bowl. Everyone looked his way.

"Sorry." He seemed calmer than all the others, content even. "It's open."

Belgrade walked over to the keyboard. Of the three guards, he had it the toughest. He went last, which left the ultimate decision in his hands. Monty didn't envy him that predicament. On the off chance they were wrong, Belgrade had the unfortunate position of being last in line to start or stop the self-destruct process.

Well, then again, any one of us three could just retype our code and unturn our key to shut it off. No decisions were final.

Belgrade, though looking just slightly more solemn than usual, didn't hesitate either. He typed in his code and turned his key. The monitors went black. No alarms blared, no fanfare sounded. The computer offered no incessant flashing or warnings. After a moment, words appeared across all the screens, reading in giant white letters, 'Facility Cleanse: 120 Minutes'.

"Facility purification process will begin momentarily," a male voice with an English accent said as peacefully as if it had just invited them all over for tea and crumpets while knitting a sweater.

"That's a pleasant way of putting it," Dr. Phillips said. He laughed, pitchy and awkward.

Then he jumped when a bullhorn went off, but Monty couldn't blame him. He jumped, too.

"Facility purification process has been initiated," the English gentleman said. "The facility will be purged in one hundred twenty minutes and counting." The bullhorn blared one more time then went silent. The noise vibrated Monty's eardrums.

"Dikembu," Monty said. "Can you kill the alarm?"

Dikembu leaned forward in her seat and brought up a data screen on a lower monitor. After a few keystrokes, she nodded at Monty. The countdown ticked off its first minute soundlessly.

"Now, can we please get the fuck out of here?" she asked.

"How do we stop it?" Dr. Werniewski asked. "You know, if for some reason we do change our minds."

"Any of the three of us can do it," Monty said. "The problem is that we'd need to come back here. And that, mate, just ain't going to happen. So, if you're all so concerned about time, perhaps we should get a move on."

"All right, everyone." Belgrade pulled a flare from a pack at his hip and ignited a small but brilliant flame. He motioned toward the tunnel entrance. "Down the hatch."

CHAPTER TWENTY-TWO

Dante wasn't the first to climb down the ladder into the dank, subterranean darkness. He declined a flashlight or road flare, opting instead for the blue-white gaslight of his flamethrower, wanting it ready to fire at all times. He volunteered himself to take the lead once everyone had assembled below. Equipped with the only other flamethrower, Belgrade brought up the rear with Monty at his side.

Dante was left with Dikembu, those with military and weapons training sandwiching those without. They broke apart into three groups, each keeping a few meters ahead or behind the others. Rather than revealing his familiarity with the site and its supposedly secret passageways, Dante let Dikembu decide their route. Not that there was much of a decision to make – the tunnel offered only two directions. One was forward, the other was back, but both led to a gate and a potential way out.

In the glow of his gaslight, he couldn't see much of Dikembu's face, and what he did see was distorted by haze and darkness. Still, something about her seemed familiar, but he couldn't remember her name from the files he'd been given. He figured maybe he was just drawn to her beauty. He'd always had a weak spot for the ladies, particularly those who could kick some ass. And with her squared shoulders and ripped physique, Dikembu looked like she could kick a whole lot of ass.

That's something I'd love to find out. Dante smirked then huffed, reminding himself to focus on more pressing matters, like staying alive while killing what shouldn't have been.

Yet he found himself staring her way again, curious to know more about her. She held a Ruger and a large heavy-duty flashlight in front of herself, wrists crisscrossed as an experienced officer or soldier would, unaffected by their weight. A loaded backpack hung tightly against her back and shoulders, but it did not appear to slow her down. Unlike him, Dikembu was focused. She kept her eyes forward, paying little attention to Dante as they proceeded deeper into the tunnel.

The shaft was approximately three meters wide and well cut, but it lacked any accommodations, be it lighting or paving. Smooth, packed dirt, frozen ground that likely had been hell to excavate, lined the walls. The frigid air turned breath to mist, but the building above must have warmed the tunnel enough at times to melt the ice contained within its walls, coating them with a layer of perspiration.

A mixture of dirt and solid rock lay underfoot. Instead of removing the rock, the tunnel's excavators had shaved it flat. As with the walls, water and ice slicked the floor.

The air tasted stale and smelled of mold, like a poorly sealed basement prone to flooding. As much as it reminded Dante of a tomb, he preferred it to the sickly sanitized eggshell-white monotony comprising the corridors above. He'd felt trapped, even after he shed his handcuffs, in those asylum-like confines, *sans* padded walls, since that morning. Even dead air tasted better to a man set free. The change in scenery was a welcome reminder that they still had ways to escape the monstrosities above, whether mankind, manmade, or not man at all.

He started to whistle a tune from *Faust*, when he heard a tiny splash up ahead. He and Dikembu stopped. "Hello?" he called. When no one answered, he let out a quick burst of flame to light the path and anything evil hiding in it.

Nothing.

"What is it?" Jordan asked, creeping up too close for comfort.

"Shhh!" Dante snapped.

Ploop.

Dikembu aimed her light in the direction of the sound. It landed on a small puddle with a rippling surface. She raised her light to the dirt roof. A jagged rock jutted from the ceiling like a tiny finger. There, moisture collected and dripped from its point down to the floor.

"It's nothing." Dante let down his guard but kept his voice to a whisper. He stepped forward.

Dikembu resumed her position by his side, with Jordan returning to his place in their makeshift formation.

Up ahead, Dante saw more puddles. Some were no bigger than a dinner plate, while others were as big as a dining-room tabletop. The ground appeared to be level, but had it gradually sloped downward, he doubted he'd have been able to detect it. *I hope it's not flooded up ahead.*

He listened more intensely then and heard more dripping in front of him. Behind him, he heard nothing but breathing and footsteps.

He approached a larger puddle, his small blue flame casting a beautiful reflection of shimmering brilliance on its still, black-mirror surface. Something about that surface was both mesmerizing and dreadful, but Dante couldn't put a finger on why. When he saw his face reflected, his eyes tired and small inside black sockets, crows' feet longer than ever, he had to look away.

Dikembu's foot came down with a soft splash. "Fuck!"

"What's happened?" Jordan again came rushing to the front of the line. "What's going on?"

Dante threw out his arm to block the scientist's approach. "Stay back!" Then, to anyone who would listen, he called for a flare.

Dr. Werniewski answered the call. He stepped up to the front of the pack and shrieked, dropping his flare onto the tunnel floor, where it cast Dikembu in a reddish glow. It illuminated her boot, which appeared to be stuck in mud – thick, black, viscous mud.

The mud was climbing.

"Dear God," the doctor muttered then proceeded to lose his shit. His breaths grew more and more rapid with each passing moment. He sounded as if he might be hyperventilating. "Oh my God, oh my God, oh my God, oh my God."

"Calm down," Dante said, trying to sound firm but calm himself. He poured flame over the cavern floor in front of them. Several of the puddles evaporated. Others ignited. They burned like oil drums in an urban campfire.

"Everyone," Dante said, "stay clear of the puddles. They're – oh shit!" A puddle beside Dante's foot shifted on its own accord, splashing around his boot and fixing it in place. He tried to rip his foot free, but the liquid seemed to suction him down. He looked to his right and saw Dikembu still trying to pull her own foot free with no success. Her foot wasn't going to budge, and worse, the black fluid had thickened into plasma and was slithering closer and closer to the top of her boot, where it could drop inside or slide up her pant leg. Tendrils crept up the leather like vines and looked like veins, black bulges over a black surface.

"Leave the boot!" Dante shouted. "It's your only chance!" He looked down to see the fluid bubbling and thickening around his own foot. "Fucker," he muttered. "I just got these boots, and already I have to give one up?"

Dikembu pulled a knife from a sheath at her hip and sliced through her laces with speed and precision. She pulled her foot out of the boot and hop-danced out of the puddle.

Dante aimed his flamethrower at the empty puddle and was just about to ignite it when Dr. Werniewski, still hyperventilating and stammering, barreled forward with submachine guns locked at his sides. Sparks flashed from the weapons in epileptic fury as he squeezed their triggers and refused to let go. He poured round after round after round into the puddle, causing it no visible damage but endangering the lives of everyone in the tunnel. The unsettling sound of out-of-control automatic machine-gun fire and ricocheting bullets echoed through the shaft until the weapons' clips clicked empty and their barrels stopped spitting.

"Drop them," Anju said. She had the muzzle of her pistol pressed flat against the back of her employer's head. Dr. Werniewski didn't appear to be listening. His mouth hung open, and he said nothing. After a moment, his arms dropped to his sides. The guns fell from his hands. He rocked on his feet and might have toppled, had Anju not been there to support him.

"A little help," she said as she struggled to hold up the doctor's deadweight. Jordan rushed to her aid.

A little help might be nice over here, too. Dante grumbled. No one seemed to want to get close, and he supposed he couldn't blame them. He set fire to the nearby puddle that had endured the barrage of bullets. Cursing his bad luck, he yanked his foot free of his ensnared boot with such ferocity that he lost his balance and fell backward onto his buttocks. He let himself rock backward so his feet wouldn't splash down in the puddle. Instead, they hovered. He pulled them in close, tucked his heels against his buttocks, and thanked God for the eight inches or so separating him from the puddle's edge.

The surface of the liquid began to roll with waves, each one headed in Dante's direction. He scooted backward and hosed the liquid monstrosity down with fire. He gritted and gnashed his teeth, grinning with rage as the puddle and his new boot burned.

"Regroup," Belgrade said, huddling everyone together and gaining control of the situation. He traced the outline of the tunnel from where they'd come with fire three times over before saying anything more.

Everyone was standing and closing toward each other in the group – everyone except Dikembu. She was down on the dirt-and-rock floor, not moving.

Anju shifted Dr. Werniewski's weight entirely onto Jordan and ran to Dikembu's side. She crouched and reached out to the fallen guard—

"Don't touch her!" Monty shouted, closing the gap between himself and the grad student in three long strides. "She may be infected."

Anju examined Dikembu without touching. "There is a bullet hole or two in her bag, and her head is bleeding, but she does not appear to have been shot, no thanks to Dr. Werniewski." She scowled at her boss, but the microbiologist had left them all for la-la land.

Anju continued her examination. "Her chest is rising and falling, so she is definitely alive. She is not seizing or mutating or blistering or doing anything else symptomatic of infection."

"Not yet," Dante muttered.

Dikembu moaned. Her fingers felt along the unforgiving floor like a blind person's reading a face. Slowly, strength seemed to return to them. She placed her hands flat against the ground and pushed herself up to her knees then staggered drunkenly to her feet. "Spinning," she mumbled. "Stop fucking spinning."

Anju stepped back. Everyone watched Dikembu closely, waiting to see what she would do next.

Wincing, she pressed her dirty palms into her eyes, trying to clear them. "My fucking head," she said, her words coming out a bit more clearly. She groaned as her fingers found the large gash, which could only have come from a collision with the wall or floor, too random and ugly to have been a graze from an errant bullet. She must have dived out of the way when Dr. Werniewski opened fire.

"It feels like the rebel shitbags back home are playing football with my head," she said, her feet looking more solid beneath her.

"You are lucky to be alive," Anju said. "At least one bullet just missed you. It tore a nice hole through your backpack, though."

"My backpack?" The words seemed to mystify Dikembu, as if they had some important meaning to her she just couldn't remember. Then her eyes jolted open, and all haziness left them. "My backpack!"

She tore her bag off her shoulders and pulled it in front of her. Like a dog digging up a bone, she ripped open the pack and shoveled through it with both hands. "The samples," she whispered, barely audible. "No, no, no, *no!*"

She looked up from her bag but made eye contact with no one. Like Dr. Werniewski, Dikembu was in her own world then. But something suspicious was going on in her world, and Dante was watching closely to find out what.

Dikembu pulled her right hand from her backpack. She raised her thumb and index finger in front of her eyes and rubbed them together. "The samples…" she muttered absently.

"Samples?" Dante asked. A realization hit him like a slap to the face. He frowned. "Your hair and name are different, but you were included in my intel. You're working for the Ugandans, aren't you? Son of a bitch!" He raised his flamethrower.

Dikembu didn't even seem to notice the weapon pointed at her. "The samples," she said again, as if she hadn't heard him, though she spoke directly to Dante. "They're broken. My hand…." She held it out to him, palm up, displaying it for all to see.

Dante couldn't see anything on it, but he knew what had been there. He knew what was inside her.

Dikembu bit down into her lip. Her eyes filled with tears. "I've been infected."

"Good," Dante said. He lit her up like a Roman candle before she could even start to seize. Her screams of agony filled the tunnel. The others watched him, some with cold eyes, but no one tried to stop him.

CHAPTER TWENTY-THREE

Clara paused and glanced at her companion. At least Alfonse was pretending not to notice her hopping, skipping, dancing, and jumping down the corridor. She didn't mean to seem so, well, happy. The use of her legs had kind of made her happy. She wanted to test her limits, to see just how much healthier she really was, not to make her travel partner think she'd gone completely insane.

Maybe she had. People were turning into monsters all around her, and she was prancing around like a coked-up monkey. *The world is a crazy place, my dear.*

Clara had been a fairly decent long jumper at university, not quite athletic enough to compete at a national level, but good enough to clear a few sandboxes. She leaped forward without exerting much effort and covered an Olympian's distance. She could have sworn her hair grazed the ten-foot ceiling. All the harder jobs, like checking around corners and remaining vigilant, went to Alfonse DiGregorio.

She paused a moment from her frolicking and stared at his back. *Alfonse DiGregorio, Alfonse the astrobiologist, Alfonse the saint.* That last distinction was a well-deserved suffix to his surname, unlike its placement in her own.

St. Pierre. Humph. She snorted. *What good have you ever done for anyone other than yourself?* Even worse, while everyone around her was experiencing loss – of friends, of loved ones, of their own minds – she couldn't understand why she'd been the only one to gain. She wore her newfound health with mixed joy and disdain, like a favored scarf half eaten by moths.

She brushed a bang out of her eye, sniffled, then stood up straight. *It's not my fault. None of this is my fault.* She was going to have to keep telling herself that if she ever expected to believe it.

"The hub is ahead, just beyond those doors." Alfonse pointed toward two glass doors fitted with mechanical locks across their top, middle, and bottom.

"Right there, huh?" Clara peered down the corridor. "It looks simple enough. Are you sure you can get this moon buggy of yours flying once we get inside?"

"Mars rover," Alfonse said flatly. "And yes, I'm sure."

"Tom*a*yto, tom*ah*to," she said, quickly dismissing the correction. Her thoughts were already past those double doors, into the hub, as she tried to foresee what kind of monsters awaited them there or lurked behind the corners or within the crevices between those doors and where they stood. She wondered what sorts of demons were crouching in the shadows.

But she saw only a few corners to hide behind and fewer shadows to lurk in. They strode down thirty meters of hallway toward the south entrance to the hub, cautious, always on guard, but without apparent cause. Their journey from the radiology lab to the hub had been delightfully free of things wanting to kill them. The ease of the trip made her more cautious, more suspicious. She tiptoed toward the double doors, expecting a trap.

When they reached the doors without incident, Alfonse shrugged. They looked at each other and turned to face a quiet, empty corridor.

He slapped his thighs. "I guess that's it, then." His shoulders noticeably relaxed and he let out a breath.

Clara wasn't ready to let her guard down. She acted as lookout while Alfonse swiped his card through the reader. A red light flashed green. One by one, starting at the top, the rectangular locks split in half, and the resulting squares slid horizontally away from each other.

Once the locks stopped moving and nothing prevented Clara from opening the doors, she reached for the handle but saw none. She heard a sound similar to that of a hydraulic pump releasing. The doors slowly swung open. Though she could see clearly through the doors that nothing was lying in wait on the other side, Clara pressed her back flat against the corridor wall in case anyone inside might be watching. Alfonse hugged the opposite wall, flexing his fingers. Neither had a weapon, and Clara lacked any combat training. She doubted that mattered though, since hand-to-hand fighting skills were useless against something one couldn't touch.

But she could touch it. She *had* touched it. More accurately, it had touched her. And as confounding and bittersweet as this apparent contradiction was becoming, she didn't question what perhaps she should have been questioning all along – whether she truly was healed.

For the first time Clara could ever recall such a thought, she wished she had a weapon. A grenade launcher came to mind even though she knew little more about grenade launchers than the fact that they launched grenades. She didn't even know what one looked like. But again, it launched grenades, and that had to count for something.

As soon as she stepped around the open door, she saw them: people, not mutated but not quite right, either. Alfonse saw them, too. He put out a hand, signaling her to stay back, the brave, defenseless fool raising his other hand and making a fist, ready to take on the enemy with strength and wits alone.

Doing so, Clara decided, would be proof positive he didn't have much of the latter. But she didn't stop him as he crept inside, her own body arresting her at the threshold, unable to do much of anything. Alfonse moved farther into the hub.

With unfocused determination, Clara managed to move one foot through the entrance. The glass doors behind her swung closed, and their weight pushed her into the room, where other people stood waiting...or doing whatever they were doing.

What the hell are they doing?

Around the helipad, seemingly stationed at random, stood three relatively human-looking humans, two males and a female. If Alfonse knew who they were, he didn't say. Instead, he kept his distance, watching their every move – a simple task, since no one was moving.

The doors clicked, locking Clara in with the statue people. She studied the closest of the infected, as she assumed they must have been, and immediately looked for signs of aggression. The female stood only ten or twelve meters away. Clara didn't recognize her. She was a short-haired, sharp-angled woman in her early forties who stood motionless except for a gentle, almost unperceivable sway. She wore a lab coat as did so many others at the center, but Clara couldn't begin to guess whose team she'd been with. She supposed that no longer mattered.

Why isn't she attacking? Is it because I'm already infected? She sneaked a glance at Alfonse. *If so, why isn't she attacking him?*

For a moment, she allowed herself to stroll down that line of thought. If Molli was intelligent, and she knew it was, then maybe it had infected

Alfonse and was playing coy in order to escape. *That makes no sense.* She tensed, angry at herself for doubting and showing such secret but altogether unwarranted ingratitude toward a man who had risked much to carry her to safety.

He's normal – talking normal, acting normal, being normal – not like Sergei Kobozev. And even if he is infected, Molli would have all the knowledge it needs to escape, from him and the others it's taken over, assuming it can retain the knowledge of its host, which an infected Alfonse would prove. It wouldn't need me. I'm deadweight. Unless…unless it wants me for something else.

"Stupid," she muttered aloud then remembered her audience, covering her mouth with her hand to try to push the sound back in.

The woman didn't move, and Clara allowed her shoulders to retreat from her neck. The human statue stood in an awkward pose, as if about to take a step when her joints had locked up, in need of oil like the Tin Man from that ridiculous, oft-parodied musical. The stance would have been impossible for any normal person to hold for more than a few minutes. The control Molli had over each of its hosts was complete and, to Clara's dismay, impressive.

The woman's eyes were blank sheets, save for tiny purple ventricles reaching like branches across a white-cloud sky. The irises and pupils had either rolled back in the sockets or had been wiped clean from the eyeball. Her skin showed signs of blisters and boils, having miraculously already scarred over, but it, her hair, and her clothing had assumed an ashen color. She appeared as if she'd been coated with lime or flash-incinerated so thoroughly her body had yet to realize it was nothing but flakes of ash to be blown apart by the slightest breeze.

Though she had no pupils, the woman still seemed to be staring in Clara's direction. She made no sign that she even knew that uninfected, or at least uncooperative, individuals were present.

"What can we do?" Clara whispered.

Alfonse had no answer. He was a few steps ahead of Clara. He looked left then right and apparently found what he'd been looking for because he crept to his right, toward what looked like a toolbox set beside some sort of drill assembly. He lingered on the corner of her peripheral vision, but she dared not take her eyes off the enemy, particularly if Alfonse had.

The woman's eyes did not follow him, remaining on Clara. Or, at least Clara felt as much, finding it difficult to tell by staring at those pupil-less sheets. They didn't so much as twitch. If they could see, they would have been able to see Clara. The fact that the woman wasn't attacking resigned her to the fact that, at the very least, the woman paid her no attention.

For now. She glanced past the women at two men, similarly frozen, watching them for any sign of deception.

A sharp, unnatural cold stung her neck. She whipped around, her hands out in front of her, but saw nothing besides the double doors they'd come through and the empty corridor beyond.

But it isn't empty, is it? Not quite.

She stepped toward it, peering closer at the glass as it began to fog up. *No, not the glass.* The air itself was condensing on the opposite side. It was taking the shape of a man.

The ghost of someone she'd seen before.

Sebastian.

Clara glanced back at Alfonse and checked again on the stiffs while she was at it. Alfonse was pulling a very large wrench from the toolbox. It came free with a *dink*, the noise causing him and Clara to cringe and momentarily freeze. None of the three ash-statue people reacted. Alfonse smiled sheepishly and crept toward the woman with the wrench firmly in his grip. The woman didn't move. Both seemed oblivious to the condensation man on the other side of the glass.

Clara said a silent prayer, thanking God that Alfonse hadn't seen the apparition behind her. When she turned to face it again, the air that composed the Sebastian replica had transformed straight from gas to solid, skipping the liquid stage. He'd become a blue-white sculpture of glacial ice.

Or permafrost.

The Sebastian-thing didn't look evil. His eyes, full of sorrow, stared at Clara through the glass.

Slowly, he raised his hand to the glass. Clara instinctively mimicked the action. Their hands inches apart, separated only by a single pane, the ice Sebastian smiled. He gave a slow, methodic wave.

Again, involuntarily and perhaps instinctively, Clara's hand waved back. But when the ice Sebastian's hand swung back, Clara's didn't follow. She pulled it away. The ice man's eyes lost the look of sorrow she'd seen therein. Disbelief and confusion, then fear, then purple-infused rage replaced it.

It slammed its palm against the glass. Clara yelped and stumbled back.

"Don't let its transparency fool you," Alfonse said, standing behind the woman with the wrench raised as if daring her to move. "It's fiberglass and not all that easy to break. What's back there? Are those things trying to get in? Is that.... Wait.... Who is that?"

"Don't come over here," Clara warned. Alfonse didn't move. His attention returned to the statue person next to him, the more immediate threat. She hoped he hadn't seen the form this monster had chosen to take, her heart filling with pity.

She turned back to the doors to find Sebastian was no longer standing behind them. Its new form made Clara want to tear out her hair and burst into sobs.

She swallowed hard. "Mom?"

"Come closer, Clarabelle," her mother's voice said in her head. The apparition smiled. *"I can take your sorrows from you. I can make you happy again. Don't you want to be happy again?"*

Clara didn't believe the frozen carbon copy outside the doors was her mother. A rage welled up in her, slowly festering but always building, until her nails dug deep into her palms and her nostrils flared. She glowered at Molli, wishing no door lay between them so she could tear that damn disease apart, molecule by molecule. *Such petty parlor tricks*. She sneered, her upper lip curling into a snarl. "How dare you?"

The ice sculpture re-formed, taking the shape of Ms. Claverie, her old swim coach, in a matter of seconds. It held a starter pistol just as in her daydream earlier, but Clara no longer thought it had been a mere daydream.

With a deadpan expression and glazed-over eyes, the Ms. Claverie copy raised its ice pistol. More angry than afraid, Clara stared defiantly into the barrel as if daring the creature to shoot. She doubted that the gun was capable of firing actual bullets even if it had been a copy of a real gun and not one designed to shoot blanks. Still, having it pointing at her face amplified her unease.

The Ms. Claverie monster shrieked, a bloodcurdling, high-pitched whine that sounded like nothing a human could make. It pulled the trigger. The sound of real gunfire filled the air.

Muffled machine-gun fire.

It hadn't come from the starter pistol but from somewhere....

Below us?

Ms. Claverie's clone placed the barrel of the pistol against its own temple and smiled. It pulled the trigger again and collapsed into a rain shower of droplets that splattered and squirmed at the door. Clara stepped back, her gaze dropping to the floor, but none appeared at her feet.

One, two, then three splashes came from behind her. She spun about to see Alfonse swinging his wrench through empty air. He squealed and stumbled away from thick, black droplets running like water down glass, except these droplets were on a horizontal surface. All three of the statue people had dissolved into showers of liquid having a consistency that reminded Clara of clotting blood.

The drops seemed to have a purpose in mind. They ran along the ground until they found a crack and disappeared into it. Soon, they were all gone.

She watched the floor run dry. The liquid critters had become someone else's problem. And Clara had an idea she knew whose.

That guard, Belgrade, the one that had helped her and Alfonse escape the creatures, had said something about an underground tunnel. She listened for the sound of gunfire, shouting, anything from the foundation beneath them, but heard nothing.

"God, I hope they're all right," she muttered. Once again, her gain had seemed to come at another's loss.

CHAPTER TWENTY-FOUR

As Dikembu's screams were ending, another's came from above, though it didn't sound human. At least, not anymore. It resembled the wail of a dying dog whose hind legs had been crushed beneath tires, and with it, the top of the walls began to bleed black plasma.

"Time to go," Dante said, igniting the walls on both sides of them and the floor in front, where more virus blobs might have been lying in wait. More mock oil drums ignited. He took pleasure in seeing them burn.

"Stay close," he ordered, "but stay behind me and clear of my flamethrower." It seemed an obvious instruction, but fear made people stupid.

"Anju!" Jordan called. "I need your help with Dr. Werniewski."

Anju started as if she'd suddenly remembered something then ran to where Jordan stood holding the semiconscious microbiologist under his armpits. "Geez." She ducked under the doctor's left arm as Jordan moved under the right. "One would think a guy who has been through med school and looks at the symptoms of disease all day long would have a stronger capacity for this nonsense."

Jordan grunted his agreement and lifted the deadweight with Anju. They followed Dante down the shaft.

Looking back to make sure Jordan still had the explosives – he did, looped around his shoulder and under Werniewski's arm – Dante was admittedly impressed to see the scientists banding together to assist their apparently mentally challenged colleague. The man was in shock, clearly, but that wasn't their problem. Dante almost told them to leave Dr. Werniewski behind, but he left the decision up to the lab rats.

Not my problem anyway. Dante was no babysitter, and his priorities were being reinforced every time he came across the disease in its oft-varying yet always terrible form. He'd seen the monster enough. He'd seen what it could do. It had to be destroyed, whatever the cost. Playing the good guy to all his newfound friends would just frustrate his purpose.

In a rare moment of unpreparedness, he was startled when Monty stepped up beside him. The ASAP guard assumed Dikembu's former position, panning his flashlight left and right to give Dante the best view possible of what was ahead.

Reds, oranges, and yellows cast eerie glows on the walls, reaching out like fingers from their source, Belgrade's flamethrower, somewhere behind Dante. He heard the gas igniting in spurts as Belgrade protected their rear. As odd as the idea would have seemed at the start of the day, Dante had allies, though he remained reluctant to admit that to himself. And some of them were proving quite useful.

But he didn't have friends, and each and every one of those allies was expendable. Dante himself was no exception, as long as it meant destroying the viruses.

The walls cried tears of water, plasma, and fire as he doused everything in flame. Fortunately, only the creature seemed to catch fire, and as long as they stayed away from the walls, which were fiery waterfalls plunging up instead of down, they were relatively safe. They could avoid the burning puddles on the floor easily enough.

"How much farther to the gate?" Dante called out to Monty over the *whoosh* of his outpouring blaze.

"Not far," Monty answered. "I just hope we have enough time to blow the charges. Obviously, those things know we're here."

But if we knock out the gate with the creatures at our heels, won't they get out too? Dante didn't like the plan so much anymore. The creatures had found the tunnel. He'd already seen one slip through a supposedly sealed door. The gaps between bars on a prison-cell door, with which he was intimately familiar, were considerably bigger. The disease would get out if it could. He was beginning to wonder if he could let anyone actually leave.

We're fucked.

Still, Dante hurried forward, shielding his face as he passed through rings of fire of his own creation. Everywhere, black plasma ignited and burned more easily than oil. The flammability of the virus was easily its most endearing factor and, as far as Dante could see, its only weakness. He vowed to exploit that weakness for as long as he could, at least until he ran out of gas.

He saw the gate twenty meters up ahead, its metal glinting every time he sprayed fire. As he moved closer, Dante saw a faint ray of light trickling through some sort of bulkhead not far beyond the gate.

The plasma emerged from the walls in greater volume, as if aware of a need for urgency. Dante had no doubt that the disease was aware in a cosmic fuck-all sense. That damn thing could think, which was what was making it so damn dangerous, more dangerous by far than all the armies and warriors and criminals and all-around scumbags he'd ever faced, combined. He wondered if he had the power to kill it, even if he had the know-how...or if a nuclear bomb would be enough.

"Dr. Phillips!" Monty shouted. "Come quickly!"

Jordan shifted all Dr. Werniewski's weight onto Anju, who nearly buckled beneath it. He hurried up to the front of the group with the duffel bag full of explosives swinging haphazardly at his side. Monty dove into the bag before Jordan could even put it down and pulled out plastic explosives not at all unlike those Dante had used in the parking garage.

He wondered if they had the same dealer as he made his move. He grabbed Monty by the wrist. "We can't," he said, appealing to the guard's sense of reason. "It'll surely get out if we do. If it's after us, the world's best chances are in our keeping its focus on us, trapping it inside until—"

Monty tore his arm free. "If we don't, we're dead." He attached a plastic explosive to the wall beside the gate. Storming back for another, he said, "My first priority is the safety of these people. That includes you, mate. The world will just have to figure out the rest for itself. Besides, there's a hundred kilometers between us and the closest village. And even if we get out, you know we're going to be quarantined. The disease ain't going anywhere because we ain't going anywhere."

Dante was about to object when Belgrade came hustling over. He helped Anju bring up Dr. Werniewski then swathed the tunnel with a blanket of fire. "Uh, guys," he said. "If you're going to do something, now's the time to do—"

"Wait!" Anju shouted. "The liquid is receding."

Belgrade went on the offensive. He followed the retreating plasma back the way they'd come, hitting it with endless bursts of flame.

"Maybe it will be easier to blow an opening under the gate," Monty said, continuing about his business. True to that thought, he placed the next plastic explosive on the ground in front of the gate.

"Do you even know anything about demolition?" Dante asked. "Your odds of blowing clear a path are overshadowed by the likelihood of you caving us in." *Which may not be such a bad thing.* He grabbed an explosive from the bag. "Here, let me—"

"Have either of you considered where we'll be standing when those bombs go off?" Jordan asked.

Dante frowned. He exchanged a glance and a shrug with Monty, making it abundantly clear to all that neither had considered that very good question.

Monty didn't waste time considering then either. "Belgrade, what's your status?"

"We're clear," the Russian answered. "It's like the black stuff just up and vanished."

"Somehow," Anju said, "I do not think we will be so lucky."

"Any liquids coming from the hatch?" Monty asked.

Dante followed Belgrade's gaze over to a ladder he hadn't noticed before. It led up to a circle wide enough for most people to fit through, a circle covered by a hatch that looked exactly like the one he'd come down. If that was the only option, he couldn't help but think they'd jumped out of the proverbial frying pan.

As if in answer to Dante's thought, Belgrade torched the ladder and cover. Nothing ignited. "It's clear."

"I'll get it open," Jordan said.

Dr. Werniewski was standing on his own, though he looked utterly confused. Still, he didn't need both Jordan and Anju watching over him.

Jordan tore off his lab coat and balled his hands up in the cloth then used it to climb the metal ladder rungs, likely still hot. When he reached the top, he pushed hard, but the cover didn't budge.

"You kind of have to twist and push at the same time," Monty said. A low rumble came from somewhere deep in the tunnel. "And hurry, mate. I think I hear something." He hustled back to placing bombs in seeming randomness save for their close proximity to the gate.

The hairs on Dante's neck stood on end. *"Who holds the devil, let him hold him well. He hardly will be caught a second time."* The quote from *Faust* had always been a favorite of his.

Jordan grunted and heaved the hatch open. He peeked his head up, and Dante couldn't help but imagine some wicked demon creature biting it off. But he came back down a moment later, looking peculiarly excited. "It looks safe. We're not far from my lab."

"Help me get Dr. Werniewski up there," Anju said.

Jordan leaped down the rest of the way and draped the zombie-like doctor over his shoulders. With Anju's help, he carried the microbiologist to the ladder then up it. The process was slow going, but not long after they'd started, Dr. Werniewski's legs were dragged up and out of sight.

All the while, the rumble grew steadily louder. Dante turned to face the source of the noise, but as he strained to see through the darkness, nothing came into view.

"The bombs are set," Monty said. "Everyone, get up the ladder." He wasted no time getting himself up, racing over even as he spoke and ascending with kangaroo quickness.

"Go, Belgrade," Dante said. "I'll cover you."

Belgrade nodded. "Thank you." He hurried over to the ladder.

Dante assumed his position and laid down suppression fire, walking backward toward the hatch, conserving gas by releasing only intermittent spurts. He backed into someone and jumped when she squealed. He'd been unaware that anyone else was still down there. He turned to see Anju, but she was staring past him, into the empty void.

She pointed her Beretta at the darkness, looking determined to shoot should anything move in it. "Hurry," she whispered.

Dante was keen to oblige. He raced to her side at the ladder's base.

The rumble grew louder still, a drumroll that kept adding drummers.

"What is it?" Dante asked.

Anju's nose crinkled. "It sounds like...running water."

Dante huffed. "You have got to be kidding me. Move!" He spun her around and hoisted her up onto the ladder before hopping on and climbing up its side. "Climb, damn it!"

Anju did just that, but she and Dante could only climb so high before they were trapped beneath Belgrade. The tank on his back made him too fat to fit through the opening, and he was struggling to shimmy through it.

"Hurry," Anju cried.

"I second that," Dante said, but his words were lost in a deluge of tar and pitch, rolling rapids of primordial ooze. Dante scrambled his way up beside Belgrade's leg. Anju did the same on the opposite side.

Belgrade's buttocks were blocking their only way out. His tank clanged against the ceiling. Dante locked eyes with Anju and saw her terror. They'd climbed as quickly and as high as they could, huddling against Belgrade as he unstuck himself, their hands and feet only a couple of rungs apart.

A wave of – *What exactly? Dissolved humans?* – broke and fizzled against the rung beneath their feet, its inertia carrying it toward the gate then through it, except where liquid ricocheted off metal. As the rushing liquid smashed against the wall and bars of the gate, it splashed, spraying backward. Anju shrunk away from that spray, but it didn't seem to be reaching her.

The disease was close to freedom. He wondered if it knew just how close it was.

The fluid rocked then flattened, leveling itself out after one final fearsome crash against the far wall. Thick sludge, like brain matter from an exit wound, spattered off the frozen dirt. Anju, fear on her face, flinched away from the splash then blinked repeatedly as if something had hit her in the eye. When Dante examined her more closely, he noticed that the area just below her eye appeared wet in the odd red glow of the flare jutting from Anju's pocket. When he looked again, it was dry.

Maybe she just had dirt in her eye or something. Maybe, but he was still wary. "Are you okay?"

Anju didn't immediately answer. She seemed far off, as if lost in a daydream.

"Anju?" Dante raised the nozzle of his flamethrower just a hair.

She snapped alert, short of breath but quickly recovering. "I am fine." She offered a smile.

I hope so, Dante thought, but he didn't say a word. He accepted her smile and offered a cheap facsimile in return. Her eyes weren't rolling back in her head, and she wasn't seizing. That had to be a good thing.

Belgrade finally shimmied his way up top.

"After you." Dante nodded in as grandiose a way as he could while scrunched into a ball and hanging from a ladder.

Anju climbed.

Dante glanced down at the silent sludge pool below him. "Stay down there, will you?" he quietly asked it. Then he turned his attention upward and proceeded through the hatch.

CHAPTER TWENTY-FIVE

Sergei had a trillion eyes. His vision was like a kaleidoscope of images, yet he was able to process them all at once. He was everywhere in the facility, watching everything, taking every conceivable form. His powers were superhuman, surreal and omnipotent, powerful yet terrifying. Having merged with approximately ninety percent of the personnel onsite in only a few hours, sharing one collective consciousness with hundreds of humans, Sergei choked on desperation as he tried and failed to talk to the other lost souls, there but not there – not like he was. Sergei was alone.

Alone with the conquering worm.

He wondered if his solitude, the warm smothering blanket of primordial ooze that swathed him, had something to do with the fact that the presence had established a mental connection – albeit in the guise of his daughter – with Sergei *before* he'd actually become infected. He'd seen a lot of people, many he'd known, swallowed by the growing plague. Yet not one of them could he find after their assimilations.

The creature had become Sergei. *Have I, too, become the creature?* If so, he couldn't understand why his will was worthless. He should have had some control over the beast or, better yet, some means to destroy it.

Where he couldn't exert his will, he instead let known his voice. *"Did it hurt?"* he asked. *"Did it hurt when those guards lit you on fire? Did it hurt when your skin melted and your blood boiled? I hope so."*

"Why does this one linger? Its time is over. Its world is no more. Its time is over!" The creature's voice hissed from countless mouths, crying in unison from all points of the research center. The human mouths it employed spoke its words fine. Other mouths garbled, gargled, and spewed guttural sounds that were at best broken-mirror reflections of human anger and frustration.

Many of Sergei's trillion eyes had become linked in body as well as spirit. The creature itself was the sum of its parts, and those parts were congregating. They were becoming one. *But one what?*

Sergei owned the creature's sight but not its mind – not yet anyway – but he wasn't ready to give up on that front. He didn't know why the beast had summoned its parts. The best he could tell was that some base need, some instinctive herding, called the parts together, making them whole. More parts were coming, the central mass growing, changing, evolving. With every new addition, an electrical cooing shot from particle to particle like synapses from nerve endings. Sergei could sense its need – no, its necessity – to be whole with those it had spawned.

A weakness? Sergei wondered if it was one that an opportunistic soul might use to his advantage if wise enough to spot it. He waited for such a soul to present himself. When that moment arose, he promised himself he wouldn't be so helpless.

No. He would be ready.

CHAPTER TWENTY-SIX

Dante stood in a hall not unlike the one he'd started in that morning, when he'd thought it a brilliant idea to head haphazardly toward a clean room containing a deadly disease that had been just waiting to get out. So far, he'd been able to outrun it. *But now, we're just running in circles.*

Also, he was standing in a circle. Across from him was that rigid Russian guard, Belgrade, crouching near the hatch cover. No one helped him as he slid the hard-to-grip weight back over the hole.

To Dante's right was Monty, not one Dante readily trusted. But the one-eyed SOB still had his shit together, which was a good thing, since Dante was short on ideas.

Except blowing everything to hell. That was and would always remain the idea of champions. *Why wait for the facility to do it for me when I have the means and the wherewithal to do it myself?*

"Had the means," he muttered under his breath. He glowered at Jordan, who paced in and out of their huddle, his hands empty.

Dante lost his cool. He rushed at the botanist, grabbed him by his god-awful green sweater, and ran him back-first into the wall. "The explosives!" he demanded. "Where are they?"

"I-I-I don't know." Jordan glanced around for help, but none came to his aid. "They must still be down there."

"You...." Dante felt a hand, firm but not threatening, land on his shoulder. *Monty.* He roared and pushed Jordan away from him. "*Merda!*"

"We have to keep moving," Anju said. She was propping up Dr. Werniewski, who still seemed out of it.

Dante watched her narrowly, daring any sign of infection to rear its pretty mutant head. He was ready to blow Anju's head clean off.

"Agreed." Belgrade said. "Monty, come help me with this."

"The detonators?" Dante asked.

"Lost," Belgrade said, grunting as he heaved the coin-shaped cover nearly back into place.

Monty stopped him within a few inches of closing it. "Don't worry," he said to Dante. "I have something just as good." He pulled an incendiary grenade from his pack.

Dante crouched and looked him dead in the eye with a mixture of concern and excitement. The facility was already set to blow. Monty risked blowing a breach in the shutter and letting those things out. *Or killing those already underground and preventing them from getting through the bulkhead.* He wished he had more time to think Monty's plan through. "You're crazy. It'll set off the other bombs—"

"I know." Monty winked. "Best get back."

"But the foundation—"

Monty's smile disappeared. "Like I said, best get back."

Dante shook his head, trying to figure out why he was debating the act. *Isn't this what you wanted?* He thought about it while he sprang to his feet and rushed toward the others. *Yes, but I want to make sure it's done right.*

"We have to move!" he shouted. "Hurry!" He gripped Anju and Jordan by the elbows and herded them away from the hatch.

Anju pulled Dr. Werniewski along with her. "Where do we go?" she asked. "Does anyone have a plan?"

Dante didn't answer. He hadn't the foggiest idea.

"To my lab!" Jordan blurted. "Come on! It's just around the corner here." He pointed up at the next intersection of corridors.

"Move!" Dante shouted. *Around a corner is a damn good start.*

"Fire in the hole!" Monty yelled then added, short of breath, "Literally."

Belgrade came sprinting up like a cheetah behind them. He shoved Dr. Werniewski around the bend as the entire building shook beneath their feet. The incendiary grenade went off with a flourish of heat and sound. A succession of roaring blasts followed, and the resulting earthquake went well above average on Richter's scale. The group huddled close together, crouching and covering their heads while the blasts crescendoed like a bass beat on a thousand speakers turned up way too high.

Glass shattered. The lights went out. Cracks appeared in the floor and continued up the walls and across the ceiling.

"Where's Monty?" Dante shouted over the roar.

Belgrade started to answer, but before he could, a barrage of flames burst across the intersection. A figure within it dove toward them and rolled across the floor, screaming. Fire ate away his clothes in several places.

Dante ripped off his vest and whacked Monty with it, smothering the small patches of fire that the man's rolling hadn't doused. Jordan followed suit with his lab coat. Black smudges of ash and grime smeared Monty's skin. His clothes were flaking and charred, matted in a few areas where they had fused against his skin. Other than those red, tender spots, which would likely need serious burn treatment, Monty seemed okay. In fact, the SOB was smiling.

"That was reckless," Dante said, helping him to his feet.

Monty took his hand and stood. "You're one to criticize, mate." He wouldn't stop grinning. "Besides, that was a whole lot of fun."

"My recklessness puts only my life in danger, not everyone else's," Dante said. "I should have let you burn."

"Aw, don't say that." Monty feigned pouting as he dusted himself off. "Anyway, no harm, no foul. At the very least, we have less of those things chasing our tails. At the most, maybe we've got a way out. Let's go back and check out the tunnel."

He started back toward the hatch cover, the others slow to follow. A burst of gas and flame blew the hatch off, sending it bulleting through the ceiling. They waited for it to come down, but it never did.

Monty ran to the hole. "The entire tunnel below is an arsonist's wet dream." He slapped his thighs. "Well, we're not going down there."

"Facility purification will commence in ninety minutes," the English gentleman's voice said over the intercom.

"Well, at least that's still online," Dante grumbled.

In a moment, so was everything else. Though dimmer, the lights came back on where the bulbs hadn't shattered. Sparks flew from those that had and from other electronics that were now malfunctioning or in pieces. Systems rebooted. All facility essentials – HVAC, lighting, data storage, et cetera – were fully operational in less than a minute. With more backup support systems than a manned satellite, the research center was designed to withstand all catastrophes short of a nuclear explosion.

Dante smirked. It was a good thing the center had that capability, too.

"So the tunnel idea didn't work," Monty said. "What say we head for this rover thing?"

Belgrade frowned. "There are other tunnels we could try. I doubt this" – he huffed – "*space vehicle* will fit all of us."

Monty laughed. "It's a long way between here and the north entrance to the hub. I have a feeling fewer seats will be needed by the time we make it there, if you catch my meaning."

"What's gotten in to you?" Dante asked. "There are civilians—"

Monty sobered. "Maybe you haven't read my shirt. I'm not army anymore. I'm guessing you ain't either. We're all *civilians*, and we're all stuck deep in this shit show. So, nothing's gotten into me. I'm just being pragmatic. And the way I see it, we're pretty damn low on options. Instead of criticizing, if you've got a better idea, then out with it."

Dante held his tongue. "The rover. Sounds like a plan."

Monty softened. "We've got one more shot of making it out of here, assuming that ship hasn't sailed. What say we make it a corker? I say, if we're going down, we do it fighting. I'm getting really tired of running."

"I might be able to increase our odds of getting to the hub alive," Jordan said, inserting himself in the danger zone between the two unspoken leaders of their group. "My lab's right there," he said, standing at the intersection and pointing two doors down on the left. "Please, follow me."

Belgrade pushed through Monty and Dante and said, "We're following," in a tone that left nothing up for debate. Jordan smiled nervously then led everyone to a door marked Botany Lab. After scanning his badge, he opened the door and let everyone inside, leaving Monty and Dante standing in the hallway, their issues not quite resolved.

After a moment, Monty punched Dante in the arm. "You win some, you lose some, mate." The guard started walking toward the lab. Dante followed.

Once inside, with the door closed behind them, Dante raised his flamethrower. He pointed it at Anju. "Don't move."

Anju gasped and froze.

"Jesus Christ!" Jordan blurted and scampered out of the way.

"You have about three seconds to explain yourself," Belgrade said. Out of the corner of his eye, Dante could see the Russian's gun aimed at his forehead. Though he could no longer see Monty with his eyes trained on the young graduate student, Dante assumed the other ASAP guard had his own gun raised.

Belgrade was right. He had some explaining to do, and the quicker the better.

"Jordan," he asked without looking for the scientist, "is your lab equipped with a scanner like that in the microbiology clean room?"

"Yes," Jordan said.

Anju stomped her foot and gnashed her teeth at Dante. "I already told you I am fine."

Dante ignored her and the guns pointed at him. "Activate it."

"But we already know the flowers carry a biological enzyme that the scanner will pick up," Jordan said. "The whole lab will register as infected."

"Just do it." Dante took his eyes off Anju long enough to shoot a fierce glare at the botanist, giving him no reason to doubt his severity. "If she's not infected, she shouldn't mind being scanned. And if she is infected, we'll know soon enough."

Belgrade's aim switched from Dante to Anju then back to Dante. He frowned. "Run the fucking scan already, Dr. Phillips."

Jordan sighed. He sat down at the computer at the center of the room. Against the wall across from where he was sitting, a giant screen blipped to life.

"I told you," Anju whined. One leg was shaking so badly that her heel was tap-dancing, clacking repeatedly against the floor. "I am not infected."

"I hope you're right," Dante said softly, but he did not lower his weapon. "I'm sorry. We have to be sure."

Anju began to sweat. She looked as though at any moment she might panic or bolt. Her reactions were becoming increasingly unpredictable.

"Look at me!" she shouted. "I am nothing like them!"

"Initiating scan for biological contamination," said that same flat computerized-woman's voice Dante had heard earlier.

Belgrade's aim shifted to Anju. Jordan swiveled in his chair to watch her. She took a step back.

When a dull tone sounded, Jordan said, "Everyone, close your eyes."

Anju didn't right way, so neither did Dante. "Don't you move," he whispered.

Ultraviolet light and heat radiated from massive lamps propped along opposite walls where they met the ceiling. Anju closed her eyes, and Dante copied her. A sound like a shaken soda bottle being opened filled the room and warmth tingled his skin.

"Scan completed," the computer said.

Dante opened his eyes. Anju's were already open, staring at him with fear and distrust. Still, she hadn't moved an inch.

"I am not infected," she said, barely audible, as tears streamed from her eyes. "I'm not."

The screen on the wall showed an x-ray of the room. "Unknown organism detected," the computer said.

Dante gave a quick glance toward the screen. Everyone's white-and-silver outlines were uncorrupted against a black-and-gray background, depicted along with everything else in the room. There wasn't any red on the screen except for a tall, reedy object with a bell-shaped head at a far corner of the lab.

"One of the lilies," Jordan said.

"Unknown organism detected." Again, an object on the screen turned red.

"Another flower." Jordan rose to his feet. He pushed his wire-rimmed glasses up the bridge of his nose and walked up to the screen for a closer look.

The scanner began to rattle off unknown organisms. The bottom half of the screen filled in quickly. The red dots and lines were progressing toward their position near the top of the screen.

Dante tried to watch both it and Anju closely. He caught the outline of one in their group beginning to shake on-screen, as if the firmness of the human form was deteriorating. He looked at Anju. It wasn't her, but her lower lip began to quiver. She raised a finger and pointed it at Dante.

"Wait, I...." Dante's confusion dispelled quickly. Anju wasn't pointing *at* him. She was pointing *past* him.

He whipped around in time to see Monty's face bubbling, purple blotches moving beneath it, as his growing maw latched on to Dr. Werniewski's neck. His teeth tore at the flesh, ripping a chunk of skin and muscle loose and spraying Monty's face in arterial blood.

Dr. Werniewski shrieked and fell to the floor. He instantly began to seize.

"Get out of the way!" Dante shouted at Jordan, who stood between him and a clear shot. The scientist froze.

Belgrade apparently had a clear shot, though not with his flamethrower. His AK-47 put several rounds into Monty's head even as his jaw continued to stretch, contorting him into something that was all mouth and sharpened teeth.

The sound of gunshots shook Jordan from his stupor. He scrambled away from Monty as the infected guard lunged toward him, snapping at the air where Jordan's head had been just a second before.

Dante unleashed fire. "I knew I should have let you burn."

Monty burst into flames, flailing wildly and ran out into the hall, an inextinguishable fireball.

In the back of Dante's mind, an idea was forming, one that made him sick to his stomach. There was no way Monty, who'd seemed perfectly normal, or human anyway, only minutes ago, who'd single-handedly wiped out a whole army of liquid creatures when he dropped that incendiary grenade into the tunnel, had become infected between the time he blew up the tunnel and the time he entered the botany lab. *Unless the disease had become airborne...or had lain dormant inside him, waiting for its opportunity to strike.*

"*Merda,*" he muttered. Either way, every last one of them could already be infected. He raised his flamethrower toward Anju. The sprayer trembled in his hands. "I'm sorry."

"What are you doing?" Belgrade shouted.

Anju screamed. In his moment of hesitation, she bolted from the lab. Dante lowered his weapon. He'd failed his mission. He'd been unable to pull the trigger when it had been hardest to pull.

"Don't you see?" he asked, his heart collapsing beneath the weight of sorrow and defeat. "We are already lost. Look at Monty. I bet we're all already infected."

Belgrade punched him hard enough across the chin to crack open his lower lip. "You goddamn idiot! If we were already infected, why would the infected still be trying to kill us?"

Dante straightened and raised a fist, but Belgrade's words hit home. His fire and rage vanished as quickly as it had consumed him. Belgrade was right. They weren't all infected, though that didn't mean all of them were clean. He had to ask himself if he was willing to burn them all to find out which were which.

A question for another time. Dante hadn't failed his mission. Not yet. But he'd failed Anju.

"We have to find her," he said. He was just coming out of his thoughts and didn't have time to recoil when Jordan tore the flamethrower from his hands.

"Well, we know *he's* infected." He doused the seizing, twitching Dr. Werniewski with a steady stream of fire until the nozzle sputtered and went out.

Jordan looked angry as he stood over the burning mound of flesh. "I guess it wasn't the oatmeal she had for breakfast."

"What?" Belgrade asked.

"Nothing," Jordan answered.

Dante dropped the empty tank from his back and let the weapon slam against the floor at his feet. He drew his pistol. "I'm going after her."

A hand locked around his wrist. He tore himself free and reeled on the botanist.

"Wait!" Jordan sputtered. "Don't hit me! We came in here for a reason, and we don't know which way she went. We can't help her if we're dead. And, though it's a longshot, I may know a way that will allow us to travel these hallways unseen."

CHAPTER TWENTY-SEVEN

With the room apparently Molli-free, Clara had time to take in her surroundings. The hub was a large, open room shaped like an octagon. In it, she saw a small office or conference room in the corner; a flight simulator; a rock wall; an obstacle course; a bevy of large pieces of equipment, the uses of which were mysteries; cranes and strange claw hands that resembled those maddening arcade games where one tries to snag a cheap, gaudy prize and transport it over to the drop box; drills of varying sizes; tools ranging from the ancient to the ultramodern arranged in some semblance of an order Clara couldn't detect; and vehicles ranging from dune buggies and ATVs to satellites and probes.

Everything was laid out around a giant helicopter pad. On it sat a rather unimpressive-looking heap of metal and junk, something out of a hoarder metallurgist's backyard, Clara's supposed ticket out of the research center, the *Herald*. Given the locations of the four keg-sized all-terrain tires she could see from the doorway, Clara assumed the *Herald* had four more identical wheels on its other side. Spindly octopus arms connected the wheels to the frame. Each of those appendages was covered with pistons, levers, and gears. She couldn't see inside the body, but it looked no bigger than the cab of a pickup truck, not big enough to fit four, at least not comfortably.

We'll table that for now. She stared down Alfonse, wondering if he could be trusted. When she looked up, she saw a blank gray dome between her and escape.

"It's retractable," Alfonse whispered, noticing her gaze.

"So how do you know the shutter's not over it?" she asked.

He smiled weakly. "It won't be."

"Are you sure you can start this thing up all by yourself?" Clara asked as Alfonse checked several computers both on and off the *Herald*, which she refused to call Edna.

"I'm sure," he said. "This isn't exactly rocket science. Well, actually, it is rocket science, but it's not like some silly spy-movie self-destruct sequence that requires eighteen passcodes and several people to initiate. One's enough." He groaned and hit the side of a monitor. "Except usually we have the luxury of seven people performing all necessary diagnostic checks simultaneously, with an astronaut member of our team leading the charge." He laughed. "Thank the Lord for cross-training."

"Huh?"

"Cross-training? Well, you see, we all need to know how to do everyone else's job in case something terribly wrong happens up there. When you're forty-eight million miles away from Earth at its closest orbital point, NASA can't exactly just send up an ambulance."

"Ah," Clara said. "I see." She did get it. She just wanted Alfonse to move a little more quickly. For whatever reason, the creature seemed to be gone. She had no way of guessing when it might return.

As if reading her thoughts, he said, "Believe me. I'm going as fast as I can."

"I'm going to look for a weapon," she said. "Just in case."

"There's plenty of those around here. As for ones that might work against the virus...." His words trailed off.

"It's not a virus," Clara muttered. She roamed around the hub, looking for the perfect weapon. She picked up Alfonse's wrench but didn't like its weight. Besides, any bludgeoning weapon would require a close encounter, which she would like to avoid if at all possible.

Some of the power drills were the normal, handheld type, while others looked as though they were meant for oil rigs. They had the same design flaw as the wrench and were equally, and in some cases much more, cumbersome.

Who am I kidding? She sighed and tossed a screwdriver down onto a rolling metal tray. *I'm no fighter.*

Her eyes caught sight of one of those face masks people in the movies or on TV always used when they were welding something, the kind that pulled down over your face and flipped back up. It was charcoal gray and had a tinted-black rectangular windshield. She didn't know what it was called, didn't know or care much about welding really, but did know it was used in conjunction with—

"A blowtorch!" She chirped like a chick as she snatched up the L-shaped tool. She turned it around in her hands, noting that she would still need to get close, but she remembered what Dr. Werniewski had said about the ASAP guards incinerating the remains of the infected. Fire seemed her best bet, particularly since she doubted she would stumble across a grenade launcher.

She heard a sound that reminded her of the conveyor belt at a grocery store. She turned to see the hood to the *Herald*'s cockpit lifting up and back, a lot like that retractable welding mask. Clapping, with the blowtorch smacking against her free palm, she hurried over to Alfonse and the Mars rover.

"*Voila!*" he said in his best French, bowing graciously. "I've set coordinates to land us in a small clearing just south of here. We could probably drive the rover straight into the nearest town from there. Won't that surprise some folks?"

"Seats four comfortably, huh?" she asked, frowning and staring at what were clearly two bucket seats, with what might have been a third crammed in like one of those foldout seats added as an afterthought in certain models of automobiles so that their manufacturers could claim higher-capacity seating. The rover seated two comfortably and one uncomfortably.

Alfonse stuck out his lower lip. He looked genuinely hurt. "We could have made it work. Sebastian could have sat between my legs, or—"

"I still can," a familiar voice said from beside them. "Take me with you."

Clara turned to see Sebastian standing only a few meters away, looking healthy and normal and sounding it, too – not made of gas and ice and all things not nice, but human flesh, whole and seemingly uninfected.

Seemingly.

"Impossible," Clara uttered. *Is it getting smarter?*

"Sebastian?" Alfonse began to unravel. His hands shook, and tears formed in his eyes. He took a step toward his partner.

Clara reached out for him, snagged the back of his shirt, and yanked him back. "Stay away from that thing. Surely, you must see through that thing's lies. It's the organism. She's...adapting. Evolving, maybe." *Or growing, maturing.* She frowned. "I don't know much, but I definitely know that isn't Sebastian."

Fiddling with the blowtorch while she spoke, Clara figured out how to turn it on. Gas hissed from its nozzle as if begging to be lit.

CHAPTER TWENTY-EIGHT

"I feel ridiculous," Belgrade said. His uniform was covered in lilies. They wove in and out of the spaces between the buttons of his shirt, protruding from every pocket and even from his boots. Jordan had even managed to loop one around his hat. "If I'm going to die, let me do it with some dignity."

Dante looked him over and chuckled before he could help himself. The guard did look ridiculous.

They continued walking. Since leaving the botany lab, they hadn't encountered a single creature, unless one counted the torched Aussie that was dead and still burning outside it. They hadn't seen any sign of Anju.

Still, Dante laughed. He couldn't help it. Something about the three of them walking down those dimly lit, horror-movie hallways clad in flowers struck him as funny, as if life itself had become one big, absurd joke.

"What are you laughing at?" Belgrade asked. "You look just as stupid as we do."

"Maybe more so." Dante forced his mouth flat. He was covered not only in flowers, but also enough dirt to pot them in. And that didn't even take into account the black cross he'd painted on his forehead. "All that matters is that it works. I can't say I quite understand the science behind it. Are the flowers releasing some kind of pheromone that confuses the creatures? Where did you say you got this idea from again?"

Jordan smiled. "Not from science. I saw something similar on this zombie show that was hugely popular like twenty years ago. Basically, the good guys would hide from the zombies by chopping one of them up – the zombies, not one of the good guys – and smearing its guts all over themselves. They would look and smell like zombies, and the real zombies wouldn't pay any attention to them."

Belgrade growled. "You're risking our lives on the basis of some silly television show?"

Dante's face lit up. "No, I've seen this show! They play it all the time in Naples. That's where I'm from. I love it! This could work!" He shook the flamethrower in his hand, which Belgrade had given him due to his demonstrated proficiency with the weapon. "But I never understood why they didn't just take one of these and light them all up."

"Probably because they would have had to light up the entire world with them, burn it all down," Jordan said.

"Small price to pay," Dante muttered.

"Anyway...." Jordan's smile quavered. "It's just a theory. I have no idea whether it will actually work. The logic seems sound, though. The infected aren't attacking Clara because they think she is already infected. Maybe these plants will help us confuse them into thinking we are as well." He shrugged.

Belgrade shook his head. "You're both idiots." His eyes fell upon Jordan's chest, which was partially covered with long, narrow, celery-thick leaves covered with tiny thorns that clung to his ugly green sweater and curled around his legs. "Why are your flowers so much less, I don't know, flowery?"

"These leaves come from a much more virile relative of *Drosera regia*, more commonly known as a king sundew," Jordan said.

Dante exchanged a raised eyebrow with Belgrade, who shook his head slightly.

Jordan let out an exaggerated sigh. "Fine. Think Venus flytrap, since that is the most popular member of its not-so-immediate family. Similar to the flytrap, it captures its prey, small rodents and insects and such, in these tentacles, which excrete mucilage, essentially gluing the food source to its leaves. But the sundew is so much more interesting than the flytrap and even the pitcher plant, though these plants have so many differences it would take me all day to name them."

"Please don't," Belgrade said.

"Anyway," Jordan continued, unfazed, "imagine our excitement when we found in Siberia seeds of a plant whose closest relative is found only in South Africa. It's both amazing and bewildering, but I am not one to question good fortune. And its versatility is amazing! It can handle a wide variety of climates, changes in atmospheric pressure, variant food sources—"

"That's great, Doc," Dante said. "What I think my friend here was asking is: Why did you get leaves from that, while we have to wear all these flowers?"

"Oh." Jordan studied his feet. "Well, it's a carnivorous plant and, as I said, hard to kill, so I didn't have a lot of dead leaves lying around, and I wouldn't want to risk using the live ones."

"It's an ancient carnivorous plant, and you're wearing its leaves as camouflage?" Dante shook his head. "For a doctor, you don't seem all that smart."

"Relax," Jordan said. "These petals are dead and detached from the rest of the plant. They're not going to be feeding on anything, let alone me."

"Hey." Belgrade whacked the botanist in the chest. "Shut up." He pointed ahead of them with the barrel of his AK-47.

The corridor bent like a boomerang. As they came to the bend, Belgrade held Dante back, pointing out the two mudskipper things they'd seen chase down that boy back on the control-room monitors. One was lying against the wall, lidless eyes rolled back in its head as if it were sleeping. The second one was lying against it, looking just as lethargic. The closer Dante watched, the more obvious it became that the second creature wasn't simply lounging against the first but merging into it.

"Time to test your theory, Doc," Dante said. He took the lead, crept silently up to the mutant mudskippers, and eased right past them. One reached out almost longingly, as if to invite them into its arms. The other didn't move at all.

Once past them, he waved the others forward. Belgrade and Jordan crept by the creatures, and they continued on their way.

In this fashion, they passed by all sorts of twisted contortions of the human anatomy and many more monstrosities that ceased to have any human resemblance at all. At one point, they approached what looked like a giant hamster wheel made from the bones of at least a half a dozen people. Inside it were three women – each with soulless, empty eyes, clothes torn and tattered – standing side by side and merging into one another. Their feet were gone, replaced by an amorphous mound of tissue.

The woman on the left had dark skin and long black hair. Dante ran to her, his heart leaping in his chest. "Anju!"

But as he got closer, he saw it wasn't Anju but some other unfortunate soul. Luckily for him and the others, his outburst had failed to shake any of the aberrations from their trance-like state. Dante couldn't tell if the flowers were keeping them safe or if the creatures were undergoing some kind of process, like a metamorphosis. He hoped not the latter, and he wasn't ready to discard the flowers just in case.

"Ow!" Jordan squawked. He slapped his back as if something had bit him there. "Ouch! Ah!" He started to wiggle and dance as if he'd been standing on a mound of fire ants.

Then he began to scream in earnest. "Get it off! Get it off! It burns! Oh God, it burns!"

Dante checked the status of the creatures around him briefly before rushing to Jordan's aid. Even the scientist's hollering at the top of his lungs had not disturbed them. Jordan was tearing at the collar of his sweater, trying to pull it off, but it appeared to be caught on something.

"Lift up your arms," Dante said. When Jordan did, Dante grabbed the shirt at the bottom and yanked it up. Jordan howled and jerked away. Dante let go, but not before he'd pulled the shirt up high enough to see that the leaves had eaten their way through the fabric and were feeding on Jordan's skin. He'd torn the lower leaves partly off. To his horror, Jordan's skin had come off with them.

"Oh fuck no," Dante said. Though not wearing the same plants, Dante no longer felt safe donned in the botanist's infected flora. He exchanged a glance with Belgrade, and they both tore the flowers off themselves and threw them as far away as they could. Once they thought they had them all, they turned back to Jordan, who stood with his arms raised, his whole body shaking, tears in his eyes, a trickle of urine pooling at his feet. His face had gone pale white. He looked too terrified to move any part of himself.

"We have to get his clothes off." Belgrade pulled a road flare from his pocket and shoved it like a bridle into Jordan's mouth. "Bite down. This is really going to hurt."

To his credit, Jordan did so and nodded. He closed his eyes. Tears popped out from their corners.

"Ready?" Belgrade asked Dante.

Dante nodded. He grabbed the bottom of the sweater from the

right side while Belgrade grabbed it on the left. "On three," Dante said. "One...two...."

They both shot their arms up quickly. Dante forced it up against the leaves' resistance. The sweater came free with the same sound duct tape made when pulled from the roll. Patches of Jordan's skin flayed off with it, exposing the red, raw muscle beneath. Yellow sap coated the skin around the wounds, interspersed on his chest and back, sticking to the sweater and skin like flypaper.

Dante and Belgrade had the sweater free from Jordan's body and were pulling it over his head when one of the petals curled inward. It attached itself to the side of Jordan's face as if it were a leech, stretching across his right eye, cheek, and most of his nose and mouth. He began to scream anew, his anguish muffled by the covering over his mouth. The one eye spared the carnivorous plant's slow digestion widened when it saw Belgrade raise his AK-47.

Jordan offered a whimper and a muffled protest.

"I'm sorry," Belgrade said. A single report echoed through the hall.

Despite all Jordan's cries of agony, the sound that had ended his suffering was responsible for stirring the creatures. White eyes filled with color then awareness. They regarded Belgrade and Dante from the trail ahead and the path behind. The mudskippers cooed. The humanoids twitched. The bone wheel rolled.

"I see you," a thousand mouths said in unison.

Dante turned to Belgrade. "Run!"

CHAPTER TWENTY-NINE

People trying to shoot me or light me on fire; weird, diseased things straight out of nightmares trying to make me one of their kind; and that lecherous, roaming-handed Dr. Werniewski....

"Ugh! Why did I even come here?"

Anju sobbed as she ran. Snot bubbled from one nostril and ran over her lip. Her heart felt as if it were about to explode in her chest. A cramp stung in her side, and she was having difficulty breathing. She did not know how far she had run, and she had no idea where she was. She had burst from the botany lab in a state of sheer terror, and as far as she could tell, she still had not calmed down a single bit.

Well, maybe enough to know that she still needed to calm the fuck down. *No sense in trying to make sense of any of this. I need to figure out what to do next.*

Leaving the group had been a bad idea. Even if that crazy Christian crusader had burned her to a crisp, it probably still would have been better than running around the research center, lost and alone, waiting for some giant purple people eater to come and gobble her up.

Well, maybe not much better. Still, she had no plan. She had no plan, not even the beginnings of an idea pertaining to one. *Come on, girl. You are smart, so think!*

Anju missed her family. She missed her little girl, Safia. She missed home.

She had always been a good person, kind and patient, never uttering a harsh word to anyone. She genuinely cared for people, regardless of their race, creed, nationality, gender, and all that other nonsense people used to make other people feel inferior. But she was being made to feel inferior, subjugated by a force that would eliminate the characteristics that made people individuals by mixing them altogether into one homogeneous mass of...*of shit!*

"You are shit, you hear me! You are nothing but shit!" Anju was not particularly proud of her insult, but the spark of rebellion did make her feel a little better, and it helped her to think just a little more clearly.

It opened the floodgates, letting in wave after wave of self-pity. She did not deserve this hell that God, or karma, or whatever force had set before her. *What have I done to warrant this torture? Am I being punished for leaving Safia home where she is warm and safe? I do this for Safia.*

That was it, the reason that had brought her to the research center, her reason to carry on: Safia. Anju had put herself through course after course and project after project to better herself and, in turn, make a better life for both her and her child. At that moment, she would have given anything to be back home with her little girl. She would wrap Safia up in her arms, blot her head with tears and kisses, and squeeze her tightly for as long as her daughter would let her. "I should never have left you, Safia."

She wiped her eyes, having found her reason to be strong, to keep on going. "I hope I get to see you again."

As if a guardian angel had heard her wish, she saw something up ahead that seemed too good to be true. A hatch cover had been removed from the floor. She remembered that guard, Belgrade, saying that there were other tunnels, other ways out. She wondered if it was wise to allow herself to hope that she was approaching one of them.

It does look like someone else tried to escape through the tunnels. Maybe they made it out.

Her heart continued to thump faster than a techno dance beat, but the discomfort in her chest diminished. She raced to the cover, crouched over the opening, and peered down into the hole. She saw nothing below except the black oblivion of darkness.

She patted her coat for the flashlight she had taken from the armory. It was gone. "Shit!" She realized she must have dropped it and did not waste time trying to figure out where. It was gone, and that was that.

She stood but continued staring into the tunnel below. She had a decision to make: run around aimlessly in the light until she found the hub or the purple people eaters found her, or brave the tunnel that, she knew, would lead to a way out that might or might not have been blocked.

When she couched her dilemma in those terms, her decision seemed easy. She closed her eyes, took a deep breath, then crawled into the hole.

CHAPTER THIRTY

"Facility purification will commence in sixty minutes," the English gentleman computer voice announced over the intercom.

Oh, shut up, Dante thought as his feet pounded across the floor. Even a man in his tip-top shape couldn't keep up forever the way he was going. He doubted he would live sixty more minutes. He would consider himself lucky to live another six. The research center's self-destruction was the least of his worries.

Belgrade ran beside him, his company a small comfort. The Russian was doing a fine job of slowing down infected with his assault rifle and staying out of the way of Dante's flame-throwing. Human flesh and hair went up like fireworks at *Carnevale di Venezia*. It stank with that acrid nastiness that only burning hair smelled like. Still, the mutant freaks kept coming.

Dante skidded to a halt. He blasted both ways down the hall.

"We have to keep moving," Belgrade said. "It's our only chance. There's way too many—"

"I have an idea," Dante said. "Actually, it was your idea. Let's pray it works better than that last guy's did." He pulled out the two smoke grenades Belgrade had stuffed into his pockets and pulled the pins on both. He tossed them down the hall, one in each direction, then covered his mouth and nose with his shirt. Belgrade lowered his mask and goggles.

A pair of newly formed conjoined twins stopped short as the canister bounced their way, spewing gray smoke that quickly filled the hallway. The twins turned and ran off in the opposite direction, no longer interested in joining Dante and Belgrade to their brood. The other critters coming up behind the pair did the same. Much like those outside the radiology lab, they fled from the gas even though it didn't seem to harm them.

Dante coughed and wheezed. His lungs burned, and his eyes watered.

As his cough became a hoarse hacking, he kneeled in search of fresher air near the ground. Belgrade crouched beside him, took a deep breath, ripped off his mask and goggles, and handed them to Dante.

Dante put them on and slowly began to recover. A minute passed, and Belgrade was still holding his breath. He seemed unaffected by the smoke, which had begun to disperse.

"That trick will only work once," Dante said between coughs. "I only had the two smoke grenades. Do you want to press forward or try to duck into one of these rooms and wait until the hallways clear a bit… if they clear a bit?"

Belgrade pulled a clip from his belt and switched it with the empty cartridge in his rifle. The new clip clicked into place. "I say we keep moving."

Dante smiled, though his Russian pal couldn't see it. He stood and saluted the guard. "It's been an honor, comrade."

Belgrade saluted him back. "The honor has been mine."

"All right. Enough sappy shit. Let's move."

A moment later, they were running full speed down the corridor. Dante's lungs were on fire, burning from smoke inhalation and exertion. His eyes no longer burned, but the goggles were fogging up except where his sweat trickled down them. Visibility was bad enough with the smoke that lingered and the tears it produced. He tore off the goggles and let them fall behind him.

His sight slowly improved, but he still nearly ran straight into the biggest creature of them all.

He tried to stop his momentum by shifting his feet sideways, much like a skier would to turn. He fell into a slide, his knuckles ringing off the hard floor, jarring his weapon loose. His momentum carried him within a few meters of a gigantic amalgamation of flesh, blood, organs, and bone, with no rhyme or reason to its makeup. A bulbous, blistering, purple-veined garbage heap of human stew, composed of easily more than a hundred people, clogged the hallway like fat in an artery. All of the creatures the smoke had chased up that way had joined the mass. Anything that made its component parts human was gone.

The way the blob pulsated and throbbed, everywhere bursting with party-balloon-sized blisters, oozing and spattering the walls and ceiling with pus, blood, and bile, was enough to make Dante want to retch. Its smell, worse than of an infected pimple wafted directly into his nose and finished the job.

He turned onto his stomach and threw up, partly on himself, as he scrambled to his feet and gathered up the nozzle. He was turning to shoot, Belgrade beckoning him back all the while, when something tripped him up. Whatever it was snapped him into the air and spun him. He crashed down onto his back, and the flamethrower's tank broke his fall. He heard a crack and felt a stabbing pain in his chest. He prayed only a rib had broken.

The impact sent him bouncing off the tank and continuing in the direction of the pull. The strap around his left arm slid down and off his flailing arms. The strap around his right caught in the crook of his elbow. The sprayer skidded across the floor somewhere behind him.

The creature had him by the leg. He raised his head to look down at the fat, pulsating tentacle that had wrapped itself around his ankle. It tightened and began to drag him toward the growing heap.

Desperate to stop his motion, he dug his free heel into the floor, but all he had on was a sock that kept slipping. Finally, something caught.

Or someone caught him. "I've got you," Belgrade said. His hand vise-gripped Dante's, but the tentacle continued to pull. Suddenly, Dante was free. The tentacle retracted with the boot and sock it had stolen from him. Belgrade helped him to his feet, and they both turned to run, Dante holding on to the strap of the flamethrower as it dragged behind him.

He was almost around a bend when the mucous tentacle slithered around his ankle once more – his *bare* ankle.

"*Merda!*"

The tentacle snapped tight and yanked him down to the ground again. As he fell, he clung to the flamethrower's strap as if it were his only lifeline. When he hit the floor, his wind escaped him. His grip on his weapon slipped. The strap slid across his fingers and was almost lost, when Dante caught it around his middle finger.

"No!" Belgrade yelled.

Dante knew the Russian would not be helping him this time. Belgrade must have known Dante had been infected, must have seen the tentacle touching his skin. Dante himself knew his fate even before he started to seize.

His eyes rolled back in his sockets. The hallway, the blob, Belgrade, his many lost boots – all ceased to exist. He was no longer part of the human world, but he was not yet part of that thing's world either.

He didn't know where he was, some dark plane of existence between reality and dream, conscious and subconscious. In it he saw night, emptiness, nothingness…and that astrobiologist, the one responsible for everything that had happened.

Dick. Dante wanted to kill the bastard all over again.

I've been waiting for someone like you, the dickhead said without moving his lips. Since no one else was there and Dante hadn't said it, the words had obviously come from him.

I've been waiting for someone who would listen, could listen, and could do something about it.

"Where am I?"

Somewhere you don't want to stay. But you can end this. In your hands is the means to destroy her.

"Who?"

You know who, Dante. She is getting smarter. You've seen it, haven't you? With the water, with Monty…. She's learning how to hide, how to deceive. The astrobiologist chuckled. *She's becoming more like us, Dante. And she'll do anything to get out.*

"I'm dying, aren't I?" Dante was strangely at peace with the idea. "What can I do?"

Destroy her, Dante, while you still can. Time moves slower here, but time is still short. You must be quick. You need to act before you're trapped here completely and your will is snuffed out. Please, Dante! Feel what's in your hand!

"What's in my hand?" Dante asked. His voice echoed through the darkness, loud and terrifying. In that dreamlike realm, he looked at his hands and saw them empty. He blinked then looked again.

In his right hand, he saw a strap.

Set us free, Dante, the astrobiologist said. *Set us all free.*

And Dante was no longer alone with the astrobiologist. Beside him stood Romanov and Monty and that asshole doctor and a whole shitload of people Dante had never seen before. Each of them stared at him with hopeful eyes as if Dante could lead them out of that limbo and into the Promised Land.

Dante had his own ass to worry about, and that was enough. He pulled the strap in his hand across his chest. A sharp pain ran through his shoulder as something jabbed into it. *The tank!* Reaching back with his left hand, he fumbled for the hose connecting the tank to the sprayer. When he found it, he tugged it toward him, closer and closer, until the sprayer knocked him in the head.

He grabbed it, rested it on his chest, and jammed the nozzle beneath his chin. The astrobiologist smiled. *Thank you.*

Dante closed his eyes. He pulled the trigger.

Blue-orange light broke through the darkness around him.

"Funny," he said. "I don't feel anything." And he continued to not feel anything as his entire body was consumed by flames. He looked down to see the tentacle around his ankle ignite. And like a chain reaction, the fire leaped down the length of the tentacle, continuing past Dante's realm of sight.

The fires of hell await. Then his thoughts began to leave him.

CHAPTER THIRTY-ONE

Clara couldn't hold Alfonse back. The man was simply too big and too strong.

"Sebastian?" Alfonse's voice quivered, sounding small and weak.

"Take me with you," Sebastian repeated.

The voice sounded right, and the man looked right, but Clara had been there when that serpent creature had wriggled its way into the real Sebastian's chest. She didn't need years of scientific study to tell her that people didn't just rebound from something like that in a matter of hours. They didn't just get better.

"That's not him, Alfonse!" she shouted, hoping to startle some sense into him.

"It is me." Sebastian took a step closer.

Clara raised her blowtorch, its nozzle glowing. "Stay back. I'm warning you...."

"How can you be so sure it's not him?" Alfonse asked. "You said so yourself, you're infected. Yet you're still you. Why can't he still be him?"

The logic was simplistic yet difficult to argue against. *'Because I didn't have a meter-long eel burrowing into my heart' doesn't seem like an answer that'll convince him.* Then again, Clara was staring into the eyes of a monster in disguise, one that could attack at any moment. She had no time for tact. Sebastian was getting closer. *Fuck considerate.*

"I don't think he's anything like me, I'm sorry to say. You're believing what you want to believe, willfully blinding yourself to the truth. The organism...it's been manipulating our form all day. Is it so strange to think that it might try to manipulate our minds? It's running out of food inside this petri dish. As horrifying as it sounds, I think its learning from us, maturing."

"That can't be." Alfonse whimpered. "Sebastian, it's really you, isn't it?"

"I doubt there's much I could say or do to convince you that that's not Sebastian at this point beyond lighting him on fire and seeing what happens. Think, Alfonse. Would the real Sebastian need to ask us to take him with us?"

"It's me, Alfonse." Sebastian stepped closer. He was smiling just a little too big to look warm and friendly.

Before she knew it was happening, Alfonse snatched the blowtorch from her hands. She tried to steal it back, but he kept her at a distance with a meaty paw. "Get in the rover," he told her, surprisingly calm. "I've got this."

"But—"

"I know. Trust me."

"Take me with you." Sebastian took another step closer.

Clara stepped back. She circled to the far side of the rover and got in, leaving the closer seat for Alfonse's easy access, should he ever choose to take it. From her seat, she could see the two members of the Mars excavation project squaring off. *Please, Alfonse, just set him on fire and jump in.*

Alfonse's massive frame was shaking. She couldn't see his face, but by the way his body was moving, she guessed he was sobbing. He slid to his right, positioning himself directly between Sebastian and the rover.

"You're not him," he said. "I know. Sebastian never used my full name."

The Sebastian-thing stopped smiling. It lunged forward with inhuman speed, too fast for Alfonse to react effectively. Caught off guard, Alfonse didn't use the blowtorch to ignite the monster. Instead he swung it with all his might at its head. The torch connected with the top of Sebastian's forehead and continued through it as though it had the consistency of pudding. Alfonse's wrist followed. When he tried to pull away, the pudding flesh solidified around his arm.

"Fuck me," Alfonse cursed, trying to tear his arm free. After a moment's resistance, he pulled out his arm with a slurp, ripping off much of Sebastian's face with it. His forearm was slick with blood and speckled with tiny mounds of purple cauliflower, which bore holes into his skin and continued up his arm underneath its cover.

Clara covered her mouth to stifle her screams. She had no weapon, no way of helping poor Alfonse now that the weapon she'd chosen for herself was covered in the biological slush of the infected.

Alfonse was nothing if not strong. He shot her a glance and smiled, trying to comfort her even while his own life was ending. He ran over to a computer and typed madly. The rover thrummed and vibrated beneath her.

The Sebastian clone's head wound closed. Its face reconstructed, no longer Sebastian's but that of….

Clara gasped. The creature turned toward her and snarled. She stared into the wild-mad eyes of her father.

"You wouldn't burn your father, would you, Clarabelle?" It grinned and raised a hand toward her. "Not again, would you?"

Before it could attack her, Alfonse charged. Whatever the spell the creature had over its shape fell away, and the form of Sebastian returned. Alfonse punched his phony partner in the chest and watched his fist come out the other side. He raised his arm and the Sebastian-thing with it, moving as quickly as he could, undoubtedly realizing his time was short.

"Hit the thruster as soon as we're behind you!" He flung himself, and the creature with him, toward the back of the rover. "Now!" he shouted, circling the final wheel. He collapsed over the back of the *Herald.* As he started to seize, he latched on to the top of what resembled a very large cone turned on its side.

"Thrusters…" Clara muttered, not knowing exactly what Alfonse had in mind. She looked everywhere before finding the clearly marked lever right beside her hand, where a stick shift would've been in a more conventional vehicle. She pushed the lever forward.

An explosion of gas and fire shot from the cone and incinerated Alfonse and his attached parasite. It also set much of the hub behind her on fire. For a long while, Clara sat frozen in shock, her mind trying to grasp exactly what she'd done. She had killed a man. Part of her had to have known that would happen. She had to know that thrusters meant the expulsion of rocket fuel, that anyone caught in that expulsion….

A second explosion, from the northern entrance, shook her from her reverie. The door blew off its hinges, and the wall crumbled and fell around it. Someone or something climbed over the debris.

A man in an ASAP guard's uniform. "Go, go, go!" he shouted.

Clara panicked. She didn't know if the man was healthy or infected. She searched for the button or lever that would close the cockpit, instead finding one that read 'Launch'.

She pushed it.

Instantly, the hood started to descend. She watched the man rushing across the hub toward her. He was fast. *Too fast?* She couldn't tell. She looked around for a weapon but found nothing. *Come on.* She tried to will the hood to close faster.

It was too slow. She raised her fist as the man dove inside with only seconds to spare. The cockpit sealed itself shut.

"You won't be needing that," the man said, glancing at her balled-up hand. "I'm not one of them."

"I've heard that before."

He ignored the remark, fiddling with knobs and equipment, looking for only he knew what. "Well?" he asked. "How do we work this thing?"

"I already hit the Launch button," Clara said. "I have no idea what I am supposed to do next."

"You mean you don't know how to fly it?" The man looked her up and down, noticing the lab coat. "Not one of the space guys?"

"Nope."

"That man you were with – I'm Visely Belgrade, by the way, the one who sealed off the passageway here for you – he was the astronaut?"

"Yep."

"And he's...?"

"Yep."

Belgrade sighed. "Nothing's ever easy."

They had another problem. Clara pointed up. The dome was closed. If they tried to launch, they would meet the same fate as birds that flew into closed glass doors.

"Great. How do we open that?"

With a thud and the sound of cranks, the dome above them began to retract. They both stared in wonder as the sky opened up before them. Even the cold, gray afternoon outside was a welcomed escape from the desolate climate within.

"The shutter really doesn't extend over the hub?" Belgrade asked. "I can't believe it."

"Some things are easy." Tears welled in her eyes. *Thank you, Alfonse.*

"About freaking time."

Clara jabbed him with her finger.

"Ow!" Belgrade frowned. "Do you want to settle down? We still have to figure out how to launch this thing."

"Sorry." But she wasn't. "I just wanted to make sure you weren't, you know, mushy."

Belgrade leveled his eyes at her. He tried on a smile, but it didn't suit his face.

Still, Clara appreciated the effort. "Are we all that's left?"

"Honest answer: I don't know. I think so."

"Are you infected?"

Belgrade sighed. "I don't know. I don't think so." His gaze ventured outside the windshield. His eyes widened. "But I know they are!"

Mutated and contorted humans and conglomerations of flesh flooded in through the broken wall. Every last one of them was converging upon the launchpad.

The cones of the thrusters folded inward, positioning for launch. Apparently, Alfonse had prepared the entire sequence when he plotted their flight plan. She wished he were coming with her. Instead, she had this stranger she didn't know and couldn't trust.

Alfonse....

A roar emitted from below them. Smoke billowed up around them. The console switched from dormant to active in the span of a second. However, the creatures were rocking the ship. Some were climbing atop it.

"We're not going to make it," Clara said as the creatures swarmed the rover.

Some looked as though they were trying to destroy it, others as though they were trying to hitch a ride. Still others were stretching and oozing and searching for ways inside the cockpit. More than one got too close to the flames below and burst into flames of their own.

Takeoff was slow, so slow Clara hadn't noticed when they'd left the ground.

"See? We are going to make it," Belgrade said as the *Herald* rose.

Something was driving the mutants toward them with even greater conviction than they'd shown in the corridors. "They chance the smoke and the fire now, and for what? Trying to escape? Do they know about the self-destruct sequence?"

"Self-destruct sequence?"

"Yes, this whole place is rigged to blow. But don't worry, we have plenty of time."

My research, Clara thought and immediately felt selfish for thinking it. She snickered. As long as she remained alive, she'd have plenty of samples to research.

A bang rattled the windshield, and she nearly jumped out of her seat. A mostly human figure stared in at them through one eye, the other eye covered by some kind of thick green husk.

"Jordan?"

His cheek slid, wet and slimy, down the windshield as his weight and gravity worked against his efforts to hold on. Blood dripped from a quarter-sized hole in his forehead. As he slid lower, Clara could see that the back half of his head was gone. Jordan Phillips was no more. What she was looking at didn't belong on the *Herald*.

She smiled when it fell.

As the thrusters sent them higher, the rocket fuel blasting everything in range of the launchpad into fiery tumbleweeds, rolling into others of their kind and spreading fire like infection, the blaze found its way up to the *Herald* over the tentacles trying to hold it down. The smaller creatures who had latched on to the rover found themselves on fire, the *Herald* shining like a meteor burning up upon entry into the Earth's atmosphere. The temperature in the cockpit rose to sweltering levels. Malfunction warnings flashed across the console as equipment failed or smoked.

Still, they continued to rise.

The fear of crashing became secondary in Clara's mind to a concern that had just occurred to her. The shelter was open. The creatures could mutate. Some could climb.

What if they can fly?

CHAPTER THIRTY-TWO

Anju stumbled around in the darkness for what seemed like an eternity. She had lost all concept of time in never-ending blindness, the last indicator of its passage having been the notification by the facility's central computer system that the facility would 'purify' itself, a description she found wholly inaccurate, in sixty minutes. That had seemed like an hour ago and had made her move faster. Still, she did not feel as though she had gotten anywhere.

Her knees were covered in bruises from all the times she had fallen. Every time she fell, she got up and carried forward. She had encountered no infected in that dark hole, which would likely become her tomb, none that she could see or that had chosen to make itself known.

Is that...? She raised a hand over her eyes as if a glare was causing her inability to see. It had no effect on her sight, but it did raise her confidence in the fact that her eyes were not deceiving her. A sliver of pale yellow broke through the darkness, like a hallway light outside a closed bedroom door. And it was only....

How far? She could not gauge the distance with no walls or floor to measure it by. She ran toward the light regardless, hoping and praying that nothing waited in her path.

She tripped. Falling forward, she braced herself with her palms and skidded then stopped on the cold, earthen floor. Her knee had again hit against something hard, another bruise for her collection. Wincing, she stood. Nothing seemed to be broken. She wiped her hands on her pants, and felt and heard little pebbles and dirt fall from the new grooves she had scratched into them.

Whatever she had tripped on was not hard like rock. It was soft like....

A body? Anju gasped then swallowed hard, trying to stop herself from making any noise. *Calm down. If it were one of those things, it would have already attacked you. You do not know what it was. It could have been anything.*

She turned to continue toward the light, at first content to never know what had tripped her. She stopped. *What if it is a person? He could need your help.* She moaned. Her conscience was her own worst enemy.

She took a deep breath. "Hello?" She crouched and felt around the tunnel floor, duck-walking slowly, cautiously closer to the place where her foot had collided with the object. Her fingertip brushed against fabric. It could have been someone's clothes. "Hello?" Her voice was barely more than a whisper.

When no answer came, she reached out and grabbed the object. It was light, big enough to be a jacket, but it definitely did not have anyone in it. If she got out, she could use a jacket. God, she was already freezing. Her teeth were chattering, and her sweat had cooled against her skin. The cold seemed to reach right through her. She wondered why she was noticing it only then.

She bundled the object in her arms and ran back toward the light. That time, she did not trip, though she did smack her shin against a metal bar of some sort, something big she had to skirt around in an area where the floor was covered with rubble. Soon, she could see her hands in front of her. She could see what was in them: a backpack with a giant black cross painted on its flap.

That man…he blew up the garage. The flap was not buckled down. She opened up the bag, hoping to find something useful inside, a lighter maybe, but found nothing.

She tossed the bag aside and continued toward the sliver of light. She began to piece together the evidence. The man had had bombs. His bombs were gone. So either he used them all in the garage, or someone else had them. And maybe….

The gate! They used them to blow up the gate! Her shin, stinging with its fresh bruise, pulsated its agreement. "Which means," she said aloud though afraid to believe it, "that there is nothing blocking my way out?"

She continued toward the light. It illuminated a stairwell leading up to a bulkhead. The light was shining through a crack where rusted metal doors met a stone basin.

Please do not be locked. Please do not be locked.

She paused, trying not to let her excitement trump her good sense, and listened for sounds outside. She heard breathing, but it came from behind her. The hairs on her neck stood on end. She was too scared to turn around and face what she knew in her heart would kill her.

But whoever or whatever was behind her fell. She turned to see an ASAP guard lying on the tunnel floor. He was clutching his stomach as black liquid poured through his fingers.

"You have been infected!" she shouted and turned to run before her brain reprocessed what she had seen. The poor lighting only made the liquid look black. The man was bleeding, and he needed help.

She hurried back to where he lay and lifted his head in her arms. He clenched both hands over his belly as he tried to hold his life force in. His face was bone white, smudged with grime, and young. He couldn't have been past his early twenties. He might have been handsome if he had not been at death's door.

He tried to speak. Blood ran from the corner of his mouth. Anju leaned closer to listen.

"Don't... go out there," he struggled to say.

But she had to go out there. The guard was losing too much blood. If the impending explosion or the creatures did not kill him first, his blood loss would. He needed qualified medical assistance and quickly. She fell short of breath, imagining what that man must have been thinking, that Anju was going to leave him all alone to die in the dark.

She lowered his head gently to the ground and stood. She hesitated briefly, but she had to leave if either of them was going to survive. "Keep pressure on the wound. I will be back with help, I promise." She climbed the steps.

"No...wait..." the young guard moaned.

Anju pushed open the bulkhead. The cold air hit her face and brought with it the smell of ferns and firs and wet earth and fresh snow. The sunlight reflecting off snow and ice was blinding at first, her eyes needing a moment to adjust. *A forest?*

"Wait, don't!" the dying man shouted. "Don't go out there!"

She walked out into the gray light, a bleak day only dazzling in comparison to the tunnel. Anything was better than the tunnel. The bulkhead had been built in a small clearing encircled by tall trees. She turned and peered through the interspersed trunks and thought she could make out the research center somewhere near the horizon.

How far did I walk? She tried to prop the bulkhead door open, hoping the sunlight would offer the guard some comfort. As she did, her hand slipped on a thick, dark substance. She sniffed it, hoping it was sap, but its coppery smell gave it away.

"Gyah!"

She wiped her hand on her leg, turning around. She stepped forward, and her foot landed in something squishy, thick like mud, and without looking, Anju knew what it was.

But she had to look. "Oh God." So much blood, crimson against the snow.

Bile rose from her stomach. It escaped when she saw the bodies lying around her, at least eight of them. Some belonged to acquaintances she had met at the research center, others to ASAP guards and facility staff members. One even belonged to the cook who had been serving the steel-carved oatmeal that morning.

All had been gunned down as they tried to make an escape.

Anju felt the first bullet rip through her even before she heard the gunshot. Before the second bullet tore through her shoulder, she started to seize.

CHAPTER THIRTY-THREE

The flight had been rocky and the landing way off the mark, but somehow they had survived it. In the distance, the Shakhova-Mendelsen Siberian Research Center was exploding. It reminded Clara of a party around a bonfire she had gone to as a teenager, with her friends setting off fireworks and enjoying a simpler time. But her celebration was tinged with a hint of sadness. All that remained of the work Clara had performed there was herself and the virus that lived inside her.

And maybe the burning bits of Molli that had fused to the rover.

Visely Belgrade – she had learned much about him during their hectic flight while they tried to distract themselves from any number of possible ways of dying, including mile-high combustion and mile-low plummeting – had kicked open the partially fried-shut cockpit hood and was watching the billowing mushroom cloud in the distance with arms crossed. A wildfire raged through the center and had made some progress downwind, east through a slightly wooded plateau. But the frozen Siberian tundra would prevent it from spreading too far. He tore himself away and returned to help Clara from the rover.

Before her feet could touch the snow-and-mud-covered ground, Belgrade scooped her into his arms as if he were some fancy-pants in a bad romance flick. She balked at being manhandled, stiffened in his grasp and pushed off him, her confusion and fear increasing her fight.

"I can walk just fine," she said. "I don't need to be carried anymore."

Belgrade probably didn't know she hadn't been able to walk a mere eight or nine hours earlier, and because of that, her imagined reasons for his carrying her grew that much more terrifying.

"I'm not going to harm you," he said.

Clara didn't relax. "Put me down!"

"The Americans, the Russians, NATO…I don't know who for sure, but someone is coming for us, and they're probably already getting close." He walked through the snow, away from the rover, carrying her as if she were his newly betrothed. "If we're the only survivors, I'm guessing first responders will be shoot-first-then-shoot-again types."

Clara's mouth dropped open. "You mean...."

"That we just went through hell only for our own governments to kill us anyway?" He shrugged. "Maybe. Maybe not. Maybe they'll just throw us in quarantine for the rest of our lives. All I'm saying is that I wouldn't trust them, I *don't* trust them, and neither should you. I used to be one of those guys."

Clara calmed. She still didn't like being carried, but she was willing to give him the benefit of the doubt. He carried her over to a large boulder and placed her atop a gradual slope. She grimaced. The rock was ice cold beneath her bare hands and even through her jeans.

"Climb to the other side of the rock and head south. We're fortunate today is warmer than yesterday, or we would die of exposure in less than twenty minutes. And if it was winter, we'd already be half-dead. Still, I'd hurry before night sets in, not only to keep your blood pumping, stay warm, and get the hell out of here, but to stave off hypothermia. If you start to feel tired, don't stop. You stop, you die."

Clara nodded. "What about you?"

He smiled. "I'll be fine. Hopefully, they'll never notice your tracks and will follow mine. The Kolyma Highway should only be a few kilometers south of here, give or take a few kilometers. You should head toward it. Despite its name, it isn't much of a road. I wouldn't expect a lot of traffic out here, and most of what you do find on it will be military or other parties interested in the research center. But no one knows you're alive or will be looking for survivors that far south, so you may be able to flag someone down and get lucky. Even if it's soldiers, I doubt they would have kill orders. These things aren't handed out like candy since the general public tends to find them controversial."

"Sounds dangerous."

"It will be, but at least you'll have a chance." He paused and stroked his chin. "Of course, if you don't find anyone, you will die of exposure, so if you'd rather just give yourself up or take your chances with me—"

"No!" she blurted, a little too forcefully than she'd intended. If the forces that be were willing to kill those they thought *might be* infected, Clara was sure to be shot and cremated by nightfall. She wanted to live. Fate had seen fit to give her her health and her *legs* back, as well as the greatest scientific discovery of the last half century in a self-contained form. She'd not let anyone take either of them from her without a fight. "I'll take my chances."

Belgrade winced when he smiled as if the action was painful. "I've got a brother, Nicoli, who lives on a boat in Magadan. If you can get there and you can find him, tell him everything and that I said he'd help you. He owes me. Stay clear of the wildlife. The bears are bad, but the ticks are worse." He shuddered.

Clara stifled a laugh. After all the man had just been through and yet needed to face, he was afraid of a tick. She stopped laughing when she saw the earnest worry written on his face.

"Life is going to be hard for you for a while, at least until this whole thing is over." He smiled as best he knew how. "I wish you the best of luck."

Clara started to cry. "Why are you doing this?"

Belgrade thought for a moment then said, "Because everyone deserves a chance at life. Too many lost that chance today under my protection. We've seen the infected and what happens to them. It's possible it may be sleeping quietly in both of us right now and could wake up and turn us into mushroom-potato people or whatever, but I'm not about to kill myself, so what right do I have to kill you?"

You poor fool. She saw no benefit in announcing the fact that she was infected and had known so all along. Instead, she focused on the flower jutting out of his boot. "What's that?" she asked, knowing full well what it was.

"Oh?" Belgrade looked where her finger was pointing. "I thought I had ripped all of these off me." He pulled the flower from his boot and handed it to her. "This thing contains the virus...I think. You're a scientist, right? I think it's safe, not like those sticky bastards. You would make better use of it than I would." He handed it out to her. "Please, take it. Use it to find a cure or destroy it or do whatever your bigger brain than mine thinks is best."

Clara took the flower and inhaled its sweet perfume. *That's the second time in one day that a man has given me flowers.* The lily was beautiful, she decided, and smiled. *Capable of healing, of improving, of evolution.* She tucked it delicately into her inner lab-coat pocket. "Thank you."

Belgrade just nodded. She leaned forward and kissed his cheek. He blushed.

Then he unzipped his fly. "Now, if you'll excuse me, I have to give them a reason why my tracks lead over here."

"Oh," Clara said flatly, then, "Oh!" when she caught his meaning.

Belgrade reached into his pants as she turned and started to climb.

EPILOGUE

"Are these the bodies from the research center?" Bogdan asked. As the coroner for the Kasparov Medical Center in Sokol, he had no military background and no crematorium, though he understood the Russian Army had somehow brought one with them when it commandeered his wing of the hospital. His staff had been sent home, though he'd been ordered to stay for unspecified reasons.

"Yes," a soldier in snow-camo fatigues said. "The general has ordered their immediate cremation. No autopsies are permitted. They are not to be touched."

Bogdan stared at the ten bodies that had each been laid out in a body bag atop its own metal slab. He felt nothing. He was used to bodies. The soldiers worried him more. *Just another day, I suppose.*

"A representative from the CDC will be here shortly to oversee disposal," the soldier said.

"CDC? As in the Americans?"

"Yes." The soldier turned on his heel and left.

The CDC? What the hell were they playing with up there, and why were the Americans involved? He sneered. "Because they stick their noses in everything," he muttered.

He shook his head. *Stay out of it, Bogdan. You don't want any part of this one.*

One of the body bags twitched, the second of the lot closest to him. Bogdan watched it through narrowed eyes. If it had really been moving, it wasn't any longer. The movement had been so slight that Bogdan thought he'd imagined it. When it twitched again, he cursed. "Goddamn rats. Oy. They tell me not to touch it. I'm not going to touch it."

He sipped from a coffee then rested the mug and his buttocks on a desk near the entrance to the morgue. He watched the body bag for more signs of the vermin.

A small, white triangular blade poked a hole through the top of the bag. It looked like a dorsal fin cutting across a black sea as the bone-colored blade sliced through the material to about its midway mark.

Bogdan leaned closer. *That is no rat.* The blade worked quickly and deftly, and he watched it in a sort of amazed stupor. When one hand popped out of the slit, then a second, he nearly fell off the desk, shaking it so violently that his mug fell to the floor and shattered. Brown liquid formed a puddle at his feet.

His mouth hung open, and his thoughts went blank with fear. He couldn't move or speak, couldn't cry for help, his mind unable to process what was happening, unable to focus or find logic until it grasped and clung to a weak possibility.

A joke? Some kind of sick, demented joke? It had to be. The dead only rose in zombie movies.

But someone was rising. The hands separated the fabric, making room for a head to emerge. It belonged to a young woman, Indian he guessed, with long hair as black as raven feathers. Her shoulders appeared next as she sat up then scooted her torso completely out of the bag. She brought her knees to her chest then pulled her feet up and out. She threw a leg over the side of the slab and stood.

Bogdan stared, still speechless, at a lovely, alive, aware, and as far as he could tell, completely unharmed woman. Her clothes were riddled with holes and stained with blood, but he could see no injuries beneath them.

"Who are you?" he demanded. "How did you get in here?"

"Getting in here was easy," the woman said, smiling and speaking perfect Russian. "As for my name, you can call me Molli."

ACKNOWLEDGMENTS

I would like to thank Kenneth Parent and Kimberly Yerina for their beta-reads, as well as my editors and publicist, whose help have been invaluable here and elsewhere. I'd also like to thank Don D'Auria, Mike Valsted, and the entire Flame Tree team for their belief in my work and for turning the words of many a fine author into something beautiful.

FLAME TREE PRESS
FICTION WITHOUT FRONTIERS
Award-Winning Authors & Original Voices

Flame Tree Press is the trade fiction imprint of Flame Tree Publishing, focusing on excellent writing in horror and the supernatural, crime and mystery, science fiction and fantasy. Our aim is to explore beyond the boundaries of the everyday, with tales from both award-winning authors and original voices.

•

You may also enjoy:
The Sentient by Nadia Afifi
American Dreams by Kenneth Bromberg
Second Lives by P.D. Cacek
The City Among the Stars by Francis Carsac
Vulcan's Forge by Robert Mitchell Evans
The Widening Gyre by Michael R. Johnston
The Blood-Dimmed Tide by Michael R. Johnston
The Sky Woman by J.D. Moyer
The Guardian by J.D. Moyer
The Goblets Immortal by Beth Overmyer
Until Summer Comes Around by Glenn Rolfe
A Killing Fire by Faye Snowden
The Bad Neighbor by David Tallerman
A Savage Generation by David Tallerman
Ten Thousand Thunders by Brian Trent
Two Lives: Tales of Life, Love & Crime by A Yi

Horror titles available include:
Snowball by Gregory Bastianelli
Thirteen Days by Sunset Beach by Ramsey Campbell
The Influence by Ramsey Campbell
The Wise Friend by Ramsey Campbell
The Haunting of Henderson Close by Catherine Cavendish
The Garden of Bewitchment by Catherine Cavendish
Boy in the Box by Marc E. Fitch
Black Wings by Megan Hart
Will Haunt You by Brian Kirk
We Are Monsters by Brian Kirk
Those Who Came Before by J.H. Moncrieff
Stoker's Wilde by Steven Hopstaken & Melissa Prusi
They Kill by Tim Waggoner
The Forever House by Tim Waggoner

•

Join our mailing list for free short stories, new release details, news about our authors and special promotions:

flametreepress.com